SEEKING SANCTUARY

THE ZAUBERI CHRONICLES

J. W. JUDGE

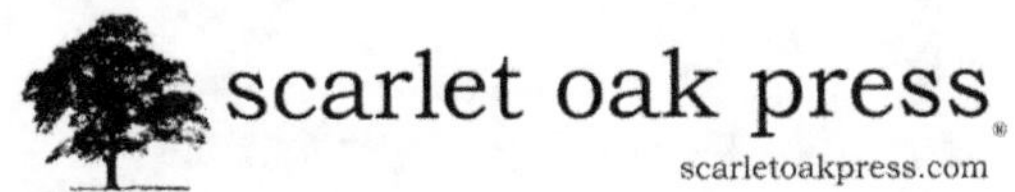

scarlet oak press

scarletoakpress.com

WORKS BY J. W. JUDGE

Fiction

Vulcan Rising (The Zauberi Chronicles, Book 1)

Seeking Sanctuary (The Zauberi Chronicles, Book 2)

Forging Bonds (The Zauberi Chronicles, Book 3)

The Murder Tree (A Short Story)

Non-Fiction

Write Your Novel One Day at a Time: How to Write a Novel While
Having a Career, a Family, and a Life

scarlet oak press

ISBN: 978-1-954974-02-9 (Paperback)

ISBN: 978-1-954974-01-2 (eBook)

ISBN: 978-1-954974-03-6 (Hard Cover)

Library of Congress Control Number: 2021921883

Published by Scarlet Oak Press (scarletoakpress.com)

And it came to pass, when men began to multiply on the face of the earth, and daughters were born unto them, that the sons of God saw the daughters of men that they were fair; and they took them wives of all which they chose.

And the Lord said, My spirit shall not always strive with man, for that he also is flesh: yet his days shall be an hundred and twenty years.

The Nephilim were on the earth in those days; and also after that, when the sons of God came in unto the daughters of men, and they bare children to them, the same became mighty men which were of old, men of renown.

And God saw that the wickedness of man was great in the earth, and that every imagination of the thoughts of his heart was only evil continually. And it repented the Lord that he had made man on the earth, and it grieved him at his heart. And the Lord said, I will destroy man whom I have created from the face of the earth; both man, and beast, and the creeping thing, and the fowls of the air; for it repenteth me that I have made them.

The Zauberi Chronicles

SEEKING
SANCTUARY

Book Two

1

AGATHA

GERMAN METEOROLOGISTS WEREN'T any better than their American counterparts. Agatha was glad she had worn her rain jacket. A twenty percent chance of rain had escalated into a deluge. She had only made it as far as Haus St. Franziskus, not even two kilometers from the house, when the skies opened up and emptied their contents on her.

So much for getting her steps in today. Back in Alabama, she would have just kept walking. Rain was pretty tolerable when it was still eighty degrees after the sun had gone down. But not here. She was lucky if the temperatures in Hornberg stayed in the sixties on her evening walks. On a night like this one, it would get down into the forties, and she might just catch her death while being soaked to the bone.

Agatha sighed and turned around. She considered waiting out the rain shower under the little barbecue pavilion nearby, but the deluge gave no indications of letting up. Instead, she took the trail that ran through the woods parallel to the train tracks, rather than continue on Rebberg and risk getting hit by a car that didn't see her. She would be a muddy mess when she got back home, but at least she'd be in one piece.

The train from Gutach rattled away somewhere on her right, impervious to and indifferent about the downpour.

She knew the trail well enough that she could nearly have walked it with her eyes closed, which she might as well have done for all the light there was. There'd have been no light at all, if it weren't for the town's lights reflecting off the low cloud cover and giving everything a ghostly glow.

The trail quickly gained elevation as she hiked, giving her an overview of the Gutach Valley that she never tired of. It hadn't taken her long to learn to love this town that nestled in a crook between mountains. Her heart had immediately recognized it as the home that it would become, and in a sense, had always been.

The goats across the road below her voiced their complaints about the weather. *I hear you, guys.* Agatha tightened the drawstrings on the hood of her jacket to keep rain from intruding.

She'd no more gotten herself situated against further trespass than the rain let up. By the time she got down to where her trail intersected with Äussere Rebberge atop the train tunnel, she let down her hood, and the moon was pushing its light through the remaining wisps of clouds.

Agatha stopped at the top of the tunnel and looked to the north, trying to discern the likelihood of getting caught in another cloudburst if she extended her walk. She moved to take a step to the left when the squishing sound in her boot brought attention to how wet her feet were. A shortcut through the trees and down to Rebbergstrasse was the most direct route home and likely her best decision.

Before she moved away from the tunnel's edge, a final cloud shuffled away, revealing a dark bulk huddled below her against the western wall of the tunnel exit. It could have been any number of things. A couple of trash bags sitting beside each other. A discarded rug. Agatha tried to think of other things it might have been, but wasn't. She knew what it was.

Agatha looked southward over her shoulder. No train was approaching. She shuffled along the embankment from the top of the tunnel down to the tracks.

"Hello?" she called to the jumbled mass. Realizing she'd spoken in English, Agatha called out in German. It wouldn't make any difference. Corpses couldn't hear. But she had to be sure.

Agatha crossed the first set of tracks. "Do you need help?"

Although the body's back was to her, she made out long hair. A bare leg protruded from the torn black dress.

Agatha made several false starts toward the body, conflicted between providing help or calling for it. Her protective nature won out. She stepped over the second set of tracks and squatted at the woman's head, listening for breath sounds. Nothing.

She grabbed the woman's shoulder and rolled her onto her back. Agatha stepped back in surprise, and an involuntary "Oh" escaped her.

The rip in the woman's dress extended up to its neckline, leaving her naked and exposed. There appeared to be something carved into her chest. It was too dark to make out. Agatha raised her right arm and produced an orb of molten lava. She grew it to the size of a grapefruit and suspended it above the dead woman.

The carving was a symbol she had seen before, though she couldn't quite place it. It looked like a six-pedaled flower with a circle around it.

Agatha tapped the screen of her watch, causing it to light up. She touched the screen several more times until a phone started ringing on the other end.

"Guten abend. Polizeidirektor Fischer."

"Markus, it's Agatha. Listen, I was out on a walk and found a body. It's a woman. Down by the train tunnel just north of town. Rebberg Tunnel. I don't think she's been here long."

"Okay. I'll be right there. Are you safe?"

Agatha hadn't considered her own safety. She looked to the

north and saw nothing along the tracks. Everything was blacks and grays. Immediately to the south was the tunnel. She flung her orb into it to disperse the darkness. A couple of rats scurried away from the fire that hissed at the wet gravel.

"Agatha?"

"Yeah. I'm fine."

"I'll be there soon. Don't touch anything."

"Ja, got it."

She punched the red button on her watch to end the call. She stepped back from the dead woman and inspected her from a distance. Her face was battered, and there was a thin red line around her throat.

Agatha produced another ball of light and directed it in a spiral that grew wider with each orbit. She looked for anything that might be out of place but didn't find anything. Still, Markus's question about her safety lingered. She extinguished her fires and waited under the tunnel, confident that she was its only non-rodent occupant. The darkness would conceal her if anyone returned before the police arrived.

With her back against the cool tunnel wall, Agatha realized she was going to be much later getting home than expected. She had told Gertrude she would stop by on her way home. If she made her mother wait, the woman would barrage her with a flurry of concerned messages. She wrote, "Be there in a bit. Got caught in the rain. Meeting up with some friends for a bite." She would have added, "Don't wait up," but Gertrude was the same night owl now that she had always been.

She didn't bother sending Thomas a message. It wouldn't occur to him that she wasn't there unless he ran out of food and paused his game long enough to go hunting for her. The odds against either of those things happening were fairly low.

When Agatha heard voices approaching, she pressed herself against the wall, all but disappearing into the darkness. They were getting closer, scampering down the hill to the tracks.

"There's the body, but where is Frau Wande?" an unfamiliar voice asked.

She pushed away from the wall. The men looked her direction, perceiving movement among the shadows. She walked out from under the tunnel.

"Gentlemen," she greeted.

"Hallo," Fischer answered, "This is Detective Pereira. He's going to assist in the investigation. In fact, Miguel, why don't you get started and I'll join you when you complete your first pass over the scene?"

Fischer stepped backward, stopping between the two sets of tracks and motioning for Agatha to follow him.

They watched as Pereira made movements with his arms that looked as if he were washing the windows of a car in slow motion. Agatha watched with curiosity.

"He can emit and see light in the ultraviolet spectrum. Think of him as a human black light. It allows him to see fluids on the body and other evidence we can't easily identify."

"Sounds like a useful skill."

"Undoubtedly. He is my most valuable detective for a variety of reasons."

Pereira was thorough. He waved his hands over the body and over every surface within ten feet of it. He reminded Agatha of a hunting dog that had caught a scent.

After completing his initial search, Pereira rejoined Agatha and Fischer. "There are no footprints to speak of. The only ones I identified appear to belong to Frau Wande. I did not find any evidence of ...." He paused, looking at Agatha and uncertain whether to proceed.

"Go on," Fischer prompted.

"No evidence of semen. We will need to collect DNA samples from her clothes and from under her nails as well. She fought."

Pereira paused, thinking through his mental notes.

Fischer asked, "If there are no other footprints, how did she get here?"

Pereira pointed at the wall above the body. "There is blood spatter on the retaining wall. It is possible she was thrown from the train."

"Geez," Agatha said.

"Do we know when the last train ran?" Fischer asked.

"It came through right before the rain stopped," Agatha recalled.

Fischer advised, "We need to pull the schedule."

Pereira looked at his watch. "It will have already stopped at Neiderwasser. It is likely that the perpetrator would have disembarked there, or perhaps Triberg."

Fischer said, "Agatha, it's not necessary for you to stay. We are going to be here for some time, and others are on their way to help photograph and collect the evidence."

"You know how to reach me if you need anything else, Polizeidirektor."

"Call me Markus, please."

She touched his hand lightly. Pereira had looked away and was occupying himself with the crime scene.

"Not while you're on the job, Polizeidirektor."

"Would you like me to have someone escort you home?"

One corner of her mouth turned up in a half-smile. "I can handle myself. Thank you for the offer."

"Of course. I didn't mean to suggest otherwise."

"I know you didn't, Polizeidirektor. See you tomorrow?"

He looked toward Pereira to see if he was paying them any mind. "Perhaps we should push it back a couple of days. I may still be dealing with this. It's rather uncommon for us to have a murder here. It's been … I don't know, several years at least."

"Fair enough," she said. "Gute nacht then."

He nodded and joined Pereira, who pointed and began talking.

2

THOMAS

THOMAS REGARDED Luka with some uncertainty. He admired Luka's lack of inhibitions and willingness to jump headfirst into shenanigans. Thomas, meanwhile, was plagued with doubts and consideration for consequences.

"What's wrong, Thomas? Are you das huhn?" Luka began clucking, bobbing his head back and forth, and flapping his arms that he'd folded in like wings. The universal accusation of cowardice.

Thomas didn't want to get dared into a contest that would devolve into something else, but he couldn't let that stand. Not in front of Emma, anyway.

"Fine," said Thomas. "I'll play your game."

The problem with Luka's games was that they always escalated. Every game of catch turned into a contest. Every bit of horseplay became a wrestling match. And whatever this started as, Luka was sure to raise the stakes to it as well.

Never one to be left out, Finn said, "I'm in, too."

"Good, good." Luka grinned at the participants. "Here are the rules. In the first round, you choose a rock and try to get closest to the middle of the knot on that fir tree."

"That seems easy enough," said Finn.

"See, Thomas? Easy," Luka teased him. "You've got nothing to worry about. Emma and Lea can judge."

"Umm, no," said Lea. "This isn't a boy's club. I will be winning this competition."

"Very well," Luka conceded. "Emma, will you be our judge?"

Before Emma could answer, Finn said, "I'm not sure she's all that impartial."

Thomas and Emma blushed deeply.

Thomas punched him in the arm. "Shut up."

"Oh, are we not talking about this yet? Move along, folks, nothing to see here."

Thomas and Emma let their eyes catch each other before darting away.

He didn't even know what this was yet. Or if it would even become anything at all. He'd like it to. She seemed to like him, too. But he was pretty sure that as fragile as it seemed right now, it could be smashed to bits by Finn prodding at it.

Thomas was ready to redirect things. "Alright, let's get to it."

They walked down to the river to pick out their rocks. Each scoured the banks for the best fit. Despite the temperature rising above eighty degrees, the water coming down from the mountains was still frigid. Thomas found what he was looking for and plunged his hand in. The rock was the size and shape of an oyster and about half an inch thick. It had been worn smooth over the years and should be perfect for throwing.

After the other three picked out their rocks, each going with a different size and shape, they trekked back to their spot about ten meters from their target.

"Any takers to go first?" Luka offered.

Thomas volunteered. There was less pressure in going first. Those who came after tended to overthink their throws. They tried to aim more than just to pitch it.

He turned sideways to the tree and raised his left leg as he went into the motion of a pitcher throwing from the stretch. Thomas let his stone fly. It clanked off the upper lip of the knot that was the size of a small plate. If he'd been David, the Israelite army would have been in real trouble with the stone bouncing harmlessly off Goliath's helmet, rather than lodging in his head.

"What was that?!" Finn was incredulous.

"What was what?"

"That thing you just did. The way you threw it."

Thomas was surprised. "Have you never seen baseball? That's how a pitcher throws it."

"I sure hope the pitchers are more accurate than that," Lea said.

"Whoa! Who knew Lea was a trash talker?" said Luka. "Let's see what you've got."

"Fine," Lea said, stalking up to the spot Thomas had occupied.

She took a more traditional approach to her throw, stepping forward with her left foot and throwing with her right hand. The triangular rock she chose embedded itself in the inner half of the knot.

The boys all looked at each other with eyebrows raised. If there hadn't been pressure to perform before, there was now.

"I'll let you follow that." Finn gestured for Luka to step forward.

"How generous of you, Finn."

Luka stepped up without further comment. He wound his arm back and launched his rock with all the force of a fire hydrant. And glanced his stone off the side of the tree.

He hung his head and slunk back beside Emma. She patted his back consolingly.

"Well, it'll be hard to do worse than that," Finn said.

He took his position. Finn adopted an underarm technique and landed his rock well short of the tree.

"What was that you said a minute ago?" Lea teased.

Finn shrugged, "Hard. But not impossible."

"On to the second round," Luka announced. "The standings are: Lea in first, Thomas in second, I am in third, and Finn is bringing shame on his family name."

"It's true. If I cannot redeem myself, I will perform seppuku rather than return home."

"What's that?" Emma asked, although she almost immediately regretted it.

"Ritual suicide," Finn explained. "It's a Japanese ceremony where you take a short sword and cut across your belly, then turn the sword knife upward. And finally, you pull your guts out."

She covered her eyes as though to keep out the image. "Oh. Please don't tell me any more."

"Anyway, as I was saying," Luka interjected, "round two involves more skill. And it will require you to demonstrate precision and control of your können. I will place a stack of rocks on the bank of the river. Your goal is to remove only the top rock from the stack."

"That sounds easy enough," said Finn.

"It does," Luka agreed. "Unfortunately, since you placed last in the previous round, you have been eliminated from the competition."

"What? Nobody said anything about elimination."

"Well, rules are rules."

Finn's cheeks reddened with frustration. "You're just making the rules up as you go."

"While that's true, it doesn't make them any less rules."

"Let's just get to it," Lea said. "Finn, be a doll and re-stack the rocks after the boys make a mess of things."

Luka made his way to the river bank and set six progressively smaller stones atop one another. The topmost stone was the size of a deflated chicken egg. He walked back to the group, who stood about thirty feet from the cairn.

"It's kind of serene looking," Thomas said.

Luka snickered. "Do you need to take a photo for your Insta feed, or can we get to knocking it over?"

"Shut up. Have at it. I assume you're up first since you were the worst one who advanced from the first round?"

Luka nodded. He lay down prostrate on the forest floor that was littered with pine needles and propped up his left elbow, looking across his upturned palm as if he were aiming a weapon. Luka closed his left eye and abutted his right hand to the heel of his left. A blast of ice burst down to the bank and overturned the top three rocks before splashing into the river.

"That was a curious technique," said Thomas.

"Wanted to keep it interesting. You're up, cowboy?"

"Cowboy?"

Luka shrugged. "You're from Alabama. Don't you still ride horses down there?"

"No, not to get around. I think the only place I ever even saw a horse was the pony at the zoo."

"Whatever. Get along, little doggy," Luka prompted in his best — but still very bad — Texas drawl.

Thomas shook his head but stepped forward.

He placed his feet shoulder width apart, offsetting his left ahead of the right, and bent at the knees. He brought his hands up in front of him, heel to heel, looking every bit the portrait of a sixteen-year-old Agatha.

Thomas took a deep breath, and as he exhaled, he released a tremendous fireball. It rocketed toward the river, obliterating the rock stack, and leaving only the bottom stone in place. His friends covered their eyes against the flash. The fireball sank into the river with a loud sizzle and a good deal of steam.

Thomas turned around to see their expressions. "So I'm …
uhh … still working on that."

Finn was the first to speak. "Tommy, I believe you have
single-handedly advanced global warming a full decade."

He hanged his head in mock shame as he returned to his
place beside Emma.

"Well, that was exciting," she said.

"I guess. My mom and I are working on it. It's not the
können I was born with. I'm trying to learn it, and it still gets
away from me a bit."

"Most people can't do that, you know," Emma said. "You
have what you were born with, and you hone it. But you can't
develop new können with any amount of skill."

"Yeah," Luka chimed in. "It should be enough that you can
talk to my cat about why she's such a jerk. Having this too is
totally unfair."

Thomas shrugged his shoulders. He didn't really know what
to make of that.

Finn found five new rocks to replace the ones Thomas had
displaced. Lea stepped up with her four friends arched
behind her.

She raised her hands high over her head and posed with all
the grace of a ballerina. As she lowered her hands in front of
her, a tendril of tornado descended from the clouds. By the time
her hands reached the level of her waist, the tornado touched
down right beside the newly reformed rock pile. The stones
shook, but none fell. Thomas' cap blew off his head.

Lea grew frustrated, having intended to land the fingerling
tornado on top of the rock pile. It was unclear whether she had
the skill to pick it up off the ground and move it over a few
inches with the precision she needed. As Lea's angst grew, the
tornado increased in magnitude and intensity.

"Lea!" Luka tried to yell over the din. She either ignored or
didn't hear him.

The tornado began slinging debris and rocks. Finn dove away. Luka took cover behind a tree. Thomas tackled Emma and covered her, his back exposed to Lea.

When Lea recognized the havoc that she was wreaking, she released the cyclone and everything stilled.

Finn uncovered his head and popped up. "That was quite a display."

Still from behind his tree, Luka called, "May have been lacking the control I'd mentioned, though."

Lea gestured rudely at him.

Thomas realized he was still laying on top of Emma. She was looking up at him with a curious expression.

"Sorry. I … uhh … sorry."

He raised himself up, trying to make as little additional contact with her as possible now that he'd become embarrassed. The rest of the group watched the extraction with knowing grins and snickers.

"That's very forward of you, Tommy," Finn said.

"Yeah, did you get consent before advancing on her like that?" Lea asked.

Thomas and Emma became scarlet versions of themselves.

"Let's not act like you're not the real story here, Lea," said Luka. "No deflecting. The government's probably going to send out agents from the Umweltbundesamt after all the damage you've done to the environment."

"Oh, please. It was just a little wind."

Luka continued brushing himself off and addressed the group. "Obviously, Lea is eliminated after round two because she just caused a natural disaster. That leaves Thomas and me to participate in the third and final round — sparring."

"No way. That's a terrible idea," said Thomas.

Luka raised his arms in a question. "What? What's the worst that could happen?"

"One of you might die," Lea said.

"Sure. I mean, I guess that's the worst that could happen. But how likely is that?"

"You can't ask *what's the worst that could happen*, then expect me to name some just moderately bad thing. If you're going to ask that question, I'm going to give you the actual answer. Besides, you just saw Thomas go scorched earth and literally kill fish."

"Fine. Whatever." Luka folded his arms across his chest. "But that's what we've got Emma for."

"Excuse me?" It was Emma's turn to be cross. *"That's* why I'm here? To put you back together? I don't think so."

Luka tried to walk back his statement. "That's not what I meant."

Finn and Thomas had a good laugh at Luka's backpedaling.

"Glad you two have my back. Are you in or not, Tommy? I guess you could always forfeit."

Thomas was still sure this was a bad idea. But he also wanted to know how he measured up against Luka. They were two of the best in their class, but that was such a controlled environment. So sterile.

Thomas noticed his toes were cold. He looked down to see that while he'd distracted himself, Luka had frozen his shoes to the ground.

"Nice." Thomas reached down and covered his shoes with his hands, thawing the ice and freeing himself. "Turnabout's fair play, I guess."

Thomas rolled a ball of magma toward Luka. It left sputtering little fires in its wake.

Luka jumped out of the way with a smile. "I guess we're doing this."

In his first attack, Luka summoned a deluge of water that he poured over Thomas, who shoved his hands upward with a sustained blast of fire. The water either evaporated or rolled off around him. Thomas was encased in a waterfall with a half-dome above him that kept him mostly dry. He jumped out from underneath the deluge and allowed his shield to dissipate.

To counter, Thomas lobbed a fiery orb toward Luka, who transformed his hand into an icy bat and swatted it. The orb flew toward Finn. He dove out of the way, yelling "Oy!" as he rolled.

Thomas realized that while he and Luka were well matched in their abilities, he was at a disadvantage. Unless he was willing to risk hurting someone, he had to play defense while he figured out a way to win without burning anyone alive or starting a forest fire.

Sensing hesitation, Luka launched another attack. He fired a blast of ice that struck Thomas in the chest and knocked him backward. As Thomas tried to regain his balance, Luka pummeled him with a torrent of hail. Thomas turned his back and crouched down to withstand the barrage.

The hail drew blood. Luka wasn't relenting. He was trying to force Thomas to surrender. But the pain angered him. He would not yield.

Thomas pushed himself up. He released a stream of fire toward Luka's feet. The hail stopped as Luka defended the counterattack. As he backpedaled, Luka raised a wall of ice in front of himself. Thomas continued to pour fire at its base until it toppled. He separated his streams of fire, casting it to the right and left of Luka, hemming him in and forcing a retreat. Luka tripped over a tree root as he scrambled.

When he landed on his back, Luka allowed his momentum to carry him into a backward somersault. He popped back up and cast a sheet of ice beneath Thomas' feet, which he followed with a ball of ice he flung at the boy's face.

Thomas dodged but slipped on the ice. His feet flew out from under him. He lost control of his hands, which rose as he fell, still emitting steams of fire.

He hit the ground with a thud, banging his head on the ice.

The last thing he heard before the blackness enveloped him was screaming.

3

———

THOMAS

THOMAS FLUTTERED HIS EYES. Gray relented to color, but focus eluded him. Something loomed over him. Beyond his feet, something wriggled and squirmed in shapes and patterns that didn't immediately make sense.

He pushed himself up onto his elbows. A wave of nausea rolled over him. He rolled onto his side, thinking he might be sick. This brought the looming mass closer.

"Thomas, if you get your sick on my boots, I will end you," Lea said.

"That might be a mercy. My head is killing me," he groaned, rubbing the back of his head and finding a sizable lump.

He shifted himself upright, testing how his body would react. Not great. Could have been worse though.

"Where are the others?"

"Emma's over there working on Luka, trying to uncook him. Finn is ... being very encouraging, but is almost entirely useless."

Thomas slowly looked up at her. She was coming into focus now. Black Doc Martens that she'd painted flowers on, gray jeans, and an Iron Maiden t-shirt. Arms folded across her chest. Unnaturally black hair. "What do you mean 'uncook him'?"

"You roasted him like a pig. Go see for yourself."

"Help me up?"

She sighed, but reached down and grabbed his outstretched hands. As he got to his feet, the ground tilted to the left, and he reeled. Lea grabbed him by the shirtsleeve.

"Come on. Get yourself together."

"Working on it. I've got something going on in my head here."

"Best I can tell, you've got very little going on in your head," Lea quipped.

Thomas gave her a hard look. Normally, Lea was just exceptionally snarky. Now she was being mean.

He walked as straight a line as he could over to where Luka was lying. What remained of his shirt was on the ground beside him. Emma was on her knees, leaning over him, her hands hovering above his chest.

Charred skin ran from his right hip up to where Emma's hands were. The skin was broken like sunbaked ground. Pink flesh seeped through the cracks. From Emma's hands up to his left shoulder, the skin was shiny and red. It looked almost like an hombre sash where the new skin met the old.

Thomas remembered that he'd heard a scream before he hit his head. This was why.

"Is he going to be okay?" Thomas asked.

"I don't know. His breathing is fast and shallow. I'm just trying to do enough that we can get him to a proper heilerin. There might be damage to his internal organs. I don't know. I'm not good enough yet to deal with that."

"Have y'all called for help?"

Finn and Emma shared an incredulous look.

"We never even thought of it," Finn said. "Hold on."

He pulled his phone out of his pocket and walked away from

the group. Emma returned to focusing on Luka's injuries. Lea watched from a distance.

Finn hung up and came back. "My brother and his friend are coming with a couple of quads. He said they have a backboard they can strap him to. I don't know why. They're weird like that."

Emma said, "Somebody will need to go back with them."

"I'll go," Lea asserted, stepping in to more fully join the group. Then more sheepishly, "I mean, if that's okay."

"That should be fine," Emma said. She asked Finn, "How long will it take them to get here?"

"About fifteen minutes."

"Okay. By then I'll have done all I can. Now give me some space so I can concentrate."

The other three walked away so Emma could tend to Luka. It was a quietly tense fifteen minutes. Thomas chewed on the side of his finger, frustrated that there was nothing for him to do to help. He still felt nauseated, but couldn't tell whether it was from the guilt or the head injury.

When Max and Yusuf pulled up on the quads, Thomas jumped at the opportunity to make himself useful. As promised, there was a backboard tied onto the rack on the rear of Yusuf's quad. The four boys gently lifted Luka and placed him on the board, securing him with straps.

Emma instructed, "Take him to Frau Vogel. She will know what to do. Lea, tell her what happened."

As Thomas and the other two watched the quads go, he turned to Finn and Emma. "My mom is going to kill me."

"Does she have to know?" Finn asked.

"Dude, there's only like four thousand people in this town. Of course she's going to know. Everybody knows everything about each other."

Emma suggested, "You should probably get ahead of it and tell her yourself."

"Yeah."

"How's your head?" she asked.

"A little foggy and a little like someone is shoving an ice pick in through my ear, but I'll be okay."

Thomas took a step forward, but Emma snagged his arm. "Let me help. Then we'll go."

Thomas didn't argue.

She reached up and placed her hands on the side of his head, her palms covering his temples. Thomas looked down at her. Despite the buzzing in his head and the situation, he had butterflies in his stomach. He'd never been this close to her before. Well, except for when he'd tackled her earlier. But other than that, he hadn't been this close to her.

"Close your eyes," she said.

He tried not to focus on how her hands felt on his face. That let his mind wander to whether Luka was going to be okay. He'd rather not go there either. It was a stupid game. He shouldn't have let himself be sucked in. His mind kept trying to come back to Emma. What was she going to think about him now? What she thought shouldn't matter this much. They weren't even ... a thing, yet. But it did matter. More than almost anyone else, he realized in that moment. It came as something of a revelation and nearly brought a smile to his lips. Until he remembered he was only here right now because Luka was on his way to see if a heilerin could fix him. That re-grounded him pretty quickly.

"Thomas?" Emma prompted gently.

"Yes?"

"You can open your eyes now."

He did. Emma and Finn were standing beside each other.

"Are you okay, man?" Finn asked.

Thomas raised his left hand to the back of his head where he'd hit it on the ground. The knot had disappeared, as had the haziness that had plagued him ever since he'd come to with Lea standing over him looking like she was contemplating smothering him.

"Do y'all think Lea has a crush on Luka?"

"What? No," Finn answered. "Maybe you're not okay. That's ridic—"

Emma raised a finger and interjected. "We are not having this conversation. We never had this conversation, and we never will. Do you understand?"

"No," Finn said.

"She's about to tell us something she's not supposed to, dummchen." Thomas translated for his friend, who was a little slow on the uptake. "But she doesn't want Lea to murder her in her sleep, so we can't let on that we know."

"Ah, now I understand."

"Good," Emma nodded. "Of course she does. She has for ages now."

Finn protested, "But she's all dark and broody. And he's all athletic and charming."

Emma shrugged. "The heart wants what it wants."

Thomas wanted to divert this conversation, afraid of where it might lead. "Are y'all ready to head back?"

"I think it's funny that you still say *y'all*." Finn had trouble pronouncing the word, and it came out more like *yaw*. "You've lived here most of your life."

Thomas put on an empty smile. Between worrying about Luka and how badly he expected his mother to respond to this situation, he was having difficulty attaching humor to anything right now.

4

AGATHA

THE FRONT DOOR CLOSED QUIETLY. Agatha expected next to hear a pronouncement from Thomas about how hungry he was. Then they would have their usual exchange that she wasn't his servant, nor was she a restaurant, so he could scrounge around in the pantry and make something for himself. But there was none of that. He was quiet as a field mouse.

"Thomas?" she called.

"It's me. I'm in here."

She walked from her room at the back of the small house to the family room. Thomas sat in the reading chair. He had propped his elbows on his knees and buried his face in his hands.

"What's wrong, buddy?"

"I messed up."

"I'm sure it's not so bad." Agatha shook her head as she sat down beside him on the arm of the chair and started patting his back lightly. *Why do parents always do that, especially when we don't yet know what the problem is?*

He still hadn't looked up, and his answers were muffled. "No, it's really bad. You're going to be mad."

"What's her name?"

Thomas popped his head up. "What?! No. This isn't about a girl. It's about Luka."

"What about him? Did y'all have a falling out?"

"Not exactly."

Agatha stopped patting his back and crossed her arms. "Well, maybe you should just tell me already instead of hem-hawing about."

Thomas scrunched his eyes. "Hem-hawing? What does that even mean?"

"It's when you won't just say something because you're afraid of what'll happen if you do. Now get to it."

"We were sparring and—"

"Sparring?!" Agatha stood up, both her volume and blood pressure rising. "How many times have we talked about this?"

Thomas pushed up from the chair. He was tall enough now that she had to look up at him.

"Sit down." She pointed at the chair. "I don't want to be looking up at you while I'm fussing at you."

He sat down and snickered. He tried to cover it up, but couldn't.

"What? What's so funny?" She was angry and red-faced now.

"Nothing," he said, a grin still pulling at the corners of his mouth. "Nothing is funny. I know this is serious. But I don't know. Something just kind of struck me funny." His expression finally sobered up. "Plus, I haven't even told you the bad part yet."

She raised her eyebrows at him. Both a question and a demand without being encumbered by words.

"I burned him. Really bad. He threw a sheet of ice under my feet, and I slipped while I was spitting fire. And I guess it flew up. I don't know. I hit my head when I landed and was out for a while."

"Is he okay?"

"I think he will be. Emma patched him up as best she could, and Finn's brother took him to Frau Vogel."

"Good. You okay?"

"I guess so. Emma took my headache away. I just feel terrible. When I went over there … I mean, I could have killed him. He's going to have a scar from his hip to his shoulder."

Agatha set her jaw, weighing how to handle this. It was so much easier when he was little. Now so much of parenting was evaluating whether to get involved and how much so. Balancing active teaching moments with allowing him to learn from his own mistakes. And the fervor that he attacked his interests with was incredible, but the lack of wisdom was astounding. She missed snuggle time, too. When he was just a tiny baby, he would nap on her chest at night before that last bottle, then go down for the night. Well, *for the night* wasn't quite right; it was usually only three to four hours at a time. When they'd gotten to six-hour sleeping stints, it was like a miracle.

But that's not where they were right now. Now, she didn't have any idea what was best.

Agatha started walking back toward her room. "Go change your clothes. We're going to visit Elle. And don't put those clothes in the hamper until you've rinsed them first. They'll ruin anything they touch."

"So … you're not mad?"

She stopped.

"Thomas, I'm fuming. You almost killed your friend because y'all were playing a stupid game. But I don't know what to do about it. And I'm hoping this weighs pretty heavy on you so we don't ever have to have a conversation like this again. So maybe that's enough. Regardless, I've got to finish getting ready so we can go visit your aunt."

"It was just an accident," Thomas offered as a half-hearted defense.

"I have no doubt that's true. But you and Luka put yourselves in a position where something terrible could accidentally happen. Now, did you really need me to explain that to you?"

Thomas dropped his eyes and shook his head.

"Good. We're leaving in twenty."

On the walk over, Thomas said, "We just saw her a couple of weeks ago."

"And?"

"Well, I mean, she doesn't even know we're there. So why does it matter if we visit her?"

"It matters to me. You and your oma and Elle are all the family I have in the world. So it doesn't matter that she can't respond. That she can't hear me. Or that she'll never know I was there. I'll know. And it's all I can do for her. So it's what I'm going to do."

"But why do I have to come?"

"Because one day family is going to be more important to you than it is now."

"Can you at least tell me what happened to her?"

Agatha sighed, "Buddy, I don't think I'm ready for that yet."

"That's what you always say."

"Well, there's something to be said for consistency, right?" she offered with a grin.

Thomas rolled his eyes. She accepted it without comment. She deserved it this time. He was old enough to hear it. She just wasn't ready to re-open those old wounds yet.

She was more than happy to turn off of Hauptstrasse onto Am Schofferpark, where the salmon facade of the Stephanus-Haus nursing home presented itself in front of them. She was less than a hundred meters away from being able to table this conversation ... again.

Thomas didn't press the issue.

They walked up to the front doors, and Agatha pressed a

doorbell. A second later, a buzzing sound informed them the magnetic lock had been disengaged and they could enter.

Inside, the receptionist at the front desk greeted them. "Guten tag, Frau Wande and Sie Thomas."

Agatha smiled. "Hallo, Emilia."

Thomas waved.

"She's in the blumengarten today. You know the way?"

"We do. Danke."

Agatha and Thomas took a left down the hallway. There were patient rooms — no, they called them residents here — on either side. Some residents adorned their doors with artwork or pictures of family. Others' doors were bare. Agatha's heart broke a little for them, abandoned here with the only attention given them coming from those paid to attend to their needs.

As they walked, the florescent lighting gave way to sunlight. A bank of full-length windows on the right revealed a cloudless sky and a well-manicured garden, housing trees, flowers, and a lush lawn.

Agatha pushed open the door, a chorus of birdsong greeting her. Really, it was more a cacophony than a choir, as if a group of small children had picked up a roomful of instruments they didn't know how to play.

Elle's attendant spotted them immediately and waved. Agatha smiled back at her and began walking in their direction. Thomas followed.

"Hallo, Marta," Agatha greeted her.

"Guten tag. Isn't it lovely out today?"

"Yes, it's very nice."

Marta shooed away a butterfly that danced on Elle's right arm. It did not flee, but instead alighted on her other arm, as if knowing it was just out of convenient reach. Marta got up and fussed at it, swatting at it with the back of her hand.

She saw Thomas looking at her quizzically and said, "Can't be letting it give our sweet Elle nightmares."

Thomas knitted his brow together.

"Don't you know about alps, Thomas?"

He shrugged. "No."

"Alps are awful creatures that bring nightmares. They sit on your chest while you're sleeping so you feel like you can't breathe, and sometimes leave a sensation of paralysis. And they particularly like to trouble women, because they like to drink the blood from their breasts."

"That's weird," Thomas said.

Marta continued, "During the daytime, the alps can turn into other animals, like butterflies. So we're not going to take any chances about that one being a nasty creature that gives our sweet Elle alpstraum tonight. Did you see her finger twitch when the butterfly landed on her arm? That's because it was an evil spirit."

Thomas was skeptical. "Maybe it just tickled?"

"Perhaps. But not a risk I'm going to take. She's got enough on her mind as it is." She patted Elle's arm reassuringly and stood up from the bench. "Shall I leave her to you?"

"Yes, that would be lovely. Danke. How has she been?"

"Very agitated the last couple of days. This is the only place she relaxes. We have been out here most of the day today."

"I hope that isn't inconvenient for you," Agatha offered.

Marta beamed at her. "I would stay outside all day of every day if I could. I just push her along the paths and tell her all about the world around her. You can see her relax as we go. She unclenches her fists. Her posture becomes less rigid. Then we sit and watch and listen for a time. These are the best parts of my workday."

"That's sweet of you to say."

"I'll come back around after while," Marta said.

As she walked away, Agatha squatted down in front of Elle. Her knees popped. "This was much easier when I was in my thirties."

Thomas shrugged. "You're getting old, Mom."

"Watch it," she warned with a smile.

"Do you think she believes all that stuff?"

"Marta? Who knows? She strikes me as a bit … fanciful."

"That's a nice way to put it," Thomas said.

"What can I say — I'm working on being nicer. How would you have said it?"

"She's nuts."

"Maybe, bud, but weirder things have happened," she said with a wink.

Agatha unclasped the straps that kept Elle's arms in place. Gently, one arm at a time, she moved Elle's arms so that her hands rested in her lap. Agatha kept her hands over her sister's, hoping against hope to sense some movement, some sign of recognition. Of life. She'd been trapped in her unresponsive body since long before Thomas had been born.

"She would hate to be sitting upright and proper all the time," Agatha remarked. "She was always such a slouch. Oma was always fussing at her about her posture. She never sat like this. Her legs were always crossed or tucked up under her. I can't tell you the number of times Oma would say, 'Elle, sit like a lady. You don't want people to see your underwear, do you?' And Elle would just lift up her dress and flash her. She thought it was hysterical. It was worth the trouble she was going to get in."

Thomas laughed. He loved hearing these stories, and she enjoyed telling them, remembering that there had been times with so much more joy and vibrancy. He had so few stories of his own about his family. It had been ripped away from him. In a life with plenty of regrets, her biggest one was agreeing to take a separate path from Joseph down in that mine shaft.

Thomas deserved to hear the family stories. Both the ones full of warmth and laughter, and the others.

Still squatting in front of Elle and holding her hands, Agatha rested her head against her sister's knees. In any other world, the older sister would have placed a reassuring hand on her little sister's head. But not in this one.

"Thomas," he looked up from his phone, "I'm going to tell you what happened to Elle."

"Really?"

"Yes. It's time."

He shoved his phone in his pocket. He'd been waiting most of his life to hear this tale.

5

AGATHA

ELLE PARKED the car at the bottom of the terraced walkway. Before she popped out, she squeezed Agatha's wrist and said, "Isn't it extraordinary?"

It was extraordinary. They sat in the car for a minute as the engine popped and cooled, taking in the scene. Flowers exploded around the Spanish Colonial manor. Its terracotta roof glimmered with dew in the soft light of the sunrise. Ivy embraced the turreted entrance, obliterating the stucco facade, and crept outward. Its tendrils tapped on the stained-glass windows seeking purchase.

After swinging her legs out of the car and standing up, Agatha hitched at the dress she'd clearly slept in, trying to give her legs another inch or two of coverage. She snagged her jacket out of the floorboard and zipped it. Despite being well into spring, the morning was unseasonably cool. She yawned loudly and stretched her arms over her head. "I mean, yeah, it's pretty. But did we have to get here so early? The wedding isn't for like eight more hours."

"Well, little miss club rat, it wouldn't feel quite as early if you hadn't been out so late."

"Whatever. And for your information, I wasn't partying. I met a boy, and we went out."

"Are you going to keep this one around for more than a couple of weeks?" Elle teased.

"I'll have you know … I'm not telling you anything until you get me inside out of the cold and I get some coffee. I don't live in Birmingham so that I can be this cold in mid-April."

Elle sighed in exasperation. "You know, for someone who's supposed to be such a badass, you're kind of high maintenance."

She snagged Agatha's elbow, and they walked arm-in-arm up the brick pavers to the front of the manor.

"So, am I acquainted with this new beau of yours?"

"Nope."

"Is he coming to the wedding?"

Agatha looked at her older sister dismissively. "Please. I mean, I like him, but there's no way I'm bringing him around all y'all. Besides, he's not zauber, so this isn't really his scene."

Elle grinned at her as they walked, "Oh, Mom's gonna love that."

Agatha stopped, grabbing Elle's hand and pulling her to a stop as well. "Can we not make anything today about me? Please. That can be your bridesmaid gift to me. Just let me be a wallflower."

"You're darn right. This day is all about me. And we're keeping it that way. Now, come on."

They walked across the Spanish tile that made up the court-yard and stopped at the red front door.

"Should we knock?" Elle asked as she raised her fist.

"No," Agatha pushed her arm down. "The key to getting away with anything is walking in like you own the place."

"I'm not trying to get away with anything. I just want to get to the dressing room."

"Whatever." Agatha opened the door and pushed in. Elle followed, her steps a little less certain.

"Where do we go?" Agatha asked as they stood in the foyer.

"I'm not sure," Elle answered quietly. "When Mom and I toured the place, we came in through a different entrance."

"Okay, so the other key to getting away with being in a place is knowing where you're going."

Elle made a sour face and shrugged.

"Well, there's only one thing to do now," Agatha said. She called out, "Hello? Anybody home?"

Elle's cheeks flushed. "I regret bringing you."

"Oh, don't think I don't regret it too. I would have been in my cozy bed for like another four hours."

Footsteps scuffed against the tile floor in a hallway hidden from their view. The proprietor rounded the corner in a pair of sweatpants and an oversized shirt with the venue's name and logo across it, Gabrella Manor. She still had rollers in her hair.

When she saw her guests, she plastered on a smile.

"Ah, Ms. Strom, how nice to see you. Pardon my appearance. We weren't expecting you for …" she checked her watch, "another couple of hours. But never mind that. Let me show you to the bridal chamber. It's all ready for you. And you must be the sister?"

"I am the sister," Agatha acknowledged. "Though right now, I'm the irritated sister." She turned to Elle. "A couple more hours?"

Elle stared back at her without remorse. "Couldn't take any chances on you being late."

"Well, you certainly cut that off at the pass. Now we just have to worry about me needing a nap."

"I'm so sorry, Mrs. Stevens," Elle said. "I'm just a little nervous."

"Don't you worry yourself about a thing. Happens often enough. Follow me."

She spun in her house shoes and led them to a staircase with an iron railing. "Just take these stairs, and you'll find your rooms at the end of the hallway. I'll be up with some mimosas and breakfast before too long."

"Breakfast sounds amazing. I'm totally starving. I could eat a horse," Agatha said.

Elle rolled her eyes. "You're such a savage. Come on before you do something really embarrassing."

Mrs. Stevens reapplied her smile and gestured for them to head up.

"I don't think she likes me," Agatha whispered as they took the stairs.

"You do lack a certain refinement. Besides, I don't even like you about half the time," Elle teased.

"Shut up. You adore me."

"Yes, but that's not the same thing as liking you."

As they ascended the stairs, Agatha said, "I've been meaning to ask you — what's it like to … you know … with a giant?"

Elle's eyes widened. "Agatha, geez! Don't be crass."

"Crass? You're my sister. Who else am I going to ask?"

"Don't you have girlfriends you hang out with?"

They reached the top of the stairs and began passing portraits of happily wedded brides that decorated the hallway leading to the bridal chambers.

Agatha answered, "Umm, no. I spend too much of my time hunting down bad guys with your humongous fiancé to be having slumber parties and pillow fights. So are you going to answer the question or keep avoiding it?"

Elle put her hand on the doorknob and stopped. She looked Agatha directly in the face with a haughty grin, "Obi is—"

"Don't call him that."

"I thought you'd be amused."

"I'm not. Martha didn't go around calling George Washington 'Prez' to all his friends."

"Fine. Athos is old-fashioned like that. We're waiting."

Agatha's jaw fell open. "So you've never?"

"No."

"Not once?"

"Not once." Elle grinned and flung her hair as she turned and opened the door with a flourish.

Even Agatha was hushed as she took in the scene. Elegant mirrors adorned the walls. Beautiful sofas offered seating around the room. They might even have been comfortable, though that didn't appear to be their primary function. Early morning light glittered through the stained-glass window on the far wall. Elle's gown hung in front of it, its simple elegance on full display. A dress intended to accent the beauty of its bride rather than bring undue attention to itself.

Agatha grabbed her sister's hand. "It's all so beautiful."

Elle's eyes sparkled with tears.

Agatha pulled her in for a hug. "I'm so happy for you."

Elle squeezed her tight. "Thanks, Sis. Love you."

"Even if you did make me get up at the butt crack of dawn."

"Uhhhh," Elle grunted in frustration and pushed Agatha away, who was clearly amused with herself. "Can't we just have one moment?"

"No. No, we can't," Agatha answered, shaking her head. "Moments aren't really my thing."

Elle's eyes landed on a chair that sat in the middle of the room. It hadn't been there when they'd toured the place looking for venues. It was made of walnut. The arms and back were overlaid with gold. Its creator had inlaid mother-of-pearl in beautiful patterns on the seat and chair back. The arm swooped down toward the seat, almost forming a brazier. The legs flare out in a convex arc. When viewed from afar, the arms and legs mimicked a woman's hips and torso.

"Look at it, Agatha. It's beautiful."

Elle stepped to the chair, trailing her hand on it as she circled it in admiration.

"Yeah, I mean, it's pretty fancy."

"It's a Savonarola."

Agatha stepped forward to plop herself down on it.

"Don't you dare," Elle warned. "I want to see it, experience it."

"Oh, my gosh. When did you get so high falutin'? Besides, it's probably not comfortable. It doesn't even have a cushion."

Enchanted by the piece of furniture, Elle shrugged the criticism away. "Do you think Athos made this for me?"

"I've never known him to do, like, woodworking, but ... maybe? Could be he just got it at an antique store."

"No," Elle argued with a strange ferocity. "He made it."

Agatha showed her palms in surrender. Once Elle decided something, it'd be easier to alter the earth's orbit than to change her mind. "Fine. Whatever. No need to get all weird and defensive about it."

If ever there was a day to concede some trivial point rather than push it to an unnecessary argument, today was that day. Elle had forgiven her a good many things, but pissing her off on her wedding day may be a bridge too far.

But she was tiring of watching Elle fawn over the thing. "Are you just going to caress that thing all morning, or are you going to actually sit in it?"

"Do you think I should?"

"It's a chair. What else would you do with it?"

"Yeah," Elle agreed. She walked back around to the front and sat timidly before fidgeting to find the most comfortable position.

"Well?" Agatha prompted.

"It's beautiful," Elle repeated, trying to leave unstated that it was uncomfortable.

Agatha inferred it anyway and started laughing.

Elle smiled in embarrassment, but her expression became troubled.

"Agatha, something's wrong," Elle struggled against the chair. "I can't …"

When she trailed off, Agatha asked, "Can't wha—"

Golden chains erupted out of the chair like serpents. They coiled around Elle's arms, legs, and chest, binding her to the chair. They inched tighter the more she fought against them.

Agatha found that she held fire in her hands and had backpedaled to the wall behind her so that nothing could sneak up on her. But there was no enemy. Nothing except the chains that fastened her sister to the chair.

Elle's breathing became ragged and uncontrolled.

Agatha extinguished her engulfed hands and rushed to her. "It's okay, Sis. It's going to be okay. I'll call Oberhaupt."

She reached for the phone in her clutch. But before she could do more, a portal opened several feet behind Elle, who saw the fear wash over Agatha's face.

"What? What is it?" she demanded.

A hulking figure stepped through the portal. He brought with him an odor of sweat and sulfur. He wore his welder's apron. His hammer hung at his waist. When he stood fully upright, his unkempt mane of hair brushed the ten-foot ceilings. Vulcan flinched at the near-impact. "That was close," he smiled as if greeting old friends.

Elle's face became ashen.

Summoning from the energy that swirled around her, Agatha called the fire back to her hands.

Vulcan wagged a finger at her. "No, ma'am. You may land a blow, but I will crush her skull before you can do more than that."

Elle whimpered.

"Dear sweet Elle," he said, "getting dragged into this through no fault of her own. A victim of circumstance. Well, circumstance and her little sister's meddling." He circled around to where Elle could see him. "Do you at least like my wedding present? I worked on it a long time. It's one of my finest pieces. Not that you'll get to have a wedding, you understand."

Elle let out a guttural groan, and her body sagged.

"Well, that's disappointing," Vulcan remarked. "I was hoping for more fight. More moxie. Guess that all went to you," he said, addressing Agatha.

She reverberated with a primal rage that she barely contained.

Recognizing the threat, even if he believed himself impervious to it as he'd said, Vulcan pointed at Agatha and moved away. He positioned himself back between Elle and the portal that he'd left open.

"I want you to appreciate my contraption. I think it's clever. And it's not the first time I've used it either. My mother abandoned me when I was a baby because I was hideous. Not that I'm beautiful now — I mean, I wouldn't score well on Hot or Not — but I'm less monstrous anyway. Imagine what that does to a child — it's not good, I can tell you. When I got older and she learned about my skills, she wanted to reclaim me. I went along with it for a while. Then I made her a chair much like this one. Left her chained to it for a couple of days so she could ruminate on her decisions. Eventually, her husband figured out how to break her out. She hasn't spoken to me since.

"You've done this to yourself, just like she did. You and your giant friend. Always hassling me. Always interfering. I've had quite enough of it. And now there's going to be hell to pay. But it won't be you who pays. I know you, and you'd think it was worth the price. It's going to be her. That way you have to bear it the rest of your miserable life."

He grabbed the back of the chair with his left hand and started dragging it toward the portal.

Agatha rushed him and lunged. She didn't have a plan, hadn't given any thought to her attack. She was going on instinct and training.

Vulcan's counterattack was faster than she could have imagined and left her with no time to react. He whipped the hammer from his belt and swung it forward, landing a crushing blow against her ribs. She landed in a heap, unconscious.

When Agatha came to, she was the room's only occupant. Elle, her chair, and Vulcan had vanished. She couldn't breathe or move without a piercing pain like she'd never experienced before.

She groped around on the floor for her phone and punched some buttons. When a deep voice answered, she croaked, "O, he took her. You need to get here quick."

Thomas was stunned, but when Agatha didn't say anything else for a while, he asked, "So what happened to her?"

"I don't know," she said hoarsely, and cleared her throat. After a quarter of a century, she still could not shake the guilt she wore about it all. She'd replayed it thousands of times looking for things she could or should have done differently. Should she have known the chair was a trap? Could she have kept Elle from sitting in it?

"What do you mean?" Thomas pried.

"The woman from Gabrella Manor called me three days later, panicking. They'd gone up to the bridal chamber to start cleaning it for the next event. And when they opened the door, Elle was sitting there on that throne he'd built. Not moving. Not responsive. Not a mark on her. Nothing." Agatha looked from Thomas back to Elle. "And this is how she's been ever since."

"What did he do to her?"

"I don't know. Part of me doesn't want to. Which is just as well, I guess, since I don't think we ever will."

"But didn't you look for her?"

"We had people scouring the earth for her in those three

days. We enlisted help from zauberi around the world. There was no hint of her anywhere. And then in the weeks and months afterward, we waged war against Vulcan's people. There was much bloodshed. But we never came close to him." Agatha hated admitting it. The failure had led to so much more heartache. "Not until many years later."

"When he kidnapped me?"

She nodded and brushed Elle's hand. It spasmed briefly. She still hadn't become immune to the hope that the spasms were conscious movements, not just some twitchy nerve thing. The doctors had long warned her away from such wishes. But hope dies hard in the heart of one desperate for redemption.

6

THOMAS

THOMAS PULLED at the front doors of Evangelische Kirche, expecting to find them locked. They weren't. He stumbled backward slightly from the ease with which the doors opened and shifted his feet to balance himself. He entered the foyer. The lights were off, but there were no signs telling him not to be there. He stepped in, allowing the door to close behind him.

The foyer was sparsely decorated. To his left was a table with some pamphlets on it. Above it was a corkboard with announcements. There was a stairwell to his right. Moderately comfortable that he wasn't about to be expelled from the church, Thomas crossed the small anteroom to the double doors that led to the sanctuary.

He peered through the window of the right-hand door. The lights were off in there as well. But the sunlight that filtered through the stained-glass windows on either side of the nave gave it a soft, warm glow. He tried this door as well. It yielded.

Thomas had lived in Hornberg since he was six, but he'd never been in a church before. There were several in town. He had friends that attended, but he and Agatha did not. It's not that she had forbidden him to do so. It was just a complete non-issue for her. He hadn't even been curious about church before, and he was uncertain what brought him here now.

The sanctuary was small. It probably wouldn't seat more than two hundred people, and then only if they were pressed shoulder-to-shoulder on the pews. The auditorium at school was larger than this. But he found it to be warm, inviting even, whereas the school auditorium was just a shell. It had no atmosphere about it.

Thomas walked toward the front, allowing his right hand to bounce against each pew as he passed it. He settled into a seat and continued looking around.

On the left side of the platform was a plain pulpit for the pastor to stand behind. Behind the pulpit was a loft for a small choir. Above it, there hung a large wooden cross. He would have expected something more ornate. So many of the churches he saw pictures of were grand and gaudy. This one was not. If anything, it was understated.

When a hand landed on Thomas' shoulder, he nearly jumped out of his skin and was yanked out of his rumination. He looked up to see a man standing over him.

The man asked, "Can I sit down beside you?"

Thomas scooted over from his place at the end of the pew. As the man sat, he asked, "You're Thomas Wande, aren't you?"

"How did you know?" Thomas asked.

The man smiled. "I am a shepherd, and you are a sheep. It's my job to know all the sheep, regardless of whether they're part of my flock."

Thomas didn't know what to say. So he said nothing.

"Also, your grandmother attends here from time to time." The man smiled again. "I am Pastor Stefan. This is my church. Well, not my church exactly. But it is where I minister. This is just a building. The church is the people."

Thomas asked, "Is it okay that I'm here?"

"Of course. It's why I keep the doors open."

Thomas nodded. He took stock of the man, wondering about him being dressed in a plaid shirt and some pants, rather than some kind of robes.

Pastor Stefan said, "I haven't seen you here before. What brings you in today?"

Thomas became shy. "I don't know. There's just a lot going on right now."

Pastor Stefan nodded. "Difficult times bring a good many people through those doors."

Thomas was uncertain how to proceed. He didn't know this man, but something about him compelled Thomas to open up to him. To share things he wouldn't tell other people. As Thomas worked through how to proceed, the pastor let him have his silence.

"I accidentally hurt my friend. We were horsing around and got carried away. Now he's hurt pretty bad."

"These things happen. Boys will be boys, as they say."

"But that's not all," Thomas added. "I learned some things about my aunt today that are pretty messed up."

"It is in the nature of family to be difficult. We do not get to choose each other. And family are often very different from one another, yet there we are all thrown into the same pot," the pastor said. "Is there anything I can do to help?"

Thomas answered, "I just came here to have some time to think."

"Would you like me to leave you alone?"

Thomas considered the question carefully before answering. Despite the man having some sort of answer for everything, which was mildly annoying, Thomas found his presence unexpectedly comforting. "I don't think so."

The pastor sat back and melded with the pew more fully now that he was being permitted to stay.

"We took my friend to Frau Vogel instead of to the hospital."

Thomas was testing the pastor to see how he would respond to the new information.

"That is sensible. She is the person best situated to handle most of the injuries that happen around here."

"Is that why we don't have a proper hospital in town?" Thomas asked.

"I suspect that has something to do with it."

Thomas asked, "Does knowing that people are zauber ... I don't really know how to ask this." Thomas shifted in his seat. He had gotten himself into an uncomfortable spot.

"You may ask your question," Pastor Stefan encouraged.

"Okay," Thomas said sheepishly, unable to make eye contact. "Does it affect your religion or God or whatever?"

Pastor Stefan grinned. "Many people want to know that. The answer is no. We are all God's creatures. We each have different gifts. And if we are believers, those gifts can be used to serve the body of Christ. We should use our können — whatever they are — to bring glory to God and not to ourselves. So your gifts as a zauber are no different from physical or intellectual gifts or gifts of empathy that another might have."

Thomas chewed on that for a minute. He didn't know enough about God to know whether he agreed or not. "Are you zauber?"

"I am not."

Thomas blinked in surprise. "I thought everybody who lived in this town was."

"They make exceptions for us clergy. We are chosen specifically based on our ability to adapt to these peculiar situations in towns like this. Seminary prepares us for many things, but not necessarily for all the situations that can arise in these unique places. Not that there aren't surprises elsewhere as well."

Something about what he said didn't ring true. It didn't jibe with his understanding of how the charms that enchanted the town worked. But something else struck him before he could dwell on that further. "There are others?"

"Towns like this one? Of course there are," Pastor Stefan answered. "Surely you didn't think this was the only place where zauberi congregate and live together?"

"I guess I hadn't really thought about it before."

Redirecting the conversation, the pastor asked, "I would like to pray for your friend, if that's okay?"

"Umm, sure, I guess. If it's not an imposition."

"Not at all. What is his name?"

Thomas hedged. He was reconsidering how much more he wanted to share. He stood up abruptly. "I just remembered I need to get home. You know, curfew."

Pastor Stefan looked at his watch with obvious amusement and skepticism. Instead of calling Thomas out, he stood as well. "Of course," he said, and sidestepped into the center aisle. "Feel free to come back whenever you like. I enjoyed our conversation."

"Yeah, okay. Thanks." Thomas entered the aisle and left the way he'd come. He paused to look back once he'd reached the back of the sanctuary. Pastor Stefan was standing in the same spot, his hand resting on a pew. Thomas waved awkwardly and pushed open the door to the foyer.

7

THOMAS

THOMAS WAITED at the front door, his nerves frayed and buzzing. When footsteps approached from inside the house, he tensed further.

Luka's mother answered. "Hallo, Thomas. It's been quiet in this house without having you around the last couple days."

Thomas looked at his feet instead of at her. "I didn't know if ... you know ... you'd want me here."

Frau Fischer placed her hands on his cheeks. "You two have been best friends for most of your lives. You're more a brother than a friend. It's going to take more than an accident like that to get you kicked out of this house."

"Okay. But I thought I had killed him."

"Killed? No. He'll be fine, and don't let him tell you otherwise."

Thomas was incredulous. He hadn't texted or called since everything had happened. And then the thing with Aunt Elle. He'd just been kind of a mess. "So he's going to be okay?"

"Ja. Ja. Come on. He's in his room." They started walking toward Luka's room. Frau Fischer stopped before they got there and turned around. "I better warn you — Lea is here. She's been

45

here *a lot*. And she may be slower to forgive than me. Are they together?"

"Honestly, I don't know. It's news to me. But it may be more her than him. She was pretty upset when … uhh … it happened."

Luka's mom asked, "Can I tell you a secret, Thomas?"

He nodded, even though the situation made him feel squeamish.

She whispered, "I don't really like her."

Thomas laughed as some of the tension fell off him, even though he was still nervous about the reception that Luka would give him.

She pushed Luka's door open and gestured for Thomas to enter. Luka and Lea sat on the bed beside each other, their backs against the far wall. Luka was shirtless, with a sash of shiny, new pink skin across his torso.

"Hey, man! How's it going?" Luka greeted.

Lea scowled at him. "What are *you* doing here?"

Thomas' nerves seized up again. But Luka laughed and put his hand on Lea's leg. "Go easy. It was just an accident. Besides, it was kind of my fault. Could've happened to anybody."

"But it didn't happen to anybody. It happened to you." Lea turned a glaring eye at a baffled Thomas.

"What the heck is going on here? It's been like forty-eight hours since I saw you. Are you two a thing?"

"No—"

"Yes," Lea affirmed, then turned on Luka. "Did you say no?"

Fear showed in his eyes.

"No. I mean, yes. But …"

He turned to Thomas, silently pleading for help. Thomas offered none, and his eyes twinkled as he watched his friend flail about.

Lea heaved a sigh. "Whatever. I have to go to the loo."

She pushed herself off the bed and brushed past Thomas on

her way out, slamming the door behind her. Thomas flinched at the noise.

"You doing okay?" he asked.

"Yeah, but my dad said he'd murder us both if we do that again. Oh, speaking of — did your mom tell you?"

"Tell me what?"

"She didn't tell you?!"

Thomas crossed his arms. "I don't have any idea what you're talking about."

"Sit down, my friend. I have a story for you. But we gotta keep it quiet for now. They're trying to keep a lid on it until they can figure some things out."

"Got it." Thomas plopped down on Luka's gaming chair.

"Your mom found a dead woman by the railroad tracks."

"What? When?" That's not what he'd been expecting.

"A few nights ago. Maybe a couple of weeks before this happened." He gestured at his chest. "Was that the night it rained?"

"I don't know," Thomas growled at Luka's propensity to get lost in inconsequential details. "But why was my mom by the railroad tracks?"

Luka shrugged. "I think she was on a walk and just saw the woman down there, so she checked it out."

"So what hap—"

Lea opened the door. Both boys stopped and gaped at her.

"What?" Lea asked.

Luka plucked up his courage. "I'm kind of telling Thomas about something."

"So. What you can tell him, you can tell me."

Luka waffled. "Umm ... not really. Not this time."

Lea's face flushed. She spun on her heel and walked out. Neither of the boys moved, waiting for what came next. The house shuddered when Lea slammed the front door.

"So," Thomas grinned, "you and Lea?"

"Shut up."

"Alright, so what happened to this woman?"

"Somebody killed her," Luka answered.

"Yeah, I got that. How?"

"Oh. Strangled her to death."

Thomas' eyes widened. "Geez. That's brutal. How did you find all this out? Because I know your dad didn't tell you."

"Nah. He came in after he dropped me off this morning. But listen, that's not the worst of it. He like branded the woman or carved some symbol into her or something."

"Weird. What was it?"

"I don't know. They figured out I was listening."

"How did you give yourself away?" Thomas asked.

Luka protested, "I didn't say I gave myself away."

Thomas silently held his position.

Luka grinned. "I farted."

Thomas shook his head. "So was it the sound or the smell that announced you? You know what, it doesn't matter. You're a dummkopf. We could have way more information about this woman who got murdered except for you being unable to control your gaseous emissions."

His friend shrugged. There was no denying it.

"So what have you been doing while I've been here on my deathbed?"

"Oh, please. You get no sympathy from me. Because apparently, you've just been making out with Lea for two days."

"Don't hold that against me. It's part of the healing process," Luka cackled. Thomas grabbed the nearest pillow and chucked it across the room.

"Emma?" Luka asked.

Thomas shook his head. "Haven't seen her." He'd have to explain not being around, but he wasn't ready to tell Luka about Elle yet. Or about going to the church. So he made up a plausible excuse. "Grounded."

A lull fell on the room as the boys navigated the crevasse between conversation topics. Thomas weighed telling him about Elle, but wasn't ready for that. Luka didn't even know about Vulcan and Thomas' history. Agatha had forbidden him to ever tell anyone, and it had become so deeply embedded that that part of his life barely breached the surface of his memories any more. Until two days ago when she'd told him about Elle, which had been like exhuming a corpse. But it was twenty corpses. Kleron and the others. His father. He had used his können to fight Vulcan, but every time his mother had made him practice since, it had felt like he was dragging their rotting corpses out of the fire and putting them on display. Beyond that, any other use of it was strictly forbidden. Verboten. He was fine with that.

He tried to bury the memory again. He visualized making flowers and placed them on the skeletons that resided in his mind, covered them in dirt, and walked away. But when he turned around, there they stood huddled together, watching him go.

A snapping sound brought Thomas back to the present. Luka was snapping his fingers. "Whoa, man, where'd you go?"

Thomas shook his head and half-smiled. "I was just thinking about something."

"No kidding. I was trying to talk to you. But you had spaced."

Frau Fischer called from the other end of the house, "Thomas, are you staying for dinner?"

Thomas looked at Luka and whispered, "What are we having?"

Luka shrugged. "Does it matter? You eat everything she makes."

Thomas nodded and bellowed, "Yes, ma'am."

"Come on then, boys. It's ready."

AGATHA

WHEN AGATHA GOT off the train in Hausach, she looked at her watch. She had about thirty minutes until dinner. The walk would take her ten if she went straight there, so she had time to meander.

She took a left out of the station onto Eisenbahnstrasse. She passed the evangelical church and a dozen businesses before she found what she was looking for and walked across the canal. A road that left the major thoroughfare. It was little more than an alleyway that ran more-or-less parallel with Eisenbahnstrasse.

The clearing to her right gave her what she wanted, an uninterrupted view of the Kinzig. It wasn't much of a river, but it was more than the Gutach, which ran through Hornberg and emptied into the Kinzig somewhere above Hausach. In whatever city she found herself, she was drawn to water. Maybe it reminded her of Joseph, who loved water so much. Maybe it was the tranquility or the reminder of the possibility of being carried away to parts unknown. She wasn't usually the introspective sort who dug into all that messiness.

Her path took her behind the mini golf park. Families laughed and squealed, enjoying the last of the warm weather before autumn crept in. Siblings squabbled over whether a stroke counted.

Agatha distanced herself from the joviality as she walked. She turned right onto a bridge that spanned the Kinzig and stopped halfway across, resting her forearm against the railing. She watched the water shuffle around the stones in its bed, wearing them away grain by grain. What the water did to the stones, time was doing to her. But today was a good day. The beginning of a new thing. She would not become overly melancholy and morose. Maybe it would be best to just head on to the restaurant. Even if she were early, at least she wouldn't be melancholy. And perhaps go easy on the wine tonight too.

When she got back to the river road, Agatha hung a right instead of going back the way she'd come. It was a more circuitous route, but it would give her more time to get in the right frame of mind. She was surprised by the caravans and shanty houses that were sandwiched between the road and the railroad tracks on her left. The people that lived there must not know what an uninterrupted night's sleep was like. Of course, she didn't either. But that's because the demons of her past chased her into her dreams, not because a train barreled down the tracks just meters from her bed.

She hung a left at Einbacher Strasse, which carried her to Hauptstrasse and the quaint Germanic storefronts and architecture she'd come to love. Whitewashed facades, exposed beams, and A-frame roofs abounded. The occasional shop-owner had the courage to paint their store a shockingly bright pink or blue that would have looked more at home in the Nyhavn district in Copenhagen.

At St. Mauritius Catholic Cathedral, she paused, wanting to go in and admire it. She consulted her watch. Another time. The Akropolis Restaurant was ahead on the left, and it wouldn't do to keep Markus waiting. It had taken him long enough to ask her to dinner; she didn't want him to think he'd been stood up.

Once at the restaurant, she checked her reflection in the window. She looked a bit windblown, but not in a good way. She started brushing out her hair with her fingers and froze, realizing that anyone inside could see her.

Agatha opened the door and saw that Markus was already seated at a table. He was perpendicular to the entrance, so maybe he hadn't seen her little display outside. She explained to the host that she was meeting someone and walked past. Markus stood as she approached.

He greeted her with a smile. "Hallo, Agatha. I am pleased you could join me."

"Oh, are we going to be all formal and awkward now, like we barely know each other?"

His smile faltered as they sat. Watching him, she thought she may need to dial back the sarcasm a bit.

"I went ahead and ordered us a couple glasses of wine. I hope that is okay," he said.

"It's lovely. Thank you," she said. "Have you been waiting a while?"

"I have, but it's my own doing. I arrived rather early. Whatever the extreme side of punctual is, that is where I find myself."

Agatha reached out and touched his hand, "Then I already have concerns about whether we are a good match. I am chronically tardy."

"That is problematic," Markus said with a smile.

"How harshly are you going to judge me if I just get a gyro? I haven't had Greek food in a stone's age, and that's what I'm craving."

Markus rubbed at the five o'clock shadow on his chin. "Only mildly."

"Fair. What about if I put some of my French fries on it like this little gyro place in Naxos that I went to?"

"I think that moves us up to moderate judgment."

"I can live with that," she said.

Markus motioned the server over and placed their orders.

When he left, Agatha raised her eyebrows at Markus. "Lamb chops. Aren't you fancy?"

"It is my favorite dish. It matters not to me whether it is plebeian or patrician."

"That's why you'll tolerate my peasant food order, then. But I do have a question for you: how offended should I be that we had to come two towns over for you to have dinner with me?" Agatha asked, needling him.

Marcus balked, "That's not fair."

Agatha covered her face and peered between her fingers. "Is it because I'm hideous to look upon?"

"Hideous? You are gorgeous, truly prächtig."

"Easy does it. You're not getting laid tonight no matter how complimentary you are and regardless of how good the lamb is."

Markus opened his mouth to say something, then closed it again. She had flustered him, and she was enjoying it. Agatha couldn't recall the last time she'd had someone to flirt with. Well, she could. But she'd rather not right now.

"Are all American women as forward as you?" Marcus asked.

"Nein. I'm a special case."

Markus raised his glass of wine. "Here's to you and all your extraordinary ways."

It was nice to be flattered. She raised her glass. "Prost."

Before Markus got his glass to his mouth, he looked at his watch.

"Am I keeping you from something?" she continued to tease.

"I'm sorry. It's Detective Pereira. I have to take this."

He stood and pushed his chair back, raising his phone to his ear as he walked toward the front of the restaurant. Agatha watched him through the street-facing window. When he frowned and started delivering instructions, she motioned the server over.

"We're going to need those entrees to go. Something's come up."

He nodded curtly. "I will have it out to you promptly."

A minute later, Markus opened the door and strutted back to the table. His demeanor had changed.

"Everything okay?"

He shook his head.

"Luka?"

"Oh. No. Nothing like that," he answered.

"Good. I almost killed Thomas over that the other day."

"Eh," he waved it off. "I would be more disappointed if they weren't a little reckless in testing their limits."

Silence sat heavy between them as he weighed what to tell her.

"I'm afraid I'm going to have to cut dinner short. They found another body."

Agatha nodded. "Well, if they're already dead, I don't guess there's any need to rush."

"Agatha," he said, chastising her flippancy.

"I'm kidding. I already told the server that we'll need to take it with us. He should be out with it soon. But if you need to go, I can wait for it by myself."

"We can wait until it gets here. The body's not going anywhere, right?"

"That's the spirit. Did you drive or ride the train?"

"Drove. Would you like a ride back to town?"

"Yes, that would be nice," she said.

When the server brought a bag with their orders, Agatha said, "I bet you're wishing you'd ordered something you could eat by hand."

They stood up together and made their way to the door, which he held for her. Once on the street, he said, "You may have the wrong impression of me. I fully intend to grab that thing by the bone and tear into it like a true carnivore."

Agatha was delighted.

Markus stopped on the sidewalk. "Let me ask you something."

"Uh-oh. Is this where you discover something that causes you not to want to see me again?"

"That seems doubtful. Here's my question: you seem a bit more complex than just somebody who works at a tourist trap shop in town."

"I should hope so. Aren't most of us a little more complicated than the occupation we hold?"

"You know what I mean," he said. "Best I can tell, you didn't flinch when you found that woman the other night."

"It wasn't my first rodeo, if that's what you mean," Agatha said, a little guarded.

"I am unfamiliar with that expression, but I think I have the context for it. Were you law enforcement before you moved here?"

"More like paramilitary. We … uhh … dispatched with bad guys."

He nodded. "That explains some things."

She cocked her head to the side and raised an eyebrow.

A corner of his mouth turned up in a smile. "Only good things, I assure you. You just carry yourself a little differently. Have you ever done any investigative work before?"

"Not like what you do. But we did intelligence work. Hang on. Are you about to take me on a date to a murder scene? Because that's gonna be a first."

"I can always drop you at your house if you prefer. But I've got a feeling you might provide some insight about whatever's happening here."

"I'm not saying no. Just commenting on the uniqueness of the offer," she said.

"Good. The car is around the side of the building."

9

———

AGATHA

MARKUS STOPPED the car when they pulled up to the park. He was reaching for the door handle when Agatha asked, "Is it okay for me to be here?"

"There's something I wasn't expecting. I hadn't picked you for a rule follower."

Even in the fading sunlight, she figured he could see her blush. "As it happens, I like to think of myself as strategically non-compliant. Besides, the stakes were a little different when I was doing my thing. Those baddies were going to end up dead anyway. So adherence to protocol was just a matter of keeping me and my boys safe. There wasn't the prospect of some murderer getting off free because of a technicality."

"Two things then. One, we have a little more leeway than most police departments because our issues tend to be unique. None of the very few folks who know about the peculiarities of this town are particularly interested in getting involved in our local affairs. And two, you will not be handling any evidence, so I'm not worried about you fouling it up. Think of yourself as a consultant. Are we good?"

"We're good," Agatha answered.

56

They got out. Detective Pereira met them at the entrance to the park. He gave Agatha a hard look that she didn't shy away from.

"She's going to be a … uh … special adviser on this one," Fischer offered.

Pereira said nothing, but raised the police tape he'd used to cordon off access to the park. Several would-be park goers had congregated nearby. They peered at the trio and did their best to see what was causing such an uncommon commotion. Fortunately, there was enough distance and foliage between them and the body to keep them from seeing anything.

The lyrics of an old country song bubbled up from the depths of Agatha's memory, "Word gets around in a small, small town…." She realized that her being a part of this — being seen going to a crime scene with Fischer and Pereira — was itself unusual and wouldn't escape notice. She recognized some folks who had gathered, and though she didn't know their names, it always seemed that people knew who she was. Maybe that was a benefit of having been from the small town; you already know everybody, so it's easy to identify (and gossip about) the new arrivals. Hopefully, that's the way it would be for Thomas. In most every way but by birth, he was from here. Whereas she had never been able to fully integrate herself.

She would have to tell Thomas about working with Fischer on this. That would definitely get back to him. The information might even beat her home tonight. She may even have to tell him they were … dating? Is that what they were doing? She'd have to find a way to deflect anything that veered in that direction. She wasn't even really ready to think too much about it yet, much less talk to her teenager about her dating life. *That's just horrifying.*

"Agatha. Ready?" Fischer asked.

"Yeah, I'm good."

"You looked like you were far away?"

"I'm fine. Just wasn't prepared for spectators."

Fischer nodded. "They're an occupational hazard, I'm afraid. Like pigeons wherever there's food around."

She smiled at the analogy.

"Pereira tells me it's a pretty grim scene up here with the body. You sure you're up for this?"

"Yes, I'll be fine."

"Okay. We have about an hour before sunset. Let's see how much we can get done before then."

Agatha looked to the west. The light was already softening, yellowing. It would have been such a nice evening. And while nice was good, a part of her was almost giddy with the excitement of the investigation. The feeling almost repulsed her, or at least, she felt like it should have.

But if she were going to be of any use here, she had to get out of her own head for a bit. She could always play psychologist later, and she had no shortage of material to work with.

The walking path curved around a hedgerow and revealed a tarp lying next to a tree. As they approached, Agatha realized that the tree, rolling landscape, and shrubbery would have combined to form some semblance of privacy in three directions.

Pereira pointed in the direction of several numbered plastic cones. "Mind the evidence markers. I've only preliminarily photographed everything on my phone. The photographer will be here shortly."

After checking to make sure no spectators had breached the police tape, Pereira picked up one corner of the tarp and looked to Fischer, who nodded. Pereira popped the tarp directly up into the air and swiveled, letting it flutter to the ground behind him.

What it revealed was so much worse than what she had stumbled upon before. The body had most of its clothing cut away. The torso was stained red from the blood that had already coagulated on its surface. Its primary source was a slash across the young woman's throat that gaped because of the angle of her head, revealing cartilage and muscle.

Images of Joseph's body, torn by the chimera and covered in blood, imposed themselves on her. Agatha nearly lost her balance from the bout of dizziness that struck her. Darkness crowded her vision from the periphery and pushed inward. She took a step backward and flung out her hand to regain her balance.

As she turned her back to the splayed body, Agatha caught the skeptical and accusing look that Pereira flung toward Fischer. She squatted down and put a hand on the ground to balance herself.

"Agatha? Are you okay?" Fischer asked with concern.

Agatha held up her free hand. "Ja, just give me a minute."

She took several deep breaths. Both the dizziness and darkness receded. She pushed herself upright. Once she was sure of her footing again, she turned back to the two men. Their expressions couldn't have been more different. Pereira contemplated her with a stony indifference that wasn't quite contempt. Fischer wore a look of paternalistic worry that she immediately reviled.

Both had in common that they were contemplating her weakness. Maybe they were right. Had the intervening years since moving here softened her? She didn't think so. This was an aberration. Hopefully.

"Maybe this was a bad idea, Agatha," Fischer said, offering her an out.

"No, I'm fine. It just ..." She wasn't ready to tell them what had triggered the episode. She had never spoken of that moment with anyone. Oberhaupt knew. He had seen her in the moment of her great loss, Joseph's blood dripping from her clothes. And that was enough. "I'm fine."

She faced the body again and maintained her composure. She assessed it with a critical eye. The woman was young, mid-twenties maybe. Agatha didn't think she recognized her, though it was hard to tell.

Tracking downward, Agatha moved to the woman's chest. There were slash marks on her breasts. Between them, the killer had carved a symbol. Agatha immediately recognized that she had seen the same symbol on the woman's body that she'd found beside the railroad tracks.

Pointing, she asked, "What is that?"

"It's a witches' mark," Fischer answered. "In the Dark Ages, people used to carve them into the walls of churches and homes to ward off evil. There are lots of different varieties of them. This one, if you follow the arcs of what looks like flower petals, you can see that this is actually the intersection of six overlapping circles."

"He carved it into the other girl, too. Does it mean something?"

Pereira answered, "I'm sure it does. We don't know what yet."

Fischer squatted down and hovered his hand above the woman's chest, outlining a circle around the mark. "What he's done here is similar to a symbol that's been around these parts for a thousand years or more, called the Sun of the Alps. But it's seven conjoined circles. The seventh one would actually be centered and touch the points of this here. I'm sure that's not unintentional. But I don't know what it means to him. Pereira, make a note for us to do some digging on that."

Pereira nodded but didn't write anything into the notepad he had been scribbling in. Agatha figured he'd probably already written as much in there. He struck her as the sort of person who was a step ahead of everyone else.

Fischer pulled a black latex glove onto his left hand and pulled back gently at one of the slashes at the curve of her breast, revealing several layers of skin and the fatty tissue beneath. He looked up at Pereira. "Those are some pretty fine cuts. What do you think he used?"

"Razor blade. Box cutter. Something like that."

"Was she raped?" Agatha asked bluntly.

Pereira nodded. "I don't think so. The coroner can confirm it."

"Is she zauberi?"

"Yes, I went to school with her," Pereira answered. "A heilerin of middling ability, at best. I think she worked as a nurse."

Fischer stood from his squatting position, his knees popping as he rose. He winced. "Sorry to hear that, Miguel."

Pereira shrugged. "It's not like we were friends. She wasn't an agreeable person."

"I thought you said she was a nurse?" Fischer said.

"Haven't you heard of Nurse Ratched?" Agatha said. "Nurse and nice aren't necessarily synonyms."

Both men looked at her blankly.

"Neither of you? *One Flew Over the Cuckoo's Nest.* Jack Nicholson. Oh, my gosh. How old am I?"

"What about the other one?" Fischer asked.

"Also a heilerin. But not from town." Pereira said, then gestured over Agatha's shoulder. She turned to see a man and woman carrying cases of equipment, presumably to document the scene.

"Alright, I guess we'll get out of your hair."

Fischer indicated to Agatha that she should follow him. He greeted the personnel who were arriving. After they'd passed, Fischer offered, "How about I drive you home?"

"That's it? Dinner, a dead body, and we're done?"

"I ... uh ... am literally dumbstruck."

"I'm teasing, of course. I know you've got plenty of work to do, and I don't need to be escorted home."

"You're sure? I don't mind."

Agatha stopped walking and looked at him squarely. "This is the second time you've insisted I need watching over. So I want you to rest assured that I can take care of myself. I'm not worried about some guy who's preying on unsuspecting women. For most of my adult life, I was the predator."

Fischer gave an exaggerated shiver. "Well, that was terrifying. Now, I'm worried for him."

Agatha grinned, "As well you should be. Guten nacht, Polizeidirektor. I'll be seeing myself home now." Agatha turned without waiting for a response. The grin fell away. She was less confident than she had let on. But she would not be coddled. She would just have to be more vigilant than usual as the sky gradually dimmed toward dusk.

10

THOMAS

THOMAS ARRIVED home to find the house dark and quiet. Not wanting to be alone, he walked next door. Although the shades were drawn in the front rooms, yellow lamplight filtered through the edges. The setting sun warmed his neck, while a breeze told the rest of his body, which was encased in shadow, that nightfall would bring with it much cooler temperatures.

He grasped the handle and twisted, opening the front door without knocking. "Oma?"

"In the kitchen," she called from another room.

Thomas followed both the sound of her voice and the aroma of whatever treats she was cooking. Flour covered her apron, and egg shells littered the counter top.

"Hey, Oma."

"Oma? That's no way to treat a woman. What are you playing at, Vik?"

Thomas stopped where he was, arm still outstretched where he had intended to side hug his grandmother.

"Oma, it's me, Thomas."

"Always messing with me. It's not just any woman that'd put up with your nonsense, Viktor. You're lucky I'm a tolerant sort.

Else I'd kick you out and raise this baby on my own." She placed her hands over her belly like a pregnant woman would. "Elle and I were doing just fine before you came along, so I 'spect another mouth won't make much difference."

Thomas took two steps backward, retreating to the cased opening between the kitchen and dining room. His face was a mess of emotions, something between confusion and shock.

"Why don't you come make it up to Gerty?" She approached Thomas with her arms outstretched, ready to wrap around his waist.

Thomas backpedaled further, bumping into a dining room chair. A wave of nausea accompanied his growing confusion. He was at risk of being overwhelmed. "I gotta go, Oma. I'll see you tomorrow."

He fled to the front door.

In a fit of sudden fury, Gertrude screamed, "Run away then, you titanic bastard! It's all you've ever done. And don't you bother coming back."

Thomas yanked the door open and pulled it closed behind him. He halted on the other side. *What the hell just happened?* He squatted down and buried his forehead in his palms. He needed a minute to collect himself.

Several deep breaths later, Thomas pushed himself up and walked home to a still-darkened house. He unlocked the front door and shoved it open. He trudged over to the chair in the corner of the room and flung himself down without turning on any lights.

When the door handle jangled sometime later, only the light from the streetlamp that filtered through the blinds provided any illumination into the room. Agatha entered and immediately turned to lock the door behind her. She flipped a switch on the wall as she turned into the room.

Agatha started, inhaling sharply when she finally saw Thomas. Her left hand flew to her heart. Thomas flicked his eyes down to her right hand. She looked down too, extinguishing the flame she found herself holding. "Sorry. Old habit. You scared me, bud. Why are you sitting here in the dark? That's kind of weird."

Thomas didn't answer her question, but instead asked his own. "Where have you been?"

Agatha bristled at what sounded more like an accusation than a question. "Out."

"That's not an answer."

Agatha's demeanor changed to match her terse answer. "Nor are you in a position to be demanding them."

Thomas didn't care that she was angry and gave no thought to any recourse for his own disposition. "Who is Vik?"

The transition from anger to confusion was immediate. Agatha narrowed her eyes. "Who?"

"Vik. Who is Vik?" he insisted.

"Bud, I don't have any idea what you're talking about. And I really can't deal with … whatever this is, right now." Agatha turned to head into the kitchen.

Thomas leapt up out of the chair and demanded, "Don't walk away from me."

He'd gone too far.

Agatha swiveled. She cleared the room in three steps. He was taller than her now, so she had to look up to meet his eyes. With a quick shove to his chest, Agatha caught him off guard and knocked him back into the chair. Thomas' eyes widened in surprise.

"I have no idea what's going on right now. But I have a vested interest in maintaining the power structure in this house. So you're gonna find that this road gets real rocky real fast if you insist on going down it."

Thomas tried to keep eye contact, but dropped his eyes and looked away when his mother didn't.

He still saw her in his periphery. She didn't gloat at having re-established her dominance. Instead, her shoulders sagged, and she seemed tired. She took a step backward so that she wasn't looming over him anymore.

Still looking down, Thomas said, "I think something's wrong with Oma. She was acting weird when I went over there tonight."

"Weird how?"

"I don't know. Just weird."

"Like, is she sick?" Agatha asked.

"No. I don't know. Forget it."

"I can't very well forget it at this point. You're gonna have to do better than *weird*. You speak two languages. Surely you can come up with something."

"Do you know how impossible you are sometimes?" Thomas fussed at her.

"Yes, now spit it out."

"Fine, but first I have a question."

Agatha relented enough to let him ask his question, but raised an eyebrow at him.

Thomas knew he had to proceed with caution. "Do you have any brothers or sisters other than Elle?"

"What? No. This feels kind of far afield from what you need to tell me about Oma."

"It's not. But this gets weird."

Agatha impatiently twirled her finger at him, telling him to proceed.

"Fine. When I went over to Oma's tonight, she was cooking in the kitchen, and when I came in she started ... like ..." Thomas' face flushed as he tried to figure out how to say it, "hitting on me."

He waited to see if Agatha was going to respond. She was a

statue, so he kept talking. "She was rubbing her belly like she was pregnant, and she kept calling me Vik. And when I said I wasn't him, she got mad and kicked me out. Then she said that she and Elle could do fine on their own without me. I mean, you know, without Vik."

"What else?"

Thomas shrugged. "That's pretty much it. I kind of freaked out and left."

Agatha sat down on the sofa, leaning forward and burying her forehead in the heels of her hands.

"Mom?" Thomas waited for her to answer, but when she didn't, he asked his question anyway. "Is this Vik guy your dad?"

Agatha gave a noncommittal response that Thomas inferred to mean she either didn't know or didn't want to talk about it. Or maybe both. He looked at his watch and tapped the screen. Nearly nine o'clock. He saw too that he had somehow missed messages from Emma and from Luka.

His pulse sped up a bit when he read Luka's. "ANOTHER BODY!!!"

He'd forgotten until now that he was angry at his mom about keeping that secret. He looked over at her. She hadn't moved. Still leaning forward, elbows on her knees, face toward the floor. Maybe they could hash that out later. He stood up.

"I'm gonna go read for a bit." He walked toward the hallway that led to his room.

"Thomas," she said softly.

"Huh?" he answered without turning.

"She never said who it was before. I always assumed she didn't know."

"Oh." Hesitantly, Thomas asked, "Should I not have told you?"

Agatha finally looked up. She looked tired. That wasn't the right word. It was deeper than that. Weary.

"No, you did right by telling me. I'll check on Oma in the morning."

"Okay. G'night."

"Come give your mama a hug."

He walked back across the room. When he stopped in front of Agatha, she held out her hands for him to pull her up. He did so with an exaggerated grunt. Agatha pulled him in for a tight embrace.

She whispered in his ear, "Buddy, I love you with all my heart … but if you ever act like I'm too heavy for you to pull up again, I will whoop you. I don't care how old you are."

She quickly let go of the embrace and tickled his armpits. Thomas squirmed and cackled before extracting himself from her grasp.

11

AGATHA

AGATHA CAME out of her room in jeans and a plain white shirt, hair still wet. Thomas was already curled on the sofa with some mammoth book. She decided to test the waters.

"What are you reading?"

Thomas held up his tome. The cover looked fantastical, but she couldn't make out anything else. She was pretty sure if she combined the last four books she'd read, they wouldn't equal the number of pages contained in the monstrosity he was reading.

Since they'd moved into this house, he'd always lain in that same spot to read. The books had gotten more bewildering and the pictures fewer over the years. Sometimes, she missed little six-year-old Thomas; he'd been more predictable and less temperamental. But if there was ever a kid who had cause for unresolved issues, it was hers.

"You want any breakfast?"

"Already ate."

Well, that wasn't any different a response than usual, so maybe we're okay for now. It was always day-to-day with a teenager in the house, but after last night, she didn't know what she'd be

69

walking into this morning. The odds were probably even on either sullen or angry, with less favorable odds sitting on agreeable. *But if there are any points in teenagers' favor over six-year-olds, it's that they can feed themselves. And that's a big plus.*

She was grateful not to have to contend with any conflict with him, since she was headed over to figure out what was going on with her mother. *Hey, Mom, are you getting crazy as a bessy bug?* This conversation was sure to go well.

Agatha scooped out some yogurt and poured muesli over it. What she wouldn't give for some bacon or sausage right now. But she'd found that being a woman of a certain age meant that her metabolism was slowing, and those extra calories kept getting harder to burn off. So she'd relegated herself to curdled milk and horse food.

When she'd finished, Agatha slid her bowl and spoon into the sink and ran some water into them. She pulled her still-wet hair up into a ponytail. Time to deal with grandma.

She headed for the front door and paused to grab her keys. "I'm going to talk to Oma, then going in to work."

Without looking up, Thomas said, "We need to talk later."

A knot formed in her stomach. She felt like the roles had been reversed, and she was the child waiting to get scolded. Her hand slid off the door handle. "Nope. Nope. We're going to do this now. I'm not carrying that around all day."

Thomas finally laid his book down and looked up. "What about Oma?"

Agatha waved her hand toward her mother's house. "She ain't going anywhere. So let's hear it."

"Well, umm ..."

She'd caught him off guard by making him have this conversation now. Good. He'd be less prepared for whatever this was about. She folded her arms across her chest and waited for him to get his words out.

"... you and Luka's dad ..."

Uh-oh. This was about to be a very different talk than what she'd expected. She wasn't ready for this one. But with no room to backpedal, she prompted, "Yes?"

"You found a dead body the other day, and you didn't tell me about it."

Agatha expelled a quick bark of laughter before she could restrain it.

"That's not funny. Why was that funny?"

Agatha held her hands out in front of her in a peaceful gesture. "It's not. I'm sorry. You surprised me. Sometimes, I have an inappropriate reaction to things. I used to get in trouble all the time for that. Alright, so the dead body. I was out for a walk one night a couple of weeks ago, and I saw something on the railroad tracks. So I went and checked it out, and it was a dead woman. She had been killed."

"Who was it?" Thomas asked.

"I don't know. Didn't recognize her. Markus wanted to keep it under wraps and asked me not to tell anyone. So I didn't. Even you."

Thomas leveled what sounded like an accusation at her. "Since when do you call Luka's dad 'Markus'?"

"We've known each other a long time. He's your best friend's dad." Agatha shrugged. "So he's Markus, even if he is the police chief. Wouldn't you think it's weird if I called his mom Ms. Fischer all the time?"

Agatha felt pretty good about her deflection.

Thomas kept eyeballing her, trying to decide whether he wanted to pry into this oddity further. He decided against it. "How did she die?"

"I don't know if I should say. It was pretty rough."

Thomas rolled his eyes in exasperation. "Oh please, Mom. You act like I'm still a kid."

Casting her better judgment to the side, she spit out, "Someone cut her throat and threw her dead body off the train.

She was laying there in a heap beside some garbage when I found her."

Thomas' face blanched. "Oh," he murmured.

Agatha regretted her reaction. He just got the better of her sometimes. "Listen, I'm sorry ..."

Thomas wordlessly waved off the apology. Though his pallor had improved little, his curiosity was stronger than his fear. "Have there been any more?"

With her arms crossed, Agatha shifted her weight to one leg and cocked her hip. "Well, obviously, you know there was. With your nosy little inside source. I can't really say anything about it. Listen. They're trying to keep things as quiet as they can for now while they investigate. Please don't be a source of gossip about this. And don't let Luka get carried away. He's a natural-born storyteller and has a propensity toward having a big mouth."

Thomas sat forward to protest in defense of his friend, but thought better of it. Agatha hadn't said anything about Luka that was unfair or incorrect.

"Okay."

"We good?" Agatha asked.

"We're good."

"Okay. I've got to go see about your grandmother now, then off to work. Love you, buddy."

"Mm-hmm." He had already returned to his book. She thought back to little Thomas again. It used to be that she got a big hug and a 'Love you, Mommy' on her way out the door. Now it was the barest of acknowledgments.

Agatha walked to the sofa and bent down. She gathered Thomas up in her arms as best she could. It was an awkward hug. His arms and book were tucked up against his torso. He was half-sitting and half-lying. She was at a peculiar angle. But she didn't care. It was good to hold the boy tight again, even if he smelled kind of musky.

Finally, she released him, tousling his hair and kissing his forehead. Now she could go.

"Don't be weird, Mom."

Agatha smirked. "It's my natural state of being. Also, take a shower. You smell funky."

She opened the door. Thomas turned a page. She turned left off the porch to go check in on her mother.

"Knock, knock," Agatha called as she opened the front door and extracted the key.

"In the kitchen."

Agatha followed the sound of frying eggs and sizzling bacon toward her mother. "Hey, Mom, how are you feeling?"

"Right as rain," Gertrude answered, sounding as chipper as ever.

Agatha wasn't convinced. "Are you sure?"

Gertrude stopped scraping the eggs onto her plate, her voice now void of its happy lilt. "Why are you prodding at me like this?"

"Thomas said he came over last night and that you were acting kind of funny. So I'm checking on you."

Gertrude shook her head. "I didn't see Thomas last night."

This would go poorly. Her mother was already edgy and defensive. It was never going to go well. No one prepares you for asking your mother if she has dementia. No one tells you how to dig up the secret your mother's been hoarding for half a century, like a dragon guarding its gold.

"Mom, he came over about the time it was getting dark. What were you doing then?"

"I don't like how you're speaking to me, Agatha."

Agatha attempted to adopt a less assertive posture. Would that help? Probably not. "What were you doing around eight o'clock last night?"

Gertrude huffed at her as she carried the still-hot pan to the sink and dropped it in. "Oh, I don't know exactly. Probably watching one of my shows or reading a book."

"Thomas said you were cooking in the kitchen."

"Well, then, you answered your own question. I was making myself some dinner."

"And you kept calling him Vik."

"Vik?" Gertrude adopted a guarded expression, and her words became clipped, terse. "Nonsense. I don't know anybody by that name. Besides, I'd know that boy anywhere. I know his face better than my own. Just look at these wrinkles," she added, patting her cheeks and feigning levity. "He wasn't here."

"He said you thought you were pregnant. And that Elle was a little girl." She took a breath before asking her next question. "Have you been getting confused lately?"

Gertrude's cheeks flushed in anger. "Don't you come in here talking to me like I'm some crazy old bitty. My mind is as right as it's ever been."

Agatha did not relent. "Thomas said when he got confused about what was going on and started to leave, you got really mad and kept calling him Vik."

Gertrude's voice was thick when she said, "I told you I don't know anybody named Vik."

Agatha heard the emotion that welled up behind the obvious lie. She'd had a lot of training in discerning when she was being told the truth. Gertrude had tried to look her in the eye as she'd said it, but she couldn't keep it up.

"Mom, did you ever have any children, other than me and Elle?"

Gertrude tried to shrug off the question and picked up her plate. "Don't be silly. You'd know if you had other siblings."

She hadn't seen the trap Agatha had set for her.

Agatha plowed ahead. "You've always told me you don't know who my father is. But if what Thomas was telling me is what happened here last night, then you thought you were preg-nant with me. And my father was somebody named Vik. Now, I need you to tell me."

Gertrude stared out the kitchen window above the sink. She set her plate down on the counter and fiddled with her apron.

"Fine," Gertrude said, turning to face Agatha. "Your father was a man named Viktor Khan. He was a lowlife scoundrel, and he ran out on us before you were born. That's the end of it. I think you need to leave. You've got me all upset. I don't even think I can eat my breakfast."

Agatha could tell this conversation would not be getting any better, and she didn't want to do any irreparable damage to an old woman. Besides, she had some things to mull over. Before she turned to go, she said. "I'll check on you again after work."

"Don't bother. I'm a grown woman, and I can take care of myself, just like I've been doing for the last sixty years."

Agatha's mind was running at breakneck speed. She was having trouble latching onto any thoughts as she covered the distance between the kitchen and the door. She laid a hand on the brass door handle but paused. Her entire life, she'd never known who her father was. And now her mother drops it on her like this, having known all along.

A flicker of thought caught at the edge of her consciousness. Almost as if it had tripped over a tree root. It stumbled and thudded to the ground, bringing everything around it to a halt. All other thoughts stopped to gawk.

Viktor Kahn. She worked the name around her mouth. It had consonance, but that wasn't what drew attention. Her mother had called him Vik. Vik Kahn. Vikkahn. It couldn't be coinci-dence. A wave of nausea struck. She yanked her hand off the door to cover her mouth. But as the sickness ebbed, fury replaced it. Agatha stormed back to the kitchen.

She didn't say a word. Gertrude wouldn't look at her. Water ran in the sink. Gertrude stopped scraping the food off the plate.

A long minute passed between them. Tears fell from Gertrude's eyes. "I didn't know," she whispered coarsely.

Agatha couldn't move.

"I didn't know! I DIDN'T KNOW!"

Gertrude smashed the plate against the counter as she screamed. Shards of ceramic exploded around her. Agatha instinctively covered her face. Her mother sobbed, mumbling repeatedly, "I didn't know."

Agatha squatted to pick up pieces of food and plate.

"Don't." Gertrude regained enough composure to deliver a quiet instruction. "Just go."

12

———

AGATHA

AGATHA ANSWERED THE PHONE, "Sol's Souvenir Shop." She continued to ring up her customer's purchases, smiling cheerily at her and nodding with great encouragement at the beautiful snow globe that was a last-minute addition.

"Agatha?" the voice inquired.

"Speaking."

"It's Poliezidir—it's Markus."

"Oh." She pulled the phone away from her face and looked at it. *Cell phone, not the work phone.* "Right. Sorry. I didn't even pay attention to what I was answering. What's up?"

"I was going to see if you wanted to meet me at the park, but I guess not."

"For a nice, romantic stroll?" she asked.

"I had more in mind going back over the crime scene and talking through some things out loud."

"Oh, that's even better." Agatha tapped the face of her watch to make it show her the time. "Sol will be here in an hour or so. How about I meet you there at three?"

"I'll be there. Ciao."

"Auf wiedersehen."

No day passed particularly quickly at the souvenir shop, but some were slower than others. Agatha spent her next hour hawking beer steins, cuckoo clocks, and wooden toys to tourists making their way through quiet Black Forest towns off the main pilgrimage. *If they only knew,* she thought.

Sol enjoyed having Agatha around the shop. So many of the tourists were American or English or just spoke English as a second language. Having an American expat greet them when they entered and available to answer their questions was its own revelation. Not to mention that she was a darn good salesperson. Revenues were always higher on the days she worked.

When Agatha asked Sol if she could duck out a little early today, he had to balance his competing desires of the increased income she represented against keeping happy his most profitable employee. He begrudgingly consented to her request with the obligatory, "Don't let this become a habit."

Agatha had the good manners to smile and thank him before turning her back and rolling her eyes. She detested having her schedule so tightly controlled by someone else, especially when that someone else spoke to her like an irreverent teenager. But what else was she going to do? Her employment history consisted exclusively of one entry that reflected core competencies of capturing or killing bad guys. A skill set for which there had been precious little demand. Until now.

Agatha made her way through town to the nearest park entrance. She walked along its rust-colored walkways, noting that they looked like the crushed brick that some groundskeeper decided would make great recycled material for a softball infield. She'd like to have a word with that guy sometime and show him the scars that her legs still bore from sliding-related abrasions that never quite returned to good-as-new.

Up ahead was the universal yellow police tape that cordoned

the scene. Markus was already there, squatting down and inspecting the grass.

"Is it still green?" Agatha asked as she approached from his blind side.

He startled and popped up from his haunches, then tried to look casual. "Except for what's speckled in red, it is."

"You think he did it here or dumped her afterward?"

Fischer gestured at several places on the ground. "The amount of blood spatter says he did it here. If he worked quickly, he could have done it without notice, which as far as we know, he did. No witnesses have come forward yet. The people who called it in found the body but didn't see anything."

Agatha looked around, trying to figure out what the sight lines would have been. The large beech tree the victim had been found under would have obstructed the view directly in front of the killer. Over Agatha's shoulder was a hedgerow that stood between them and the roadway on its other side. And the way the path curved down and away on either side of them meant that this place was its own little peninsula of privacy unless someone happened to be in close proximity.

Fischer watched her. "He picked a good spot, didn't he?"

She nodded. "I've always thought of this park as being so open, but there's just this one little nook that's not." An idea alighted on Agatha. "You think he's from here?"

Fischer waggled the notebook he'd been scratching things into. "Either from town or at least familiar enough with it to know this spot was ideal for what he had in mind. Although we can't entirely rule out the possibility that he's not familiar with it and picked a random place to do his work."

The lack of conviction in the last statement told Agatha he put little stock in the theory.

Fischer continued working through the problems out loud. "But that leads to the question of whether he was waiting for her particularly, or are the victims random?"

"You think he knew her?"

"Don't know. Can't say. But nobody reported hearing a scream or any commotion."

Agatha considered the implications of that. "So if she didn't know him, then what?"

Fischer started to answer the question, but Agatha interrupted by holding up a finger. "If she didn't know him, then … he was a stranger that she wouldn't have been alarmed to have been stopped by. Right?"

Fischer smiled. "I agree. You sure you haven't done this before?"

Agatha arched an eyebrow at him. "Don't patronize me," she warned.

Fischer raised both hands to protest his innocence. "I'm being serious. I came to the same conclusion. She either knew him or at minimum was familiar with him. Or he was in some sort of uniform that would have disarmed her."

"Or he pounced and caught her completely by surprise," Agatha suggested.

Fischer shrugged noncommittally.

"You don't think so?"

"It seems less likely to me. First," he said, holding out his right index finger, "it is very risky. If he doesn't immediately cover her mouth or knock her out, there's too much likelihood that she screams. Second, where does he come from? While the area is somewhat secluded, there's not a lot of cover. There's too much distance between the tree trunk and path or hedges and path for him to clear quickly, without her getting alarmed."

Agatha looked up. It also seemed improbable that he would have dropped down off a tree branch. Too much there could go wrong.

"So we're left with her either being acquainted with him or him being in uniform?"

He agreed. "Those seem like the most probable scenarios, though I'm still open to something else. Too early to rule much out."

"That doesn't give us very much, does it?"

"Not standing alone, maybe. But when we apply the same theories to the girl on the train, then we might make some progress."

Agatha smacked herself lightly on the forehead. "I hadn't even thought of her yet. Did anyone see anything?"

"Problem is, we don't know what car she was in. Seats aren't assigned, and there are no security cameras, so—"

"Really, no video cameras?"

Fischer nodded. "Germans value nothing so much as our privacy. That means limited CCTV, no Google street view, and if you even suggest using facial recognition programs, you need to start looking for a new job. But we have caught up with a few people who remember her. No one saw or heard anything. Could be she was in a car by herself."

"What about the two girls? Is there any connection between them?"

"Aside from both being heilerin, nothing obvious. We're still doing background on the new girl."

"So what's next?" Agatha asked.

"We're collecting DNA samples off the second vic, fingerprints, checking for fibers. Anything that might match up with the first one and give us more information. That'll take a couple of weeks to process, depending on how backed up the lab is."

"Umm ..." Agatha didn't let her next thought get further, thinking better of being critical this early on.

"Let's hear it," Fischer said. "I didn't ask you to consult with us so you would be prim and restrained."

"Fine. A couple of weeks? We might have another body by then."

Fischer shrugged grimly. "We only have access to the one lab."

"Can't you pull some strings or something?"

"Agatha," he chastised. "Do you know nothing of German bureaucracy? Everything in order, all the time."

"Well, I guess that'll give me time to deal with my addle-brained mother, who decided yesterday to tell me who my father is after telling me my entire life that she didn't know his identity."

Agatha watched with some amusement as Markus tried to figure out what the response was to the information she had unloaded on him. It was like watching Thomas doing his math homework and come up with the wrong solution over and over again.

She decided to let him off the hook. "Don't worry about it. It's not a big deal. I shouldn't have said anything."

"Of course it's a big deal," he said earnestly. "It's a part of who you are. Would you like to talk about it?"

"Not really. I'm not ready to scare you off yet. But I do appreciate you offering, even if you were terrified that I would take you up on it."

Markus nodded. "He is a fool who proceeds without trepidation into the matters of a woman's heart."

"That's pretty deep, Fischer. I didn't know Germans were romantics."

"I had a wise mother."

"I did too once upon a time. Now I just think she's going to get to the point where her brain stops waving long before her heart stops ticking."

Fischer cocked his head and wrinkled his brow. He said slowly, "I don't think—"

"Shh," Agatha interrupted with a smile. "It doesn't have to be scientifically accurate. It conveyed my meaning."

Fischer's demeanor changed as he said, "Before you go, there's something I need to tell you."

"I don't like the sound of that. Something about you?"

"No. About this town." He looked down at his feet, then at the place where the second victim's body had lain, before meeting Agatha's eyes again. "This is not the first time these kinds of killings have happened here."

13

THOMAS

WHILE FINN GATHERED sticks for a fire, and Lea and Luka snuggled up with each other in a way that was kind of nauseating. Thomas couldn't help but search the ground for scorch marks from his recent duel with Luka. The group had come to think of this spot as their own over the years, but right now, the one terrible memory heavily outweighed all the accumulated good ones.

Emma walked up beside him and slid her hand into his. He clasped her fingers and looked at her in surprise. She smiled sheepishly and gave her shoulders a barely perceptible shrug. *I guess we're doing this.*

Distracted by his previous concerns, Thomas didn't immediately notice that the wings of the butterflies that now filled his belly had fluttered away the shadow that had been wearing him down.

Finn completed the stacking of his kindling that took the shape of a topless pyramid and asked Thomas, "Would you do the honors?"

When Thomas realized that the other three were looking at him, he abruptly released Emma's hand. He was flustered and said quietly, "Sorry. I don't know why I did that." Trying to recover, he said formally with a mock bow, "It would be my honor, sir."

Thomas sat down, and Emma sat right beside him, her shoulder pushed up against his. One of the things he most liked about her was how quick she was to forgive. And since he was prone to screw-ups, that was a particularly appreciable quality.

He cupped his hands together, and a glow emerged between them. The minor miracle took a little longer than normal to produce, as he found it difficult to focus entirely on his können. Some of his attention remained diverted to Emma and the feeling of her leg resting against and slightly under his own. *Focus*, he instructed himself.

Thomas uncovered his right hand and revealed a molten globe. He tipped his hand forward and rolled it toward the carefully arranged sticks. The fiery little bowling ball left a wake of glowing pine straw and smoldering leaves as it progressed toward its set of pins. Finn had left an opening large enough for it to enter through, if Thomas aimed it carefully.

Finn hovered over his tower of sticks, trying to protect it from the small rocks that Luka had been lobbing over his shoulder. But Luka switched tactics and began making silent gestures of explosions to Thomas, holding his hands together, then spreading them apart. Thomas shook him off, like a pitcher to a catcher who's signaling unwanted pitches.

Thomas guided the orb into the pyramid, igniting it and casting the group in a glow that matched the orange sky. Thomas smiled at Luka. "You're out of your mind. If I sent somebody else to be cared for by Frau Vogel, the next time y'all get together would be for my funeral after Agatha murders me."

Before moving back toward his place in the circle, Finn said, "Speaking of Agatha, have we ever talked about how hot your mom is?"

Thomas made a quick gesture with his hand, and the small

fire became an inferno. Finn jumped backward and went sprawling on the ground as the flames chased him. The distinct smell of singed hair filled the air. Finn jumped up and felt at his face and head. His eyes were the size of dinner plates. He found that the mustache he'd been curating most of the summer had been irreparably damaged, as had the few whiskers that adorned his cheeks.

Thomas sat back with a smirk and said, "No, we haven't talked about that. Do you think you would like to?"

Lea and Luka rolled with laughter. Emma took a more reserved approach, covering her mouth as she laughed.

"Even you?" Finn said to her as he recovered himself to a sitting position.

She shrugged. "You talked about his mom. What did you think was going to happen?"

Finn scolded them. "All of you are bad friends. Bad friends. But you're the only ones I've got, and I have a story to tell. So I guess I'll tell it anyway. Who here knows the tale of the Beast of the Black Forest?"

Only Lea raised her hand.

Luka was skeptical. "Beast of the Black Forest? Sounds like a dumb story to scare little kids."

"Not to give away any spoilers," Finn said, wanting to divulge as little information as possible before telling his story, "but he was a serial killer in the 1950s."

"How do you know about it?" Luka asked with less skepticism, while trying to catch Thomas' attention.

"My oma used to tell me that Heinrich Pommerenke — that's his name — was going to get me if I wasn't a good boy. She wasn't a very nice woman."

Luka hadn't finished his inquisition. He turned his attention to Lea, who was leaning against him. "And how do *you* know?"

"All the old newspapers are archived on the computers at the library. It's pretty gruesome."

"Whoa! I didn't know you were a nerdy library kid," Luka said.

Lea reached up and pinched the back of his arm. Luka flinched and jerked his arm away. "Ow! What'd you do that for?"

Lea looked straight ahead and tried to wear a disinterested expression. "Name-calling isn't nice. I also had a grandmother who was a mean old witch, and she used to teach me little hexes to use on the kids who picked on me. We can try that instead of pinching if you'd like. They're mostly harmless, but I think you'll find them uncomfortable. I've modified a few of them over the years to suit my tastes."

"Well, that's scary. I think maybe *you're* the Beast." Luka pulled his arm across his body as he said it to keep it out of pinching distance.

Luka jumped up and yanked his Yankees cap off his head and started swiping at his left leg while dancing as if he were on hot coals. "There's a giant spid—"

He stopped mid-swing and looked down. Lea stared back at him with as much innocence as she could muster. The rest of the crew laughed with a mixture of hilarity and horror.

Luka pointed at her, "That's mean. You know how I feel about those things." Addressing the other three, he said, "And you all should be ashamed of yourselves for not helping me out."

Their laughter resumed in full. Without a word, Lea patted the ground beside her, inviting Luka to sit back down. He did so with trepidation, and Lea leaned against him as though nothing had happened. Luka cut his eyes over to Thomas, who clearly didn't want to get involved.

"Can we get back to the story now?" Finn proposed.

"Let's," Lea answered for the group.

"On a deep, dark night in the Winter of 1959, Heinrich Pommerenke went to the movie theater to see *The Ten Command-*

ments. During the movie, there's a scene where women are dancing around a golden calf, and Heinrich got all ..." Finn floundered, trying to maintain his sense of propriety, "... worked up."

"Wait," said Luka, waving his arms. "You couldn't figure out how to say it in front of the girls, so you thought *'worked up'* was the best choice?"

Finn blushed, "I froze."

"Oh, please," Lea interjected. "You don't have to be prudish around us. We know you boys are no better than animals when it comes to your schniedel."

Finn buried his face in his hands and continued in a muffled tone before looking up again. "He was aroused, okay? He was aroused. And he was crazy. Because he decided right then that women are the root of evil—"

"Are we sure he was wrong about that?" Luka said, laughing at his own wit, until he caught the look Lea gave him and felt her fingers pinch the back of his arm again. "I'm sorry. Please don't hurt me."

"Anyway, he decided women are the root of all evil, and it was his calling to punish them for it. So that night, as he was walking home through the park, he started following a woman and abducted her. When they found her body the next day at the train station in Durlach, her throat had been cut and she had been raped."

"Oh my gosh," Thomas whispered.

Emma pushed up against him a little tighter.

"It gets worse. A few days later, outside of town—"

"What town?" Emma asked, despite the evidence on her face being that she might not want to know the answer.

"Our town. Hornberg. He did all this in Hornberg."

Luka and Thomas exchanged horrified looks that Lea intercepted.

"What?" she demanded. "What do you two know?"

"Nothing," Thomas said too soon and with an urgency that defied belief.

Lea sat upright and repeated herself, looking directly at Luka. "What do you know?"

Luka stole a look to his left where Thomas was shaking his head with all the subtlety of a wildebeest. He turned back to Lea. Her arms were crossed and her eyes glaring. "Just let Finn tell his story, and then I'll tell you what I can."

He tried to coax Lea to snuggle back up to him. She didn't budge, but turned her gaze to Finn, who took his cue.

"A few days later, he was stalking around outside of town and happened upon a teenage girl. He dragged her into a wooden hut that was nearby, and ... you know ... raped her too. And then he smashed her head in with a rock and threw her body in the river. They found her washed up the next day."

Emma stood up. "I can't. I can't listen to any more." She turned to Finn. "Is there more?"

He nodded but offered, "It was a long time ago, Emma."

Lea popped up and went to Emma, standing arm in arm. "Now, your turn."

"Hang on," he said. "Finn, what happened next?"

"He, uh, tried to strangle a girl, but she got away."

"Oh man," Thomas said, less quietly than he'd intended.

Finn was confused. "What's going on?"

"Nothing," Thomas said, pushing himself up. "Are y'all ready to go?"

Lea let go of Emma's arm. When Luka started to stand up, Lea flung her hand in his direction. A gust of wind swept across the campfire and hit Luka in the chest, knocking him back down. Luka was wide-eyed. "We're not going anywhere until you two talk."

"Just tell them," Thomas conceded.

All eyes were on Luka. He stammered and tried to figure out

how to start, how to break into it, before finally just taking the plunge. "There might be another serial killer."

"You mean the girl in the park?" Lea asked dismissively. "Everybody knows about her. Just because it was weird doesn't mean it's a serial killer."

Thomas shook his head. "There was another one a couple of weeks ago. He strangled her on the train and then threw her off. My mom found her body by the railroad tracks. How did he kill the girl in the park, Luka?"

"Cut her throat."

"You two are connecting dots that may not go together," Lea said.

"There's more," Thomas said without enthusiasm. He had thought it would be fun to tell his friends about this. None of them knew the women who had died, or at least he didn't think so. It should have been just like telling a ghost story. But it wasn't. It was too real.

"He carved a symbol into their chests after he killed them," Luka continued, moving over beside Thomas so that he'd be on the same side of the campfire as everyone else. He leaned forward and drew six intersecting circles in the dirt. The dancing flames caused shifting shadows among the ridges Luka had caused. The symbol appeared to be undulating rhythmically.

Finn tilted his head as he looked at Luka's drawing. He squatted down and traced a circle within the interior of the circles, at the points where they conjoined. "It's the Flower of Life," he said.

"I heard my dad call it something else, I think."

"The Sun of the Alps?"

Luka nodded.

"That's another name for it. But people have been using this symbol long before anyone ever migrated to the Alps. Archaeologists have found it inscribed on things dating as far back as the Bronze Age."

"How do you know all this?" Thomas asked.

Finn shrugged. "I'm curious."

"About what?"

"Just … generally."

Lea was still salty about having been kept in the dark this long. "What else have you not told us?"

"There is one more thing." Thomas looked Emma in the face when he said it. "It may just be coincidence, but both of the women so far have been heilerin.

Emma groaned, and her eyes welled with tears. Lea pulled her in for a tight hug and glared at Thomas. "It's going to be fine. Nothing's going to happen to you."

The three guys alternated between looking at the ground and into the fire, uncomfortable but not knowing what to do.

Emma pulled herself together and said to Lea, "I want to go home."

"Me too," Lea agreed and took control of the situation. "Luka put out the fire. Then you three will walk us home. Emma first, then me. After that you're on your own. But no one's going to mess with any of you unless they know what a collection of dummkopfs you are."

The boys looked at each other. Thomas considered suggesting that Lea stomp the fire out with one of her giant Doc Martens and with the other she could … but he didn't. He cowed to her, as did the other two. No one argued with Lea about the insult. They didn't have much of a leg to stand on with the way the night had gone.

Luka summoned a basketball-sized sphere of water from the river and dropped it onto the fire. It extinguished the blaze but covered his and Thomas' lower legs in a slush of ash and mud. He looked up with a guilty grin.

"Ugh." Thomas looked down in disgust, not that he could see much with their source of light having been drowned.

Lea shook her head. "Not that I needed you to make my point for me, but I believe you might just have done that."

Thomas formed a glowing orb in his hands for them to see their way back through the woods to town.

"It may be best if we don't draw too much attention to ourselves," Finn suggested, digging through his backpack and extracting a couple of flashlights. He handed one to Emma and kept the other for himself. Thomas allowed his fire to fall like a dying flare.

14

———

THOMAS

THE WALK through the woods was subdued. At least for the members of the group. The forest itself came alive after the sun went down. The din of cicadas and crickets oscillated with a rhythm orchestrated by the forest. With every crash of a branch and rustle of leaves magnified by the darkness, Emma clutched more tightly to Lea.

Finn headed the procession, trying to twirl his flashlight like he was a majorette, which resulted in his having to bend down and pick it up every few paces. Lea had restrained herself from commenting as long as she could. "If you break it, we'll be down to just one light. And you'll be an even more useless point man if you can't see where you're going."

"Okay. Sorry." Finn pointed his light at the ground ahead of him.

As obnoxious as his nonsense had been, its cessation somehow made things worse.

"Finn, I didn't mean that you were us—"

"It's fine," he interrupted, waving her off.

At the rear of the procession, Luka muttered to Thomas, "We didn't handle that very well."

"You think?"

"Well, to be fair, there was never going to be a good time," Luka attempted to defend them.

"Sure, but maybe ghost story time in the woods after Finn had just told us about another serial killer was … not ideal."

Luka had no rebuttal.

"How did you not know that?" Thomas asked.

"I don't know. Maybe it's something the town wants to forget. I mean, you've lived here for …"

"Twelve years."

"… for twelve years, and you've never heard of it either."

"Yeah, but that's not the same thing. People still look at us like we're the new folks in town."

Luka paused to think about it. "You are the new folks in town. Like relatively speaking. People don't come and go around here. Tourists pass through. But the rest of us are … I don't know … embedded here or something. Like part of the landscape."

"Can you leave?"

"Yeah, man. Nobody's being held hostage. But out there—" Luka didn't even trail off. He just stopped talking.

"Out there — what?"

"I don't know. It's kind of scary. Going on holiday is fun, but my mom always lectures me about not using my können. When we'd go to the beach in Spain when I was little, she spent half the trip telling me not to make the waves bigger or do anything fun or people would notice. It kind of trains your brain that it's scary out there. I'm in a little cocoon here, and it's cozy and I like it. Out there, I'm a freak."

"To be fair," Thomas grinned at him, "we all think you're kind of a freak in here too."

Luka gave him a sideways shove. Thomas recovered his balance before he would have spilled off the path and into the woods.

The trail dumped them out onto a meadow with an over-looking view of Hornberg and the Gutach Valley. The sky was still purple to the west with a faint orange hue at the horizon, though it was quickly relinquishing its color and being replaced by a plethora of constellations. Lights twinkled on in town and in the homes scattered throughout the valley. Hotel Schloss Hornberg and its tower burned brightly on the mountainside opposite them, as if they were bastions of light whose mission was to dispel the darkness.

It was hard to imagine that somewhere down below, there might be a killer stalking his next victim. He couldn't help but to worry about Emma and Lea and his mom. He almost smiled. If the killer attacked his mom, he'd be lucky to escape alive. She'd never told him exactly what had happened the night that his father died. And while he hadn't seen her kill the Warden, he had seen what was left of him. On their way out of those tunnels, she'd tried to distract him, but the carnage she and his dad had left in their wake coming to find him was everywhere.

Not only that, but on the couple of occasions that Oberhaupt had visited over the years since they'd moved to Hornberg, he and Agatha would reminisce about old times and old missions, after she'd sent Thomas to bed. He used to sit against the wall beside the door that was cracked to let some light in and listen to them until he fell asleep. Agatha could take care of herself.

Thomas heard his name called at the same time that a flash-light beam struck him in the face. He grimaced and put up his hand to block the light. "Knock it off, man."

"Just checking on you," Finn said, redirecting the light to the ground. "Looked like you were off in your own little world there."

Thomas gave a thin smile. "Now I can't see a thing, so thanks for that."

Addressing the group, Finn suggested, "Let's get going. We

can drop Emma and Lea off first. Then the guys will be on their own."

"Yeah, I already said that," Lea chafed.

"Maybe you can each message us after you get home. Just so we can all sleep a little better," Emma offered.

No one objected.

Finn took his place at the head of the procession, but the arrangement behind him had shifted. Luka and Lea fell in after him, draped over each other like wet blankets. Thomas and Emma brought up the rear. She kept the flashlight pointed a few steps ahead of them so they could avoid obstacles. Thomas reached out his left hand to where he knew he would find her right. Their palms and fingertips touched, and she clasped her hand to his.

"Can you believe those two? It's totally weird," Thomas whispered.

"It won't last," she answered. "They're just … geil."

"Geil?"

He could sense that she didn't want to explain the word. She was probably blushing right now. He loved how reserved she was, so unlike any of the other people in his life, who were all so assertive.

"You know, randy."

Thomas laughed. "Oh, that's definitely true. What happens when it's over?"

"It's going to be a mess."

He laughed again.

Thomas slowed and stopped, letting go of Emma's hand. He turned to the side and squatted down. He had an idea.

"What is it?" Emma asked.

"I thought I saw something."

She turned on her flashlight and saw that his hands hovered over the ground. The light mostly landed across his back and kept her from seeing much. When Thomas stood again, he held out to her a bunch of flowers. They looked like little white starbursts. She held out her free hand to receive the offering.

"Is that edelweiss?" she asked, her voice incredulous. "I thought it only grew up in the mountains."

Thomas shrugged, but his grin belied his gesture of ignorance.

"Danke schoen. That's very sweet." She handed him the flashlight and switched the flowers to her left hand. While he was normally obtuse about these things, Thomas took his cue and reached out his hand again for hers.

"Now let's see if I can get down the mountain with these things without falling and ruining them."

Thomas and Emma picked up the pace to catch back up to the group. Thomas beamed in the darkness. It had felt good to create again. It was kind of reckless, and Agatha would tan his hide if she found out. But he almost didn't care. Even the waking nightmares that were imprinted on his brain had kept themselves at bay.

The path carried them to the outskirts of town, and from there, they walked to Emma's house. The rest of the group arrived slightly ahead of Thomas and Emma. When the trio turned around to wait on them, Thomas dropped her hand. More than dropped, he all but pushed it away. Luka snickered. Lea elbowed him hard in the ribs, eliciting a grunt and more laughter. Emma turned to Thomas with a raised eyebrow.

They came to a stop at the walkway in front of her house. "Sorry," Thomas said, "I just ..." He just didn't know what to say and didn't finish his sentence.

Emma put her hands under his chin and pulled his face down to hers. She kissed him confidently but sweetly. The edelweiss fluttered against his cheek. She closed her eyes, but Thomas' were wide open in surprise and disbelief. A flush of heat coursed through him. His hands were out to his side, not knowing what to do with themselves. It wasn't a long kiss, but it was long enough. When she let go of his face and took a half-step back, Emma patted Thomas on the chest. "There," she said. "Maybe that will help get some of your jitters out."

"I'm not sure *that's* the effect it had," Luka muttered, receiving another elbow to the ribs.

Emma said, "Good night, Thomas." She waved to the others and turned to walk to the front.

"G'night," Thomas said belatedly. Emma opened the door and gave him a last smile before going in.

Thomas turned to his three friends, looking half-drunk.

"Who would have seen that coming?" asked Finn.

"All of you should have," Lea answered with an exaggerated sigh. "You all are the most oblivious — maybe I should walk myself home. As obtuse as you are, the killer will carve me up and make a pelt of my skin like Buffalo Bill before you notice I'm gone."

"Who's Buffalo Bill?" Finn asked.

Thomas shrugged, but Luka declared, "I would notice."

"Yes, that's very reassuring." She grabbed his arm and led them to her ramshackle house by the railroad tracks.

Finn called up to Lea, "Are you going to get in trouble for being out this late?"

She turned her head as she walked. "Did Aunt May and Uncle Ben hassle Peter Parker about where he was all the time?"

"I don't ... what?" Finn screwed up his face in confusion. "You know we aren't superheroes, right?"

"Aren't we though?" To make her point, Lea raised her arms over her head and called down a small tornado that wound around her. It whipped at the boys' clothes and started picking up debris. The boys raised their arms or turned their backs to protect themselves. Lea cackled as lightning cracked around her before releasing the cyclone and allowing a silence to descend around them. It was only then that she answered Finn's question. "My aunt and uncle have already raised their kids; though 'raised' may be giving them more credit than they deserve. I think they were a little surprised when my parents dumped me on their steps and bailed. But whatever. They're too hopped up on their drug of choice for the week to keep up with me. As long as I'm not having sex with dudes in the living room, they mostly leave me alone."

Luka wore a hopeful expression as he walked her to the front door. He put his hands on her hips and pulled her toward him. "Do I get a kiss too?"

Lea leaned in and tapped him lightly on the nose. "No you do not, dummy." She twisted out of his grasp and went inside.

Luka turned to Finn and Thomas, mouth agape. "Did you see that? She just like totally … that was harsh."

Thomas and Finn burst into laughter and became unable to answer. There is no misfortune too big to bring mirth to teenage boys. With a sigh, Luka stalked off into the darkness and out from under the glow of the streetlight.

"Where are you going?" Finn called.

"Home," Luka said as his form disappeared into the gloom. Thomas lived a couple of streets over from Luka, but Finn lived in the opposite direction. The two boys shrugged at each other as each worked out the logistics. Someone was going to end up walking home alone, regardless.

Thomas suggested, "I'll catch up to Luka. Just send a group text once you're home?"

"Yeah. Sure." The joy had drained from Finn's face.

"Want me to walk with you?"

"No. It's cool. I'll be fine."

"One more thing," Thomas said, stopping Finn mid-turn. He spoke into the night the thing they were both trying to avoid and which was inescapable. "What ever happened to that guy? The serial killer?"

"They caught him after he'd killed like seven people, and he spent the rest of his life in prison. Died in 2008, I think."

"Okay. See? Nothing to worry about. We probably just got carried away."

"Yeah. Alright. I'll see you."

Thomas waved, wondering if he should walk with Finn. Fear had pierced their fragile shell of teenage invulnerability. More than fear. Dread. Thomas trotted to catch up to Luka. He pulled up alongside his friend, and they settled into a comfortable silence for the next few streets. When they turned onto Reichenbacher Strasse with only a couple hundred meters to go before reaching Luka's house, Luka all but whispered, "I thought she was going to invite me in."

Thomas laughed curtly before cutting it off. "For what? Coffee?"

"No, man. To, you know … hang out."

"You're probably better off. There's probably discarded needles all over that house. Who knows what you might catch," Thomas said.

"I've had my tetanus shot."

"Yeah, that's not what I was worried about." Thomas was about to tread some treacherous ground that was loaded with land mines. "I thought y'all were just kind of messing around?"

"We were. We are. But it's … you know."

"That was eloquently stated. You're a regular Otto von Bismarck."

"Shut up," Luka said. "I don't know who that is. Never mind. Don't tell me. I don't care."

Within view of Luka's house, Thomas said, "You know if you push this too far, you're not going to be able to … uhh … extract yourself from the situation. Then one of you will be mad, and we'll have to choose who we're siding with. It'll be a mess, and we're all too old to go finding new friends."

Luka's shoulders slumped. "Yeah, I guess you're right. But what if it works out?" he asked with some optimism.

"Works out how? Are y'all going to keep dating for the next two years?"

The optimism dissipated. "Oh, yeah. Probably not. She's not very nice sometimes."

Thomas was bewildered. They'd been friends with Lea basically their whole lives. She'd never been particularly nice, but Luka was acting like this was a revelation. But they'd have to finish this later. At the corner of Mühlenpeterweg, Thomas hooked a thumb to the left said, "This is where we part."

Luka nodded, then grinned. "Want to race?"

"Only if you want to lose."

"What are the rules?"

"Text as soon as you touch the front door. First one to get their message out wins," Thomas said.

"Fair," Luka agreed. "Ready. Set. Go!" Thomas stuck out his foot to step on the heel of Luka's sneaker as he took off. Luka's foot lifted up and out of the shoe, which flipped away. Thomas cackled as he sprinted away. He needed the extra time since he lived further away. By the time Luka got his shoe back on and yelled "Cheater!" after him, among other expletives, Thomas was nearing his right turn onto Gartenstrasse.

Before Thomas reached his front door, his watch chirped at him again. He'd already received Finn's message. This could only be Luka. The message contained no words, just a short video of Luka dancing victoriously. *Dagummit.* Thomas was reminded of his dad. He hadn't retained many memories of him that hadn't faded with time, but that word had stuck.

When he walked into the house, Agatha was sitting in her corner chair reading a book. She offered a small smile before saying, "We need to talk."

Thomas' stomach tangled into inextricable knots. "Did I do something?"

"Not that I know of. Sit down," she said, gesturing at the couch.

He complied. "Is it about the dead girls?"

"Women. No. It's about my father."

<h1 style="text-align:center">15</h1>

THOMAS

THOMAS STAYED in bed until after his mother left for work. He had been awake for a long time, having not slept much that night. He heard when she got up and started moving around the house, and smelled the eggs and bacon she had made for herself. It was as if she were trying to lure him out of bed with bacon, and it had nearly worked. But he wasn't ready to face her again. Not yet. So when she had opened the door to check on him before leaving for the day, he had feigned sleep. Seconds later, his door closed, followed by the front door being opened and closed.

He waited to make sure she hadn't forgotten something, then kicked his covers off. Agatha had always laughed at the way he got out of bed. She said he looked like a kangaroo lying on its back the way he curled his legs and punched the sheets and blanket with his feet, sending them sprawling away from his body. She'd gone so far as to try to fix it by demonstrating how a *normal human* uses their hand to peel back the sheet from the corner, like opening a can of tuna. The lesson didn't take.

He shuffled to the kitchen and opened the refrigerator. After a minute of cold air wafting over his skin, he just grabbed the jug of milk. He couldn't think yet, or didn't want to. His brain was still a fog from the night before. Thomas had a visual of his brain imploding with the new information. *Hey, just so you know, your grandfather is a super villain who's responsible for your father's death. And remember that one time he kidnapped you because your superpowers might help him rule the world or something? Oh, and by the way, your grandmother might be losing her mind to dementia, and we might have to put her in the nursing home with your aunt who's so messed up she doesn't know what planet she's on. Yea family!*

With a shiver, he closed the door to the refrigerator. He opened the pantry and grabbed Nutella and a loaf of bread. He flung the bread onto the counter a few feet away. Toast and Nutella. The breakfast of champions. Was it still considered breakfast at ten o'clock?

Thomas had no idea what he was going to do with his day. But he couldn't sit around the house all day. He'd make himself crazy. *Then I could go live at the nursing home too. We could be one happy, little insane family together.*

He had to get out of the house. He was already dark and broody. That was only going to worsen if he sat around here.

After wolfing down his breakfast, Thomas threw on some clothes that smelled mostly clean and weren't overly wrinkled. He stepped out the front door with no clear idea of where he intended to go. He looked to his left at his grandmother's house, but couldn't stomach the idea of seeing her right now. Instead, he turned right and headed toward town.

Ten minutes of walking carried him to the heart of Hornberg. He had an urge to yell to the tourists who'd descended on the town as a part of their tour of the lesser seen parts of Germany. *Hey, have you heard about our serial killer?* The urge passed without any action on his part.

After navigating through and past the human obstacles on the sidewalks, he realized how little he wanted to be around other people right now, which really limited his options.

At the river, he propped his elbows on the white fence that kept the unwary from tumbling the two meters down into the Gutach. He looked around. No one was paying him any attention. Thomas hopped the fence and lowered himself down the retaining wall and sat on the exposed rock beside the running water.

He sat with his arms behind him, holding him up. Already, the rocks were a good bit warmer than he'd expected. He took off his shoes, wadded his socks up and shoved them into his sneakers, then plunged his feet into the river. The contrast of the frigid mountain water against his feet was startling. He gave a shiver that resonated all the way up to his ears.

"Thomas!"

He looked around, trying to locate the voice. Whoever it was sounded displeased.

"Behind you."

Turning around, Thomas placed his hailer. Polizeidirektor Fischer stood with both hands atop the white fence. Thomas greeted him and got waved over in response. He grabbed up his shoes and loped to the retaining wall.

"You can't be down there," he said.

"Okay." Thomas looked down, where water was still running off his legs. "Can I throw my shoes up to you?"

Fischer gestured for Thomas to toss them up, which he did without incident. He placed his hands atop the wall and pulled himself up, swinging his right leg up and using his exposed toes like a monkey would, to get leverage. He vaulted himself over the fence and swung himself around to face the man he was never quite sure how to address. Thomas had known Fischer most of his life. He was his best friend's dad, but he'd never been around all that much. When they were younger, he'd been working all the time. Later, he and Luka's mom had gotten divorced. So mostly, Thomas tried to avoid addressing him by name or title.

"What were you doing down there, Thomas?"

He shrugged. "You know, just hanging out."

Fischer scrutinized him for a long minute before shaking his head, as if Thomas were some inexplicable alien life form. "Are you doing okay, Thomas?"

He had no idea how to respond. He tried to remember if they'd ever had a personal conversation in his entire life. Nothing came to mind. He considered going with, *Yeah, it turns out I might be a demigod or something like that, so that's been weighing on me a bit.* Instead, he said, "Yes, everything is fine." He didn't want to seem like he was blowing off the question, but he didn't know what else to say.

"And Agatha, how is she doing? I saw her yesterday, and she seemed … out of sorts."

Thomas dropped his eyes to the ground. How to be evasive but responsive. Tell partial truths. He looked back up. "I think it's been a rough week. There was the thing with Luka." Thomas ran his hand from left hip up to his right shoulder. Fischer nodded his understanding. "And her mother isn't doing very well. Then there's the ser—"

"Nein," Fischer cut him off, looking around at the passers-by to see if anyone was paying them any undue attention. "Nein, Thomas. Please be discreet."

This last bit seemed to have the desired effect. Fischer had lost his appetite for further questions.

"I have to make my way back to the polizeiwache. Mind the signs and stay out of the river in town. I can't have tourists following your lead and getting washed away."

Thomas nodded his compliance. As Fischer walked past him, Thomas spied the steeple of Evangelische Kirche peeking over the tops of the buildings along the waterfront. He decided to go visit Pastor Stefan again. Maybe the minister wouldn't mind seeing him twice within a week. Thomas was uncertain whether he wanted company, but he was sure he didn't want to be in his own head any more right now.

Inside the sanctuary, Pastor Stefan was working at some sort of ornate table that stood below the podium at the front of the church. He arranged a loaf of flatbread and a carafe of wine. Upon hearing a noise behind him, the pastor peered over his shoulder. "Thomas!" he greeted as Thomas entered through rear doors.

Thomas waved sheepishly. "Is it okay that I'm here?"

"Yes, of course. Just getting some things ready for service tomorrow."

Thomas made his way up the center aisle. "Are y'all eating lunch in church tomorrow?"

Pastor Stefan laughed but stopped himself when Thomas' cheeks flushed in embarrassment. "It's for communion."

Thomas didn't recognize the meaning of the words. He'd never been exposed to any kind of religion and had no idea what Pastor Stefan was talking about. He had only the most primitive understanding of Christianity.

"Sometimes it's called the Lord's Supper," the minister offered, clearly hoping to make a connection.

Thomas shook his head.

Pastor Stefan opened his mouth again. Thomas thought he was going to give a whole exposition about this supper thing, but he appeared to think better of it and redirected. "Did you have a particular reason for stopping by today?"

He honestly didn't know. But weirdly, it seemed easier to talk to someone who was more or less a stranger than anyone else he could think of.

"Things have been kind of tough at home."

Pastor Stefan nodded. "The teenage years can be difficult, under the best of circumstances."

Thomas shook his head. "Not like that. It's family stuff still."

"Ah. That never gets easier, regardless of age."

An uncomfortable silence fell between them. Thomas filled the gap. "When I was little — before we moved here — I was kidnapped. My mom and dad had to rescue me, but my dad ..." Thomas didn't normally get upset about what happened to his dad anymore, but his throat got thick, and he stopped talking.

"I'm sorry, Thomas. I did not know."

He collected himself and took a big breath, preparing himself for the next part. He hadn't said it out loud yet. "I just found out that the man who kidnapped me is my grandfather."

Pastor Stefan sat with that quietly for a long time before asking, "Can I tell you a story?"

"Sure," Thomas answered.

"It is a dark and unhappy one."

"Okay." *What could be darker than your own grandfather kidnapping you?*

"Have you heard of Heinrich Pommerenke?"

Thomas nearly choked and fell into a coughing fit. "No," he lied. He was curious where this was going and didn't want to spoil it by telling the truth. "Should I have?"

"Not necessarily. Many people in town know the name, but they do not speak of him. He was a deeply troubled young man who lived here in Hornberg. His father had been killed in the Second World War, and his mother abandoned him when he was a boy. In February 1959, he went to a showing of the movie, *The Ten Commandments* — have you seen it?"

Thomas shook his head.

Pastor Stefan waved it off. "That is neither here nor there. After the movie, he went out and bought a razor at a shop in town. Then he stalked a woman until she was alone on a street, where he attacked her and dragged her to a nearby park. He raped her, then cut her throat. According to reports, he later said the movie made him realize that women were the root of all evil in the world, and he was put here to punish them. But he was only 21 years old and had already raped several women before this, so I do not believe it.

"Anyway, over the course of the next three and a half months, he killed three more people, attempted seven other murders. And he raped or attempted to rape more than twenty women. He was caught in June of that year and is remembered by many as the Beast of the Black Forest."

"That's really awful," Thomas said, maintaining his facade. "But why are you telling me this?"

"Because one woman that he raped — but failed to kill — became pregnant with a baby girl."

"Oh. That's ... she kept the baby?"

"Yes, and she loved the girl as if she was the child she had always intended to have. That child was my mother, Thomas. My opa is the Heinrich Pommerenke."

"Oh," Thomas said. He thought for a while before asking his next question. "Are you worried that you carry inside you the ability to, you know, do what he did?"

"That is a very poignant question, Thomas. And I understand why both of us have circumstances that cause you to ask it. Is that something you've been concerned about since you learned about your grandfather?"

"I saw him do some terrible stuff. Like, as bad as Pommerenke. And he's been alive for hundreds of years, maybe thousands — I don't know. There's no telling what he's done." Thomas fidgeted and scratched at his arm. "His blood is in me. It's a part of me."

Pastor Stefan looked like someone who had had this same conversation with himself innumerable times. He reached out and put a hand on Thomas' hands. Thomas hadn't been looking at him anymore and flinched at the unexpected gesture. How long had it been since a man had touched him? The hands weren't as soft as he would have expected of a minister. The palms felt like fine grit sandpaper. *No, more like a cat's tongue.*

Pastor Stefan called him out of his analogy, "Thomas, to answer your question — no, I don't worry about that."

"Really?"

"Really," Pastor Stefan smiled to reassure him. "We are not our heritage or what happens to us. We do not bear the sins of our fathers before us. Who we are and what we become is the accumulation, the culmination of the choices we make. Who my opa was has no bearing on who I am. It took me many years to come to that realization. For most of my life, I was ashamed of who I was, who he was. How could I not be? But I have since found a peace about it."

Thomas tried to memorize what he said. He needed to chew on it for a while. But he had a more pressing curiosity. "Did you ever meet him?"

"Yes, once. After I became a minister, I went and visited him at the Hohenasperg Fortress, where he was imprisoned. He was a sick, old man at this point."

The pastor laughed abruptly and clapped his hands.

Thomas was confused. None of this seemed humorous to him.

Reading Thomas' expression, Pastor Stefan said. "My apologies. It just occurred to me that I called him an old man, but he was only seventy or so. And the older I get, the younger that becomes. He had spent nearly fifty years in prison. Time had been hard for him, and he looked to be much older than his age suggested."

"What was it like?"

"I did not tell him who I was. I expect he just assumed I was a chaplain coming to visit a dying inmate. But I wanted to look in the eyes of a man who was capable of the things he did."

"What did you see?"

The pastor shrugged. "He was a man. Not a demon. I saw

many things. But I do not know what they meant. Maybe he was evil. Or maybe all men are evil, but he succumbed to his baser desires in a way that most of us do not. I don't know."

Thomas looked down at his watch, which vibrated against his wrist with an incoming message from Emma. A kaleidoscope of butterflies erupted in his belly. When he looked up, he knew the interruption had broken the spell of their conversation. He regretted it, though he wasn't sure how much more bizarre information he could take in right now.

Pastor Stefan reached out and put a hand on Thomas' shoulder. "Indulge an old man for a moment longer before you go. I want you to understand this, to truly grok it — are you familiar with that term?"

Thomas was not.

"It's from a book called *Stranger in a Strange Land*. You should read it. Something tells me you'd appreciate it more than most. Back to my point, hear me on this and take it to heart — you are not your grandfather's misdeeds any more than you might lay claim to being a good person because of some good works your mother has done. Only you can choose your path. There will be many deviations, and you will not know where they lead when you make the choice of which route to follow. You can, and should, rely on the wisdom of those you have surrounded yourself with, but your choices are your own. Do you understand?"

Thomas shrugged. "I don't know. I mean, yes, some. But I'll think about it some more."

"Good enough," Pastor Stefan said, standing up. "Please stop by again, Thomas. While our conversations are difficult topics, I do enjoy your company."

The boy smiled and followed the pastor's lead in standing to leave.

16

THE SHEPHERD

EVERY NIGHT, she went for a walk. At the same time. Along the same stretch of road. Regardless of the weather being good or ill. On this night, which was to be her last, the wind howled through the valley. Low cloud cover obscured the moon and stars, but reflected the lights of the town, covering everything in a diffuse gray glow.

The Shepherd's lantern creaked gently as it swayed with his gait. He made his way down Schwanenbacher Strasse and stood at the end of its driveway, wondering how many generations of her family had pattered through this farmhouse.

He ambled up the drive and sat down on the front steps, setting his lantern beside him. Knowing he had some time, he stood back up and began looking around the front of the house for a stone. It needed to be large enough to inflict damage when swung, but small enough that he could wield it in his hand. Before long, he found what he was looking for, a roughly dome-shaped rock that wasn't so smooth as to be difficult to grip. He tested it in his hand. It was larger than a grapefruit and had significant heft. It ought to do nicely.

The Shepherd returned to the steps, lantern on the left,

stone to his right. There he waited, not impatiently. He had been waiting for this one particularly. Anticipating it. A few more minutes were of no consequence.

When he heard the crunching gravel at the end of the drive, conflicting emotions crescendoed within him — dread and eagerness, joy and revulsion. He thought he might be sick and leaned over to retch. Nothing came. It was the same every time.

Her steps slowed. She would have seen him now. She was still outside the circle of illumination cast by her porch lights. "Guten abend, Frau Vogel," he greeted, trying to keep the giddiness out of his voice.

The gravel resumed its underfoot crunching. She entered the light and looked concerned. "How nice to see you this evening."

But he heard the strain that she was attempting to mask with formal language. His presence was a surprise to her, but perhaps not a pleasant one. She had every right to be surprised. He had never made a social call on her before. He should only be here if something were wrong.

Something was wrong. But he intended to rectify it. One zauberi at a time.

Frau Vogel's approach slowed as she drew closer to him. At this rate, she would come to a stop well before she reached him. He stood to greet her, pulling the lantern in front of him at waist level to hide the stone he was picking up and tucking behind his right leg. When he started walking toward her, she stopped altogether, about three meters from him.

"Is everything alright, pastor?"

He adopted a reassuring smile, knowing that his being backlit by the porch lights would render him mostly a silhouette. "Everything is fine. Or at least, we will make it so soon, Wölfin."

She wrinkled her brow, likely in confusion about being called a she-wolf. She had little opportunity to mull it over though. He continued his approach, not hurriedly, not setting off a flight response. Steadily. After the pastor had closed to within arm's reach, he swung his right arm with the flat side of the stone facing outward. He struck the side of her with enough force to render her unconscious, but not kill her ... hopefully. He had things she needed to hear.

Really, though, it wasn't so much that she needed to hear them as it was that he needed to say them. He hadn't told the others, and it was time they understood why he was doing this to them. For them.

She slumped forward as soon as he hit her. He dropped the rock as his arm recoiled from the impact, immediately reaching forward to catch her under the armpits. It wouldn't do for her to fall and smash her head on the ground. She was a more stout woman than he had realized, and he nearly dropped her. By adjusting his feet, he maintained his balance and lowered her slowly to the ground.

He ought to have started this work when he was a younger man. His age was certainly an impediment at times. The natural degeneration of his strength and equilibrium had certainly factored into the equation tonight, though they were not outcome determinant. He found that the work was giving him renewed vigor in ways that he had not expected, without requiring him to resort to ... other means.

He grabbed her hands and dragged her up the driveway toward the house. He took the steps backwards, tugging on Frau Vogel, her torso thumping against each step in turn. Undoubtedly, this means of transporting her would lead to some abrasions and bruising, but it wouldn't make any difference.

Releasing her right wrist and letting her hand slap the wooden boards, the pastor reached behind him and twisted the door handle. When the door unlatched, he used his hip to pop it open. As he pulled her across the threshold, it occurred to him that if they were newlyweds, he would carry her across and to the bedroom for a consummation. Instead, he was preparing for a disunion. There was no redemption for her. She was a wolf, and he had a flock to protect from her and her ilk. She must be dispatched with.

After closing the front door, Pastor Stefan resumed dragging Vogel through the house and into the dining room. He swiveled the armchair at the head of the table so that it faced away from the table. He squatted down, knees popping as he went, to pull Vogel into a sitting position so he could grab her under the arms. Stefan pulled her in close to his chest — under other circumstances, they may have appeared to be embracing — and wrestled her into the chair.

He stopped for a minute to collect his breath, but when she showed small signs of coming to, the pastor hurriedly grabbed the zip ties out of his pocket and began securing her to the chair. One arm to each chair arm. One leg to each of the front chair legs. He liked the symmetry of that. Walking over to the kitchen sink, he picked up a thinning dish rag, rang it out as thoroughly as he could, and returned to Vogel. He placed his thumb on her chin and applied pressure downward, forcing her mouth open and filling it with the damp cloth.

Now it was a waiting game. Stefan had been so hurried with the others. He hadn't had the luxury of time. Tonight was different. He would have her know why this was happening to her. The gardener was weeding his land, and she was a thistle. He stood again and walked around the front of the house, finding windows and closing their treatments. They weren't likely to have visitors this far out of town and at this time of night, but it wouldn't do to be interrupted. He had so much pent-up excitement now that a disruption might ... what? He might kill people he hadn't planned on killing? If eradication was the goal, what did the specifics of the plan's execution matter? It wouldn't be ceremonious, but the ritual was just for his own gratification anyway.

When he returned to his chair opposite Frau Vogel, her eyes

were open, glassy but open. "Welcome back, Wölfin." She murmured and worked her tongue against the dish rag.

Stefan reached across to her, and she flinched. He took hold of a corner of the cloth that extruded from her mouth. "I will take it out, but if you raise a fuss, I will hurt you. Do you understand?"

Her eyes flared, but she nodded her compliance. He gave the cloth a yank and dropped it at her feet.

"Water," she croaked.

Stefan sat back, crossed his right leg over his left, and waved dismissively. "You will not be thirsty all that long."

Her chest heaved as a sob escaped from it. The sound was strangled, as though she were trying to restrain it but could not.

"Do you want to know what this is about?"

Vogel took her time answering. He cocked his head, amused that she was giving it this much consideration. "No. It does not matter."

He stuck his lip out in a pout, feeling playful now. "You are right that it does not matter, in that the outcome will not change the final result. You will be dead either way. But in another way, the reasoning matters far more than the result. So I will tell you to satisfy my own need to say it, even if your resolve is stronger than your curiosity. Are you familiar with the Old Testament in the Bible?"

She looked him squarely in the face but did not respond.

"Fine, I'll recite a passage to you, then. This is from Genesis 6. 'And it came to pass, when men began to multiply on the face of the earth, and daughters were born unto them, that the sons of God saw the daughters of men that they were fair; and they took them wives of all which they chose.' For context here, the *sons of God* are Lucifer's fallen angels."

He watched her for any reaction, but receiving none, he continued with the narrative he'd been waiting a long time to deliver. "'And the Lord said, My spirit shall not always strive with man, for that he also is flesh: yet his days shall be an hundred and twenty years.' Now, pay attention because this is where the zauberi enter the scene. 'The Nephilim were on the earth in those days; and also after that, when the sons of God came in unto the daughters of men, and they bare children to them, the same became mighty men which were of old, men of renown.

"'And God saw that the wickedness of man was great in the earth, and that every imagination of the thoughts of his heart was only evil continually. And it repented the Lord that he had made man on the earth, and it grieved him at his heart. And the Lord said, I will destroy man whom I have created from the face of the earth; both man, and beast, and the creeping thing, and the fowls of the air; for it repenteth me that I have made them.'

"Later in Genesis 6 and 7, God destroyed the earth with a worldwide flood, all except Noah and his family and the animals that boarded the ark with him. You," he shoved a finger in Vogel's face and his eyes blazed with passion, "were supposed to be part of that destruction. The Nephilim — those offspring of the demons who were tempted into relations with women — were such a vile abomination that they brought on the destruction of the earth. But here you are thousands of years later. A remnant. An abominable remnant. My calling, my crusade, is to rid the earth of as many of you as hell will accept. To vanquish the wolves and protect the flock."

Still, Vogel gave him no reaction. Not even further recognition that she understood her fate. When she chose to speak, her words struck hard. "You are nothing. You self-aggrandize your preying on women by claiming it is divine work. But you are no different from any other inadequate man who has taken to attacking those he sees as weaker than himself. But I know I won't dissuade you. You'll call me a temptress and explain away—"

The pastor slapped her with enough force that her head

turned with the impact. His fingers tingled with pain. Heat coursed through his hand.

When she squared up again, she resumed looking him directly in the face, her eyes welling with tears and her cheek bright red with a handprint. It was a recrimination of his failure to remain dispassionate. But how was he supposed to remain composed when he was eradicating the remnant? Not only was it right, but he had found that the work exhilarated him.

He took a step back, giving himself time to recompose himself. "Where are your scissors?" he asked Vogel, who said nothing further. Stefan held up a finger and walked toward the kitchen. He rummaged through drawers until he spied a pair of shears in the knife block.

When he returned to Vogel, he knelt in front of her. She pushed herself into the back of the chair and strained against the zip ties, but had nowhere to go. The trickles of blood that had made their way through hair onto her cheek and down her neck behind her ear exacerbated her wild expression.

Stefan grabbed the bottom of her shirt and roughly cut upward through the collar. He let the shirt fall to the sides, exposing her chest and undergarments. He looked at her for a long time. She was shaking now.

He reached out his right hand and touched her breast lightly, before yanking it back as if from a flame. "My apologies. I should not have done that. I will deal with myself for that. But you should not have tempted me."

Vogel spit in his face. He stood slowly, her saliva running down his cheek. Again, he slapped her. "You will not enjoy this next part, but it is necessary. Just as God marked Cain for his transgressions, I will mark you." He pulled a handkerchief out of the rear pocket of his pants and wiped the spit from his face. He balled up the cloth and instructed her to open her mouth. When she didn't immediately comply, he growled, "I will break your teeth and shove it in through the gap. Open."

She opened her mouth slowly.

"Thank you," he said, pushing the handkerchief in. He pulled out a small roll of duct tape. He applied it over her mouth and wrapped it around her head. Vogel's bravado finally failed her. Tears streamed down her cheeks, fell over the tape, and dripped down her chest.

The pastor knelt in front of her and pulled a razor out of his pocket. A muffled "No, no, no" arose from behind Vogel's restraints. He made the first semi-circular incision, and the protest became a muted scream. She bucked in the chair, and her blood ran freely.

"Stop," Stefan commanded. She did not. Between her bleeding and bucking, it was going to make a mess of the mark. He smeared the blood away from the incision with the handkerchief, but every heartbeat pushed more out. He folded the razor and returned it to his pocket.

He put his hand on her right leg, just above the knee, and began pushing himself up, using her as a support. Before he could regain his footing, she jerked her knee to the side, causing his load to shift unexpectedly. As he fell downward, she forced her left knee up with as much force as she could manage while the zip tie bit into her ankle. Her knee caught him on the cheekbone, opening a small gash under his eye. Once he got himself upright and standing, Stefan looked down at her. She returned the stare, all defiance and loathing. The fear remained, but it was not what defined her last minutes.

Blood trickled down his cheek as he turned wordlessly and walked out the front door, leaving Vogel to wonder what was about to befall her next. Stefan walked far enough down the gravel driveway to retrieve the stone he had first subdued her with. He returned and stood beside her chair.

After the first blow, she grunted involuntarily, but it was the last noise she vocalized. Each successive strike was less solid and more wet. He only stopped when the left side of her head was a concave mess. Stefan leaned forward with his hands on his knees, wheezing and out of breath. Once he had recovered his breathing, he walked around to the back of Vogel's chair and lowered it gently to the floor. He pulled both his knife and handkerchief from his pockets. He moved her shirt aside from where it had fluttered and stuck to the still-wet blood, then thought better of it and used the shirt to dab away the excess blood from his incision.

"Now," he said, as a father who has put the children to bed and finally has a minute to himself. He set about finishing his mark.

17

AGATHA

AGATHA'S PHONE rang at her. She pilfered through the pile of clean laundry she was folding trying to find it. How can two people have so many dirty clothes so often? One of the great regrets of her lifetime was that no one had made a robot like the one on *The Jetsons*. Giving up the search for her phone, she looked at her watch. Markus.

She went to her bedroom to take the call, to be out of earshot of Thomas. She tapped the screen. "Guten tag, Polizeidirektor Fischer," she greeted him in lilting German.

"What are you doing?" he asked, but it did not sound like casual conversation filler. There was intention behind it.

"Are you about to ask me on an impromptu date?"

"Not unless your idea of a date involves a dead body."

Oh. Well, missed that cue. "It would certainly be non-standard for most, but it would be our second such occasion. So I guess I can't rule it out," she said, still a little playfully, despite sensing that the moment wasn't appropriate for it. When Fischer's silence on the other end confirmed it, she asked, "Is it someone we know?"

"Yes ... Frau Vogel."

"Scheisse," Agatha whispered, sitting against the edge of the bed. The heilerin was one of the first to welcome her here. She had brought over a platter of rindsrouladen and become fast friends with Gertrude. Together they had cooked and gossiped to their hearts' content. As the town's most accomplished healer, Vogel always had plenty of news — they liked to call it "news" because it connoted an air of dignity, rather than just two old ladies airing everyone's dirty laundry — to share about Hornberg's residents while they made meals for the sick and unwell. Agatha asked, "What happened?"

"One of her appointments found her this morning. It's bad, Agatha. Very bad. I'll send a car around for you. How soon can you be ready?"

Agatha looked down at herself, trying to remember under pressure when she had last showered ... was it last night? The day before? She smelled at herself. Mostly fine. Nothing a wash-cloth and some dry shampoo couldn't fix.

By the time the car arrived, Agatha had thrown on jeans and a dark shirt and was sitting on the steps waiting for it. Thomas hadn't been overly inquisitive about her departure. She thought he seemed curiously disinterested. *There's no accounting for that boy.*

Agatha had the foresight to grab a snack on her way out the door, not knowing how long they'd be at the scene. It had only taken her into her mid-forties to start thinking ahead like that. She smirked at herself. She was making big strides in personal development.

She opened the front door of the blue-and-yellow Audi to find Pereira in the driver's seat. "Guten—" He paused to look at an incoming message on his watch before resuming his perfunctory greeting. "Guten tag, Frau Wande."

"Howdy, Pereira." She added an extra dash of chipper since

he was clearly unenthusiastic about this assignment. "I'm surprised to see you behind the wheel."

"Not half so surprised as I was at the request, Frau Wande."

Agatha noted that the usually reserved — or at least passive-aggressive — detective must have been really salty about it to go so far as being snarky. Oberhaupt had always told her she had a way with people; it's just that her way was often not dissimilar from a particularly vexing rash. She needed to check in with him again. She had allowed too much time to slide past since the last time.

"You want to use this time to catch me up on what happened to Frau Vogel, or should we just enjoy the silence?"

Before turning up the volume on the news station that had been murmuring in the background, Pereira said, "The Polizeidirektor will tell you what you need to know." They conducted the rest of the drive through and out of Hornberg with a marked lack of conversation. Trees canopied the roadway after they left town. A creek dipped in and out of view to the left. Before long, a cluster of cars appeared ahead. Their lights and bright paint obliterated the surrounding serenity. Pereira turned off the roadway and pulled to a stop in the gravel drive.

He got out without another word, leaving Agatha to decide for herself what to do. She unbuckled her seatbelt while glaring at the receding form of Pereira. She attempted to put her irritation behind her as she got out and took in the scene. Evidence cones were breadcrumbs leading up to the front door and into the house. Agatha steeled herself for whatever she was about to see. As bad as the first two murders had been, at least they were strangers. Maybe they'd already taken the body away. A part of her hoped they had.

She wasn't even sure what she was doing here, or what Markus expected her to contribute. All these folks were far more experienced than her. She had no police training. All she had to go on — what she'd run on most of her life — was intuition and a proclivity toward action. And look where that had gotten her. A widowed bastard with a senile mother. And how much should she really trust herself now anyway, knowing that her father was a monster? That was really messing with her head. How could it not? She'd never been one for self-doubt before. A side effect of an abundance of confidence and near total lack of inhibitions. Was she fundamentally different now that she knew something about herself that had been true all along? Of course not. The only difference was her lack of ignorance. But she couldn't shake the mistrust that the knowledge had sown.

"Agatha," Fischer called.

He motioned for her to come up the steps and onto the cottage's front stoop. She gestured past him inside the house. "How are you?"

He shook his head and looked at the ground. "Not good. No one can teach you how to investigate the murder of a friend. A woman I've known my whole life. She has treated most everyone in this town at some point. I mean, Luka was here just a few weeks ago." Fischer motioned from his belt up to his shoulder. Agatha remembered that day all too well. But it seemed impossible that it was such a short time ago. So much had happened in the interim.

"I'm so sorry, Markus. She really was a treasure."

He nodded. "It is very bad in there. Worse than the others. You don't have to go in."

"You're doing it again," she warned. The hair on her neck stood up, and the belligerence within her bubbled to the surface. Nothing like someone else coddling her to bring out the ornery Agatha she was so much more comfortable with than the doubtful version with whom she'd been contending more recently.

She took the steps, and as she attempted to brush past Fischer, he put a hand on her forearm. "It's quite bad."

She looked him in the eye and pulled her arm away wordlessly as she bustled into the house. She pulled up like a horse that had seen a rattlesnake. The way Frau Vogel was tied to the chair caused Agatha to flashback to Elle all those years ago. She fought to push it aside and stay in the moment. She worked her way up from the naked chest with the bloody witches' mark inscribed in it to the malformed head that slumped forward. The skull was cratered on the left side. Shards stuck into the brain at odd angles, like chips in a bowl of gray guacamole. She realized that the clumps on the floor beside Vogel were blood-covered brain matter as well. Flies had already discovered it.

Agatha's stomach lurched, and she raised a hand to her mouth. She fleetingly realized for the first time the officers who were working the scene. She spun on her heel and made for the front door. Fischer stood where she'd left him. He sidestepped, clearing the pathway to the door as she hurried his way. She leaned over against the left railing in case anything in her needed to make a hasty exit.

After collecting herself but before turning around, she said, "When I turn around, if you have a smug look on your face, I'm going to punch you."

"Others reacted similarly," he said. "Besides, I will leave the smugness to Pereira."

She turned around to face Fischer. "You should have warned me about what I was walking into."

He raised an eyebrow. "Ja, that would have been good of me. Can you go back in?"

"I think I'm okay now."

Agatha entered Vogel's home for a second time. An officer that she recognized from the park photographed the body, being careful to step around anything on the floor that might be evidence. Pereira spoke with another officer, but his eyes stayed on Agatha. Appraising her, judging her. Agatha asked quietly, "Is he always so ... I don't know what the right word is ... detached?"

"I sometimes wonder if he's a robot and his creators forgot to program him to have anything more than the most primitive emotions."

"They at least coded him for dislike because he seems to find me intolerable."

"Yes, I agree. He does. And he is normally an inscrutable judge of character. So does that say more about you or him?"

Agatha flicked her eyes at him and caught the smirk on his lips. "Careful, Polizeidirektor, or they may be investigating two murders."

When Fischer saw that Pereira was still watching them, his demeanor reverted to business. "Here are some things we've put together so far. This killing is obviously different from the others. The first two, we think he was hunting, but he didn't have those two women in mind particularly. He just happened upon them. They were in relatively public places while still being secluded. He had to work quickly. But not here. This was more like trapping. He specifically chose the victim and the setting."

"So what does that mean?"

"I think he's getting more comfortable with it. Sometimes, these things are a compulsion that they're acting on. At first, these killers are inexperienced. They don't know what they're doing. But as they evolve and mature, their tactics change. Some don't. But the more cerebral ones tend to. Our killer seems to be one of those. But there's something else too. He seems to be copying — and we weren't sure of this until now — the murders and attempted murders by a serial killer from seventy years ago, named Heinrich Pommerenke. Do you know of him?"

"I didn't until recently. But I do now. I was checking on Thomas' search history—"

"You what?" Fischer was affronted at her admission. "That is a violation of his privacy, Agatha."

The hackles on her neck raised for a second time, and her

cheeks flushed at being chastised. "Privacy schmivacy. He lives under my roof. I get to know what he's looking at. And I'm glad to report it's nothing too weird or unexpected from a boy of his age with the whole of the internet at his disposal. But maybe this isn't the time to get into parenting techniques."

Fischer went from shaking his head in moderate disbelief to nodding in agreement that it was a good time to return to the subject at hand. "Right. So the murder on the train, the throat slashing at the park, this," he said, gesturing at Frau Vogel. "They were all means of killing or attempted kills that Pommerenke employed."

"What's next then?" Agatha asked.

"I don't know. Pereira just made the connection. I'm not terribly familiar with the details of the Pommerenke murders. There is one significant difference though."

Agatha pulled her gaze away from the windows that overlooked the woods and creek that ran behind Vogel's house, and looked at Fischer.

"Pommerenke raped all his victims. He raped a lot of women, even women he did not kill. Our man isn't doing that. It's an important distinction, but I don't yet know what it means. We may have to consult with a criminal psychologist."

Agatha flung her eyes back to the windows. "I think we're being watched."

Fischer turned his head in the same direction but didn't see anything. "Perhaps it was a rabbit?"

"It wasn't."

"A deer then. These woods are filled with red deer."

"No," she said flatly. "It didn't move like a deer. Too cumbersome. I'm going to step out the back door."

"Agatha, that's not a good ..." He didn't finish his sentence because his words were falling on her backside. Agatha circumnavigated the folks collecting evidence around Frau Vogel. She kept her gaze fixed out the windows, making her way to the back door. Fischer followed.

She stopped on the grass behind the house. All was still. Fischer pulled to a stop beside her. "How sure are you?"

Agatha's skin tingled. Something out there was watching her. Someone. Had their killer come back to watch the show? Had he done the same thing at the park? And at the train tracks? She realized that he could have. One was a public place. The other was at night. Not only had he been ahead of them. He'd been spectating like he was at a football game. A chill crept over her as she remembered how long she'd been alone with that first body. What he could have done — or more like, could have attempted to do — to her, if he'd wanted.

She clenched her jaw, molars grinding against each other.

Agatha snatched the ponytail holder off her wrist and put her hair up. Fischer looked first at her wrist, then her head. "I always thought that was just some peculiar bracelet."

When she glanced back at him, excitement blazed in her eyes. She hadn't been the predator in a long time. Her blood ran hot with the prospect of it. Agatha took another step forward, then another. She readied her hands at her side. She and Fischer closed the gap between themselves and the creek.

Something burst from the underbrush on the far side of the creek and into the dense shadows of the forest canopy.

18

AGATHA

WHATEVER HAD BOLTED WAS large and moved quickly. She couldn't get a good look at it through the growth on the forest floor. Agatha broke into a run. She was at risk of her prey escaping. Fischer yelled after her, but she heard his footsteps quicken as well.

She eyed the creek as she approached. Could she clear it with a leap? Twenty-something Agatha probably could. Middle-aged Agatha absolutely couldn't. She was going to have to contend with wet sneakers for the duration.

Agatha launched from full stride at the edge of the bank, landing in the cold mountain stream with a grunt and a splash. Not just wet shoes, but wet jeans too. As Fischer splashed down beside her, she bounded out and onto the other side. She kept her eyes up, hoping for the best, so that she didn't lose sight of the dark, awkward-moving shape heading further into the forest.

She was losing ground to the suspect. Before it disappeared entirely into the gloom of the forest canopy, she watched it split itself in two and go around a tree. Her mind briefly turned itself inside out in the process of working out what it just witnessed. *Occam's razor*, she thought.

"There are two of them," she called to Fischer. "You go left. I'll go right. If we can catch up to them, maybe we can hem them between us."

He nodded, catching up to her just in time to take off again.

The uphill grade convinced Agatha that her daily walks weren't sufficient exercise to keep her in shape for chasing bad guys. Her breathing coarsened, coming in great gusts as she ran. She consoled herself that if she were just running a straight line, she'd have been fine. But not with monitoring for stones and deadfall to trip over. Then there were the low-hanging limbs attempting to clothesline her that added to the degree of difficulty.

She didn't know how long they'd been running through the woods when she began to have doubts. She couldn't very well check her watch. A while though, that was for sure. But what did the time matter anyway? Either she could maintain the current level of exertion or not. She used her forearm to wipe the sweat out of her eyes and off her forehead with one swipe.

Agatha's sole encouragement was the steady gains she made on the dark-clad figures up ahead. Her resolve to catch them exceeded their ability to escape. Fischer was just as driven. He kept pace with her some twenty meters to her left.

What's the plan here? We can't just go on chasing them indefinitely. In answer to her question, the subjects ducked behind an ancient beech tree and vanished. Agatha stumbled forward several more strides before slowing to a walk. As she worked to get her breathing under control, she looked to Fischer. She pointed at her own eyes, inquiring whether he had a sightline. He shook his head and raised his arms in a question. He didn't know where they'd gone either.

Fischer moved his hands in two wide arcs that met in the middle. Agatha nodded. She focused on the massive tree, not wanting to confuse it with one of its siblings and converge in the wrong place.

She was grateful that stealth was more important than speed now. The perennially damp forest floor provided suitable cover and allowed her to move mostly soundlessly. She was less appreciative of the humidity. Her hair was a mop, and her dark shirt clung to her like a fourth layer of skin. She peeled it up and away to wipe the sweat off her face, but managed only to distribute it more evenly. Agatha yanked the shirt away from her face. Maybe she should have taken that shower after all. Not that it would have mattered all that much in this soup she was navigating through.

She looked to her left to check on Fischer. He had begun his inward arc to meet her on the other side of the tree. She wished he'd pull his gun out of its holster. Maybe American cops were too aggressive on that front, but the Germans were too reticent. If ever there was a time to have your sidearm handy, it was chasing someone from a murder scene. Not someone. Two someones. Had they missed some cue that these were tandem killings? Surely not. How rare was that anyway? The Menendez brothers came to mind, but they hadn't been serial killers.

Focus, she fussed at herself. These questions would answer themselves in due time. Now was the time not to get killed because she was distracting herself.

A blast of something came from the direction of the beech. It smashed into the tree in front of her and brought a large limb crashing down at her feet. Ice encrusted the broken end of the tree limb. On her left, a wall of fire drove toward Fischer, trying to back him down. He nonchalantly encased himself in a translucent, glimmering shield as the inferno washed over him. She hadn't known what his können was until now.

Agatha's heart rate had been accelerated before. Now it was redlining. She charged toward their attackers. A loud curse from ahead. The figures burst from behind the tree, running away again.

As they ran, she saw ahead that the men were approaching a giant boulder. Agatha formed an orb of molten fire in her hand and flung it ahead of the subjects. It landed to their right at the base of the boulder and burst into a conflagration, driving them left. Pushing them toward Fischer, hopefully. She hadn't been able to look or even listen to determine whether he was in place.

She received her affirmation when the two subjects collapsed to the ground. They fell under the weight of some sort of shimmering blanket that Fischer had projected outward. It looked to be the same substance he had surrounded himself with moments before. The men on the ground struggled in vain against the constraint.

Agatha dropped her hands to her knees to catch her breath. That last sprint was rough. Then remembering a lesson from youth sports many years — *Scratch that, several decades before. Geez, I'm getting old* — she stood up and clasped her hands over her head to open her lungs.

Fischer approached their subjects, no longer with any caution. They had mostly stopped writhing, and as he stood over them, they stilled completely. He looked to her in an expression laden with fury. When she noticed the shoes of the nearest subject, she knew why. Her blood boiled. She would recognize those doodle-covered Chuck Taylors anywhere.

Fischer allowed his shield to dissipate. Luka and Thomas sat up. They looked at each other in fear, then at the forest floor. Agatha snatched Thomas off the ground by the front of the shirt. She may be feeling old, but she was still strong, especially when her mama-bear instincts had been awakened. She slammed Thomas against a tree. His head bounced lightly off the sodden, moss-covered trunk.

Agatha kept his shirt balled in her fists and crowded his

space. She looked up at the boy who had outgrown her. Thomas averted his eyes.

"What were you thinking?!"

Despite the words, it was clearly not a question. Thomas attempted to answer anyway. "I—"

"Don't talk," Agatha interrupted. Thomas closed his mouth that had still been attempting to form a word. "You could have been hurt. Or even killed."

"We—"

"I said don't talk." Agatha shoved him as she spoke, pressing him harder against the tree. "You threw fire at Markus!" her indignation reaching a new level.

"Not—" Thomas cut himself off this time and looked sheepishly, apologetically in the Fischer's direction.

"Agatha," Fischer coaxed, placing a hand on her left shoulder. Instinctively, she swatted it away. But the sequence seemed to break the spell of her fury. She released Thomas' shirt and stepped backward.

"Frau Wande?" Luka said, knowingly placing himself in the line of fire by interceding for his friend.

She responded by looking at him, saying nothing.

"We just wanted to see what was going on."

His father asked, "Why did you run?"

Luka shrugged.

"That is not an answer."

Thomas picked up the mantle. "We thought ..." he hesitated to see if Agatha was going to cut him off again. "We thought we'd get in trouble for being there."

"You *thought*?" Agatha scoffed. "That sure is giving yourself a lot of credit for whatever the unilaterally stupid decision-making process you used should be called."

Thomas' eyes welled with tears. He attempted to hide it by clearing his throat and wiping his face on his shirtsleeve. Agatha recognized the gesture. He'd done the same thing since he was small. *The boy may be a moron, but at least he's still sensitive to getting in trouble. He's certainly had plenty of opportunities lately.* She wished she knew more about what Joseph was like as a teenager. Her mother's words, spoken whenever Thomas was acting out, kept replaying themselves in her head, "You're paying for your raising." Remembering that Thomas wasn't all that much different from herself brought Agatha some much-needed calm, and a little bit of regret.

Fischer took the lead. "The two of you go check to make sure the fires have died out. Douse them thoroughly, Luka." He added with an edge, "And maybe do all of that without bringing any trees down on our heads."

The boys slunk away.

Agatha and Markus turned to face each other. Both had more questions than answers. Markus led with one of his, "What are we supposed to do with them?"

"Were you like Luka?"

Fischer smiled grimly, "It is like looking in a mirror."

"What did your folks do when you got in trouble?"

"My father got drunk and hit me."

Agatha tilted her head from one side to the other. "I guess that's not an option?"

"Decidedly not."

Agatha shrugged, "I don't know then. My parenting manual doesn't cover the part where your kid sneaks off to a crime scene and makes you chase him through the forest."

"You have a manual?"

Agatha raised her eyebrows at him.

"Oh, I see."

Thomas and Luka returned, and the group stood in an uncomfortable circle. Looking at the ground between everyone's feet, Thomas asked quietly, "Did y'all figure out what our punishment would be?"

"Your punishment," Fischer repeated. "Let me ask this first — Luka, how did you get here today?"

Luka directed his eyes at the same space that Thomas' gaze occupied, and it was beginning to feel crowded. "I … uhh …"

"We," Thomas said, showing solidarity.

Luka glanced at his friend with appreciation, then reverted to looking at the ground while answering the question. "We borrowed your car. Parked it a little ways down the road so no one would notice it." Luka dug through his right front pocket for the key and offered it to Fischer.

"That's what I thought. Let me recap your actions and help us get some perspective. You started with theft of a motor vehicle and graduated to battery with a deadly weapon against a police officer — that's you, Thomas. You, Luka, engaged in assault with a deadly weapon when you attempted to drop a tree limb on Agatha. I think we could easily make charges stick for evading or resisting arrest as well. Did I miss anything, Agatha?"

She shook her head.

"I didn't think so. So when you ask me about your punishment, here's my answer: Any prison in Germany would be happy to house you."

The boys looked sideways at each other, their eyes widened. They dared not look up.

19

THOMAS

AS THEY BUMPED along in the back seat of Fischer's police car, making their way back to town from Frau Vogel's house, Luka whispered, "What do you think is going to happen?"

"I don't think we're going to see sunlight again until school starts," Thomas said.

Luka nodded.

What they had done was dumb. All of it. Dumb was an understatement. Taking the car had been dumb. Everything after that had escalated into something that *dumb* was inadequate to describe.

To pass the time, Thomas guessed at what his punishment would be. He thought back to when he had burned Luka. What had Agatha prescribed then? He realized, to his surprise, that she hadn't legislated any punishment. It occurred to him that might actually make things worse. Maybe he'd get a double helping of it now. By the time his mom let him out of the house again, Emma would have probably found some other guy to date. Thomas slumped further into his seat. Not that she had a ton of options in Hornberg. There just weren't that many kids their age. But a girl like her had whatever options she wanted.

Fischer stopped the car in front of their house on Garten-strasse. Thomas and Agatha both unbuckled themselves and looked to their respective companions for a show of support before getting out.

Agatha was closest to the curb and waited for Thomas to round the back of the car and go ahead of her toward the house. Thomas took this as confirmation that she wouldn't be letting him out of her sight for a while. He had the urge to explain himself again to see if it would help. But he usually talked too much in these situations, so he tried a different tack and held his tongue. After trudging up the driveway, he leaned against the house with one hand while reaching down with the other to pull off his sodden sneaker.

"Don't take your shoes off," Agatha instructed.

It was the first time she'd spoken to him since they'd been in the woods. After the four of them had hiked back to Frau Vogel's house, Thomas and Luka had waited while she and Fischer had explained the situation to Pereira and the others, followed by Fischer giving instructions to his crew. Thomas was empathetic enough to recognize that the embarrassment they'd caused on top of the strain of the circumstances had intensified things nearly to their breaking point. But as a teenager, he was also just narcissistic enough to think that whatever punishment they got was unjust. They just wanted to know what was going on. Besides, it wasn't even his idea. Luka had texted him, telling him to be ready in five minutes, and that was it. He didn't know where they were going until they were on their way. Of course, he did know that Luka wasn't driving age yet. His plea of inno-cence wasn't without its holes.

"They're muddy," he said.

Agatha waved to Fischer as he pulled off. "We're not going inside."

"Okay." He would not ask like she wanted him to. If she was going to be coy, he'd just wait her out.

"You wait here. I'm going in to grab some towels, food, and water. Then I'll be back out."

Forget it. He couldn't not ask. "For what?"

"We're going to practice."

The color slid out of Thomas' face. "No. I'm not doing that." His tone was more resolute than defiant. He reached down for his shoe again.

Agatha's voice was calm as water. "If you take that shoe off, you'll go barefoot."

He whined, "I'm tired and hungry and gross." Thomas pulled at his shirt. "And I don't want to do this."

"I couldn't possibly care less. You want to play games with the können that I taught you so that we could hide your true gift? Fine. But now we're going to see what you can do. Have you been practicing?"

Thomas fixated his attention on his shoes. They were more brown now than the faded black that they had been when the day began. He shook his head.

"That's what I thought. You've been lazy. But that's alright. Now we'll practice. I'll get the stuff."

"I have to pee," Thomas offered his final protest.

Agatha opened the front door. "When we get there, you can pee wherever you want. That's one of the luxuries the great outdoors provides."

He sighed. It was all the protest he had left. He was resigned to what they were doing. He wanted to tell her it wasn't laziness. That's not why he didn't practice. Every time he used his true können, he saw their faces. All the corpses he'd reanimated. Their gray skin with the fur and feathers sloughing off. Their deflated eyeballs that kept trying to slip out of their sockets. And the stink. These monstrosities revisited whenever he used his schöpfer abilities. The visions left him nauseated and haunted him for days whenever he closed his eyes. But he hadn't told her. Couldn't tell her.

Thomas slid down the wall. When Agatha came back out, his folded arms rested against his knees and propped up his head.

"Let's go," she said, walking to the car that she'd backed into the driveway. He'd once asked her about why she always backed into parking spots. She'd said only, "Habit from another life a long time ago. Sometimes you gotta get out of a place quick, fast, and in a hurry," and hadn't elaborated further.

They got into the car in two very different mental spaces. Where Agatha appeared to be determined, Thomas had acquiesced to the inevitable. They turned left out of the driveway, right onto Mühlenpeterweg, and immediately right again on Reichenbacher Strasse. He knew the route by heart. He thought he could probably get them to their destination with his eyes closed, although avoiding pedestrians in town could get a little tricky.

Frau Vogel had told them about this place eight years ago. While they'd been at her house one day, Agatha had asked her about a secluded place they might practice. It was the closest his mother had come to disclosing their secret to anyone. While Vogel was the keeper of many of the town's secrets — and perhaps, because of this — she had the discretion not to inquire further. She described this place, and they'd been going ever since.

Agatha drove into town and turned north. They kept the river Gutach on their right until they reached the Thai massage place and took a left on the next road. That road may have had a name, or it may not. It was little more than a pig trail that ran parallel to a creek called Wonnenbach, as it carried them into the depths of the forest and eventually petered out, having lost its motivation to blaze its trail any further. Rather than pulling off to the side of the road, Agatha picked a place to park. They were just outside of nowhere, surrounded on three-and-a-half sides by forest, and they'd never seen evidence of other human traffic out this far, so it's not as if her haphazard parking was inconsiderate.

When Agatha stopped the car, Thomas breathed slowly and deeply several times, clearing his mind of everything else. It was a process, and he had several minutes of hiking ahead of him that would allow time for, and even enable, the transfiguration. Maybe with enough concentration, he could keep the ghosts away.

The Wonnenbach diverged from the road they had traveled in on and wound into the trees. Thomas and Agatha stepped into its mostly dry bed and followed it into the forest. A green canopy enveloped them, requiring their eyes to adjust to the comparative dimness. The landmarks here were subtle. There were no waterfalls, no extraordinary features. The place's beauty lay in its relative homeliness. Thomas knew it intimately.

The further they walked, the less tense he felt about the day's events. It was as though the tension were being drawn to the surface and wicked away. He even realized a certain lightness about himself when he found that he was hopping from one boulder to the next, rather than plodding through or beside the creek bed.

Thirty minutes in, they neared their destination. On the approach, Thomas saw exotic plants interspersed with the native foliage. His handiwork. When he was young, he thought it was fun to grow hibiscus and Venus flytraps and every other wild thing he could think of. At his mother's request, there were even strands of passion fruit vines strung here and there. As much as he once loved his creations, he now recognized them for the alien invaders they were.

With every step now, the water beneath their feet became clearer. The plants a more vibrant green, hosting flowers that exploded with color. Then there were the animals that had been drawn to this modern Garden of Eden. Mice, squirrels, and rabbits could be found peering out from behind leaves. In the same way the first creatures did not fear Adam and Eve, they did not run from Thomas and Agatha. Deer nibbled at the lush grass. Goats tempted each other to try daring jumps from one boulder to another. He hadn't spotted any predators yet. But with this congregation of food sources, they must be nearby.

Thomas stopped and closed his eyes. He inhaled through his nose. While the musky odors of the animals reached him, the sweet aromas of nectar and pollen in a garden of perennial springtime overwhelmed his senses. His creations cried out and drew him toward them. Their call wasn't audible; instead, it reverberated through him, intensifying as he entered the garden and was surrounded on all sides by the works of his hands.

Thomas only opened his eyes again when Kleron's crushed and rotting head invaded his reverie and whinnied.

Agatha tilted her head inquiringly. He didn't know that she had been watching. "Same thing?"

"Yep," he answered, making sure she couldn't miss his contempt at being forced to be here. "Always the same thing."

"Things are happening, Thomas. All around us. We must be ready. You don't know when you're the one who will be next."

Thomas shook his head. "You're just paranoid."

"Paranoid?! Are you kidding me? Vulcan wants to be your puppet master. There are dead bodies turning up all over this town. I have half a mind to up and leave. If it weren't for your grandmother and aunt, we'd be in Croatia by now."

"You might. I'm not going anywhere," Thomas said.

"Of course not. You won't practice your abilities. Refuse to use them offensively. Tell me you won't run. You'll wind up dead like the rest of them, leaving me here alone. Just like …" Agatha ran out of steam and her voice faltered.

"Say it," Thomas pushed.

She shook her head.

"Say it."

Green tendrils reached out of the ground and grabbed

Agatha's wrists, bound her ankles. She tried to snatch her hands away from them. But the vines were too strong. The half dozen or so that had affixed themselves to each appendage held her firmly. Their siblings wound around them, forming ropes and slithering up past her wrists and ankles, up her arms and legs.

"Say it," Thomas demanded again. His eyes glittered with anger.

The vines rushed up her torso, coiling themselves as they went, until finally they reached her neck. Their roots took hold of her throat and snugged against it.

"You'll wind up dead just like your father. He wasn't zauber and got in over his head. If you won't get yourself together, you'll be just like him." Agatha's anger matched his own. "And I'll be left here to bury you. Is that what you want to hear?"

"You don't know what it's like!" Thomas yelled back at her, further constricting the vines that encased her.

20

AGATHA

AGATHA SOFTENED HER TONE. "Baby boy, I may be the only person in the entire world who does know what it's like."

The living bonds that held Agatha became brown and brittle before falling away, as Thomas collapsed to the forest floor. She hurriedly brushed at her arms and legs, shedding herself of the remaining vines, now little more than withered husks. She rushed to where Thomas crouched and wrapped her arms around him in a smothering hug.

After a minute, she lowered herself to the ground and sat with her back against a tree. She pulled at Thomas and coaxed him into her arms and onto her lap. She whispered, "It's okay, baby boy," into his straw-colored hair until she was sure that he had heard her, and the swell of his sobs receded.

When Thomas finally sat upright, Agatha grunted as his weight redistributed itself. "You're a little bigger now than the last time you sat in my lap and had a cry."

A chortled laugh escaped Thomas before the embarrassment and shame colored his expression. Agatha placed her hands on his cheeks and wiped away the more stubborn tears with her thumbs. She pulled him forward and kissed his forehead. He looked away sharply as she let him go. "Don't be embarrassed. You're never too old to have a come-apart."

Shame gave way to guilt, and still Thomas couldn't meet her eyes. He asked quietly, "Did you think I was going to … you know?"

Agatha's lips turned up. "Hurt me? Kill me? Umm … no. Matricide takes a whole lot of gumption, and — and I mean this in the best possible way — I don't think you have the stones for that."

He flashed a defiant look at her. He wanted her to think he was tough. She raised an eyebrow at him, watching his inner turmoil continue to play out on his face. But maybe being tough enough to kill your mother wasn't a bone worth picking.

"Can I be real with you for a minute though?" she asked.

Thomas nodded.

"I made peace with my mortality a long time ago. And there are some days that it would be a relief. Life is so much harder than I thought it would be. I just thought things would get easier, be easier. But there's been so little reprieve. I feel like I've been moving from one tragedy to the next for the last thirty years. And I'm tired. Down to my bones. I'm just exhausted."

Thomas' eyes were the size of dinner plates.

Agatha grimaced. "Was that too much? That was too much."

Nodding, he asked, "Are you, like, suicidal or something?"

Now Agatha was ashamed. She'd laid too much on the boy. And as hard a hand as he'd been dealt, he wasn't yet in a position to understand what she was talking about. She had to keep this bottled up and not pour it out on him. A boy isn't prepared to hear that kind of truth from his mother. She reached out and tousled his hair. "No, buddy, that's not something you need to worry about. I have my struggles, but that's not one of them."

"Okay," he said, getting to his feet.

Agatha held out her hands. "Help your momma up." Thomas grabbed hold and pulled.

"I guess we need to practice now?" Thomas asked.

"Practice? You just weaponized your können in a way I haven't seen you do before. So I'd say we can pretty well call that today's lesson."

The boy smiled sheepishly.

"What we need to do is talk about why it is you dread coming out here so much."

The smile faded, and he let out a noise that was somewhere between a grunt and a sigh. "I don't want to talk about it."

"And I don't care what you want." *That was a little harsher than intended, but whatever.* She knew he would rather cut off his own hand than talk about his feelings, and she could identify with that. But it had to be done. Agatha crossed her arms and waited. She had no doubt that she could wait him out. She'd had much more training with tactical patience. Besides that, she had the car keys.

"Fine," Thomas conceded with a fluster. "I can feel it, all of it. Everything I made. It's like it's pressing in on me. And all the animals want to talk to me, all at the same time. I can't keep it all out. It makes me crazy, like a ... I don't know ... like a hive of bees got let loose inside of me."

"Oh," she murmured.

Thomas shook his head. He wasn't finished. "But mostly, it's because I see *them*."

"Them who?" Agatha asked.

Thomas massaged his temples with his fingertips like doing so would help to erase the images he was frustrated to have to describe. "Them. Kleron and them from when I was a kid. I can't keep it out."

"Oh," she said softly. "Buddy, you did what you had to do. You saved my life. It was the bravest thing I've ever seen."

"I know. I know. It's not even that I feel bad or guilty about it. It's just that ... I'm not explaining it very well."

"Take your time," Agatha suggested, and held her arms out

at her sides. The weather was perfect, as were their surroundings. Flowers and foliage in the foothills of the mountains, with a creek meandering lazily alongside them. In Birmingham, it would have still been ninety degrees with ninety-five percent humidity, the kind of stifling air that nearly suffocates you. But not here, not in their corner of the Black Forest, at least not since the morning haze had burned away. "We don't have anywhere to be other than here."

"Okay. It's whenever I use my schöpfer ability, whatever I create kind of imprints itself on me." His eyes lit up, and he started talking faster. "Alright, you remember how in Spider-Man the spider bites Peter Parker and changes his DNA and that's how he becomes Spider-Man. It's like that, but not really."

Thomas had a very expectant look on his face. Agatha didn't want to break it to him that his was one of the worst explanations of anything she'd ever heard in her life. "That was ... very descriptive."

He appeared to be pleased with himself. "So you understand now?"

"Maybe? Not really. But I think it's less important that I follow what you're saying, than that we figure out a way to help you deal with it."

"Yeah, I guess," Thomas said, a little crestfallen.

"Maybe we should get you started with a prayer and meditation practice."

Thomas' jaw nearly unhinged itself. "What are you talking about? You're not even religious."

Agatha said, "I'm open to it."

"Since when?"

She opened her mouth to answer, but didn't have one immediately ready. "Okay, so I haven't been, but I'd like to think of myself as the kind of person who can be."

Thomas looked at her skeptically, then decided to test these new waters. "Fine. I'll talk to Pastor Stefan about it."

"Who?" Agatha felt like the tables had suddenly turned, or she'd been lulled into some kind of trap.

"Pastor Stefan. He's the minister at Evangelische Kirche. I've talked to him a few times. I like him. Maybe he can help me with this prayer and meditation thing."

Agatha swallowed her first instinct to buck against it. She didn't like that he was spending time with a man she didn't know and not telling her about it. But as the sunlight glittered through the trees and landed on his cheek, it lit up the stubble on his face. He was nearly a man himself now. He was going to have — and should have — his own life, his own secrets that she wasn't privy to. "Okay. Maybe he can."

"Really? That's your answer?"

"Mm-hmm."

"I can see you have more to say," Thomas offered provocatively.

Agatha pasted on her best smile, though it didn't quite reach her eyes, "Like I said, Thomas, I'm open to new things." But that didn't mean she wasn't going to be introducing herself to this Pastor Stefan cat.

21

AGATHA

As Agatha opened the door, she wandered back through her memories, trying to figure when was the last time she had been inside a police station, if ever. She wondered whether a town the size of Hornberg would normally have warranted its own polezeiposten — the nearest state police station was in Triberg — but Hornberg's exceptional existence had required certain other exceptions as well. Policing was among them. Some things just happened here that were beyond the ken of the standard-issue police officer.

Even calling it a police station was being generous. It was an unassuming space that sat on the eastern end of Werderstrasse at the end of a row of buildings. The only full-time employees were Fischer, Pereira, and the receptionist who greeted her efficiently and directed her to the conference room. Fischer had explained that the other folks working the scenes were deputized part-time support.

When Agatha walked into the room, Pereira and Fischer were pouring over crime scene photographs that had been distributed over a table. Fischer looked up at her and asked, "Do we have another murder on our hands?"

"What? Already?" Agatha asked, a sinking feeling in her belly. She looked back and forth between them a little wildly.

Pereira looked confused, which was a rarity for him.

Realizing his mistake, Fischer waved both hands in front of himself. "No, no. My apologies. I was making a joke. I meant, did you kill Thomas after yesterday's episode?"

"Oh. No. We had a real long talk about things, so he probably would have rather I killed him than have that conversation."

Fischer said, "How very German of you."

"Let's get started," Pereira suggested.

Agatha thought the unspoken remainder of that sentence was "… because the sooner we get her out of here, the better."

"Where do you want to start?" Fischer asked.

"With Pommerenke. In February 1959, he rapes a woman and slits her throat. He had committed some other crimes, including sex crimes before that one, but as far as we know, that was his first murder. In March, he kills a woman with a stone and leaves her body on a railway embankment. Two months later he breaks into a home and attempts to strangle a woman. But she's able to call for help, and he flees. The next day, he boards a train and stabs a woman in the chest. He throws her body off the train, then disembarks the train himself, goes back to the body, and commits sexual acts with it."

"This is all sounding darkly familiar," Fischer said.

"Except for the sex stuff. Our guy isn't doing that," Agatha said.

Pereira reluctantly pointed to her in acknowledgment of her observation. "Ja. Over the next month, he commits multiple rapes and attempts several murders by stabbing. His last murder is in June 1959. He rapes and strangles a 16-year-old girl and dumps her body in the woods."

Fischer nodded grimly. "Who has access to this information?"

Pereira shrugged and frowned. "Anyone with access to a search engine. There are pages dedicated to him in multiple languages all over the web. He has encyclopedia pages, serial killer fan pages." Pereira shrugged again, emphasizing the ease with which detailed knowledge of the Pommerenke murders could be obtained.

"How did they catch him?" Agatha asked.

"He was foolish, like most of them. He committed a robbery and left a footprint that matched a footprint he had left at one of the murder scenes. When a man provided a description of the culprit from the robbery, Pommerenke was recognized in Hornberg the next day and arrested. Shortly afterward, he confessed to dozens of crimes. Even many he had not yet been linked to."

When Fischer opened his mouth to ask his next question, Pereira held up a finger to cut him off. "There are two things though that are not on any of the websites and, as far as I can tell, are only found in the polizei files. First is the witches' mark." Pereira opened a folder that had been sitting on the table beside him. It was thick with documents that had yellowed over the years. But on top were black-and-white photographs of the victims. Pereira laid the photographs he had cultivated side-by-side in front of Fischer and Agatha. "Pommerenke carved the same witches' mark into his victims that our man is doing."

Agatha inhaled sharply at the grisly close-ups. The knife-cuts were almost surgical in their precision. She prompted, "And the other?"

"It follows the first. All Pommerenke's victims were zauberi. In his confessions, he is reported as saying that he had come to believe women were the root of all evil, and he was on a mission to punish them. But I think that was only a partial truth. It may have been more specific to zauberin."

"I can't believe they were able to keep that under wraps like that," Agatha said.

Fischer found himself able to contribute to the conversation finally. "Remember, in 1959, they would have only been fifteen years removed from World War 2. Much of Germany was still being rebuilt. The wounds were still fresh for us here. They would have been very sensitive to any killings being done to eradicate a certain portion of the population." Fischer placed his palms on the table and hovered over the photographs of the victims who had been stabbed, strangled, slit open, or stoned, before having their clothes torn away so they could have a mark carved into their chests. "They were quite motivated to keep things quiet." Agatha was ready with her next query. "If the information about the mark and the zauberin was never reported, then who could have known?"

Pereira nodded as though he'd been anticipating the question. "That is a more difficult question. It appears that even the prosecutors and those who adjudicated him did not know; either that, or nothing was ever reduced to writing. This folder," Pereira nudged the one that had contained the photographs, "was not with the primary investigatory materials."

"Is that unusual?" Agatha asked, assuming the answer.

"Quite so. Usually in investigative files, everything is kept together and organized so no information is lost. But if there were some information that you wanted to be ... partitioned, you would put it elsewhere."

"Like we are doing with our current investigation?" suggested Fischer.

"Indeed."

Agatha raised her hand like a schoolgirl with a question. "I'm feeling a bit out of the loop here."

Fischer filled the gap. "The state policing agencies can access our investigatory materials, just as we can theirs. So given our particular circumstances, there are some things stored locally and not accessible beyond this building."

Makes sense, Agatha thought. *You didn't want some knucklehead in Munich accidentally learning there's a contingent of magical folk in a small town in western Germany. Oh, and they're being picked off one by one.*

"So back to Pommerenke," Fischer said, "we only know for sure that he and the police who investigated the crime knew. Who else could have known?"

Pereira answered, "That is hard to say. He was imprisoned for nearly fifty years. Guards he became close to, cell mates, visitors — who knows who he might have confided in during that time?"

"Let's start there then. I want a list of every Gefängniswärter that was assigned to him, every visitor that he had, everyone he shared a cell with, and every warden that oversaw Bruchsal prison during his tenure."

The word *warden* sent a shiver down Agatha's spine. When both men looked at her in response to the twitchy movement, she said, "Guess a possum walked over my grave."

Pereira ignored the interruption as best he could, refusing to ask the obvious follow-up question about what that meant, and nodded his compliance to Fischer before adding, "Many of these people will be dead now."

"Good," Fischer replied. "It will truncate the work we have to do in interviewing people."

Agatha asked, "Is there anything I can do? I don't seem to have a lot of utility at the moment."

Pereira's smug expression that he'd worn throughout his little seminar became even more self-satisfied. Agatha would have paid good money to punch him in the throat. He looked her directly in the face. "I have been saying as much to Polizeidirektor Fisch—"

"Enough," Fischer said, waving him off. "Your time will come back around, Agatha. In the meantime, we must consider what proactive measures we can take. Our killer's timeline seems to be accelerating. There is already an underlying panic creeping through the town. It will become hysteria if we turn up a couple more dead bodies. I was thinking about imposing a curfew for the next few weeks."

"You don't think the tourists will notice that?" Agatha said.

Fischer frowned. "Ah. I hadn't yet considered that." His frown flipped, and he gestured to Agatha. "See? Already, you are contributing again."

Pereira rolled his eyes.

Agatha's cheeks flushed with anger. She leaned toward Fischer and said in a quiet, steady voice — the one that Thomas was always so scared of — "If you ever patronize me like that again, your boy Pereira there is going to have the quickest and easiest murder investigation of his career, because he's going to be a witness to it."

"Uh, noted. My apologies."

She nodded graciously.

"Perhaps, we could tell the tourists there have been bear sightings?"

Pereira furrowed his brow. "There haven't been bears in these forests in the last hundred and fifty years."

Fischer shrugged. "I do not anticipate the tourists will be aware of that. But I am open to better suggestions." He looked back and forth between Agatha and Pereira. "If none are forthcoming, we will proceed with a curfew due to bears. Please get that under way."

Pereira looked uncomfortable for a minute before speaking again. "There is one thing I haven't figured out yet."

"Who the killer is?" Agatha asked innocently. She couldn't help herself.

"No. Well, yes …." Pereira cut himself off, glaring at Agatha and trying to figure out how to answer the question.

"Agatha, please," said Fischer.

Agatha raised her hands in mock surrender. "Okay, what is it you haven't figured out?"

"I don't know whether it is significant or not, but he's only killing heilerin. It's statistically improbable that it would be happenstance."

"That is puzzling," Fisher said.

Agatha looked at them in disbelief. "Have you two never done any tactical training? The reason should be readily apparent to both of you."

The two men exchanged glances, but neither had an answer. They returned their focus to Agatha.

"If you were cutting your teeth on doing some murders and you were attacking people who had können, who is the least likely to be able to hurt you? The ones whose abilities are as healers. Not the ones who are human weapons." She saw the light click on for each of them. "He wants to minimize risk while attacking. He is going to choose prey that poses the smallest threat to him. He's basically a mountain lion. Ferocious and stealthy. But it's not going to attack a bear. They hunt deer, rabbits, mice. That's our guy. Preying on field mice."

"If Agatha's theory is correct," Fischer said, "and our killer is targeting heilerin, what information can we extrapolate from that?"

"He is local," Pereira answered, problem-solving aloud. "And not new in town. To know their können, he has to know these people. Or know of them. Perhaps a public official."

Agatha added, "Or a business owner. Someone with a client-facing business."

"Good. Good. Let's start compiling a list of anyone who could fit the mold. Then we can do background on them and begin building a profile."

Agatha looked at her watch. "Guys, I've got to go to work. I'll text you names as I think of them."

"Won't that create overlap with names we've already written down as we work on it from here?" Pereira grumbled.

Agatha winked at him — only to irritate him further, "Just think of it as affirmative operational redundancy."

22

THE SHEPHERD

BLOOD POURED from the pastor's forearm as he shuffled into the darkness between buildings, the sounds of the woman's screaming becoming fainter. He clutched his arm to his chest. He couldn't let the blood fall to the ground. They might identify him or follow his trail. He held the arm upright so the blood would have a lot of traveling to do before being able to free itself from either skin or clothing.

You are a stupid, stupid man. Unworthy of this. You reprehensible, vile filth.

No. Don't say those things.

None of us are worthy of our callings.

Yes, but not all of us are so imbecilic.

He calls us despite our failings. The Pastor continued to coax himself. *Moses thought himself unsuitable for his position as the representative of Israel who would free them from their bondage. Even after Yahweh had appeared to him in a burning bush. He begged God to allow Aaron to assist him. And look how that turned out. With a golden calf. Aaron led the people astray. Moses should have had faith.*

You must carry the faith. Of course, you are not worthy. But that does not mean you have not been called. Nor does it relieve you of your burden.

Just like the Apostle Paul. He considered himself chief among sinners. Yes. Had even taken part in the murder of Stephen. A saint and a martyr. Then persecuted the Christians with imprisonment and … worse. Still, he was called out of it.

Just as you have been. He killed God's children. You are exterminating abominations. These Nephilim. And you must not fail. Will not fail.

You failed tonight. You will punish yourself for your weakness.

No. Please. No.

Yes, you will reprimand your flesh. Then you will find another. And you will redeem yourself.

Yes. There is only one path to redemption. Opa Heinrich knew the way. The Redeemer of the Black Forest, not its Beast. Even the death angel serves the purpose of reconciliation.

Or damnation. But that is not your decision to make. Your lot is only to arrange the meeting.

With that resolved for now, he had to figure out where to go. He would not have the necessary cleaning supplies in the parsonage. He would have to go to the sanctuary.

He hadn't figured out yet exactly where things had gone sideways tonight. It was time for another eradication. He could feel it. Had come to lust for it. He knew he should be more objective, maybe even disinterested, but shouldn't a man derive pleasure from his work? Perhaps not. This work was necessary, but not enviable. He should not get such a thrill from the warm blood being pumped out from the Nephilim over his hands. But he did. And that's what his acts of contrition were for, to negate his own failings and infirmities.

Tonight, he had been ready to graduate upward. To increase his degree of difficulty. He would not limit his options to heilerin any longer. *Wrong. I only thought I was.*

He had walked down to the Gutach on Leimattenstrasse. It was late enough that most of the shops were already closed, and the restaurants were closing. A few stragglers navigated the lamplit streets, enjoying the last night they'd be able to do so before the curfew went into effect.

His curfew. It was going to significantly affect his ability to do his work. He was not prepared to attempt this in the daylight. He had to come up with a new solution. But that could wait. He needed to focus on the task before him tonight.

He spied a woman walking alone. She would walk past him momentarily. He panned from left to right. The street had emptied. He looked toward the woman again. Not conspicuously, not eagerly. She was in her twenties. He recognized her as local, but did not know her. That was risky. Risk was necessary. He may not have another chance, and he wanted this. Needed it.

After she passed by, the pastor slumped to the ground and wedged himself against the bench and railing.

"Fraulein," he called in a raspy voice. "Fraulein."

She paused and turned her head slowly. He clutched at his chest with his left hand and reached out with his right.

"Hilfe, fraulein," allowing his voice to falter as he pleaded for help. He let his left hand fall to his lap.

The woman turned around, looking up and down the street, considering her options. She walked toward him, warily. "I will call for an ambulance," she said as she reached into her bag.

"No," he said too aggressively. The young woman paused mid-stride and looked around again. The street was still empty. *Easy. Do not scare her off.* "Please, fraulein. If you could help me onto the bench, I will be okay. It was only a fall." He lent more strength to his voice as he spoke, belying his desperation.

She stepped toward him again. Slowly still. He could almost see her inner admonishment. *You should have listened to the part that told you to walk away. But at least you will be a worthy sacrifice.*

When she was within a meter, he reached up both hands for her to grasp and pull him up. Her last uncomfortable glance around told him the streets were still empty on both sides of the river. At last, her tender hands with their extraordinary skin clasped his weathered palms. His heart fluttered.

The pastor yanked the woman downward and swept her feet. She crashed to the ground on her left hip, grunting. He rolled onto her and pushed her downward onto her back. Her eyes blazed with realization, exhibiting the same addicting terror the others had. He sat on her pelvis, keeping her pinned. He was not a large man, but he significantly outweighed this petite waif.

He had managed to maintain a hold on her wrists, which he forced above her head. He transferred them to one hand and squeezed, grinding her bones against each other. She opened her mouth to scream. He covered it with his free hand, muffling the noise she emitted. She fought to free her hands. He squeezed tighter. She winced in pain. Tears came to her eyes. Still, she resisted, using her legs to try to buck him off, but unable to get the leverage to do so. They were at a stalemate.

Pastor Stefan's knife was tucked into a sheath at the small of his back. To get to it, he'd have to let go of either her mouth or her hands. Her mouth was the more immediate threat. It was more likely than not that her können was inert and unable to harm him. He took a chance. Keeping her mouth smothered, he released her hands and arched his arm backward for the knife.

He had misjudged. A glint in her eyes forewarned him of the danger he'd placed himself in. She struck him in the chest with her palms before he could unsheathe the knife. The problem was not the initial contact, though that was sharply uncomfortable. Her hands released a blast of ... something ... that shoved him backward and off of her.

She scrambled to her feet as he rolled onto all fours and pushed up. They squared off. She had her right hand in the bag that was slung to the left side. His bare hands were out at his sides. He had lost his knife in the tumult. It was somewhere behind him. He couldn't look away. All he could do now was attack and maul her, hoping he could find it along the way. This had already gone on too long. It was a miracle they were still alone.

He lurched forward to grab her. She ripped her hand out of the bag and swung wildly toward his face. Light glanced off a blade. He swung his arm up to protect his face. The knife bit through skin and muscle, scraping its steel against bone. The sound set his teeth on edge. He flinched backward and lost his balance.

By the time he had recovered himself, she was half a building away and yelled for help. Stefan would not catch up before she reached the intersection. He could not pursue, only flee. He scoured the ground around him, spotting his knife. With his mangled arm pulled tight to his torso, he grabbed the knife with the other and ran, going south until he reached the river bridge and turning west. He was going the wrong direction. The church was north and east, but he couldn't very well go in the same direction that she had. Most important now was vacating the area and remaining unseen.

By walking along the edge of the forest behind the buildings on Hauptstrasse, Pastor Stefan found a balance between staying concealed and hurrying back to the church. He was fortunate the quarter moon was out. A cloud-covered night would have rendered his path nearly unnavigable. The longer he remained exposed, the more likely he was to be caught, and the entire house of cards would come tumbling down on him. He wondered about the likelihood of being incarcerated in the same prison that had held his grandfather. And for continuing his grandfather's work. No, not his grandfather's. A holy work they'd both been called to.

He stopped when he came to the Gasthof Rose hotel. From here, he could cross the street, squeeze between buildings, and arrive at the footbridge that would take him to the church courtyard.

Every voice he heard on the street set off alarm bells in his head. Were they already searching for the girl's assailant? How quickly could that be orchestrated? *Just get to the sanctuary.* Water burbled below him as he crossed the footbridge, masking both his sounds and those that might alert him to danger. He focused on what was in front of him. He did not want to appear suspicious to anyone who might observe him by jumping at every noise.

Stepping off the bridge and onto the gravel walkway set off a flutter in his stomach. He was so close now. He paused to listen. Stillness all around him. *Good. So close.* He strode across the courtyard, heading to the side of the church. A small section of open ground, before brickworks and darkness would shield him.

He reached into his pocket for the keycard.

"Pastor Stefan?" a voice called from his left.

He swore softly and turned to locate the source of the summons. A boy sat at the foot of the history fountain.

"What are you doing here?" Stefan asked sharply, but added in a more tender tone, "Shouldn't you be home already?"

"I like it here," Finn answered. "It's where I come to—" He cut himself off when the headlights from a passing car caught enough of the pastor to expose his blood-sodden arm and shirt. "What happened to you? Did you get attacked? I'll go get help."

The pastor hurried across the cobblestones to where the boy was now standing. His heart banged against his ribs. Bile rose in his throat at the prospect of being found out this way. By a naïve boy.

"Finn, I am fine. It looks worse than it is," he offered reassuringly. Stefan pointed at the fountain, "May I show you something you may not have noticed before?"

Finn inspected the arm with morbid curiosity before nodding. When the boy returned his attention to the fountain, the pastor slid behind him. He wrapped his left arm around Finn's throat and grabbed the back of the boy's head with his right arm. Stefan winced at the pain. He flexed his arms to secure the choke hold. More blood flowed out of the wound. A wave a lightheadedness washed over him. Finn struggled against him and grabbed at the left arm. But the hold was good and secure.

Stefan pivoted and thrust his left hip into the small of the boy's back to apply greater pressure. He silently counted backward from twenty. With each passing second, the resistance lessened. By the time he reached eight, the boy's body had gone entirely slack. He allowed the body to slide to the ground and scanned the area. Still quiet. He had been lucky on that front tonight. Or perhaps it was divine providence.

Stefan squatted down and, with his left hand, pushed the boy into a sitting position. Finn's phone slide out of his pocket and lit up like a beacon when it hit the ground. Stefan snatched it up and shoved it into his own pocket.

The boy's timing couldn't have been worse. What would he do with him?

The pastor folded his right arm in like a broken wing as he wrapped his left arm around the boy again, this time hooking him under the armpit. He dragged the limp body the ten meters to the church door. He used his right hand to depress the lever and pull the door open enough to catch it with his foot and prop it while he wrangled Finn inside.

The door swung shut, and the pastor slid down the wall and collapsed against it. He raised his hands, one palm white and the other red, and covered his face.

23

———

THE SHEPHERD

AFTER A MINUTE of recovering on the floor, the pastor forced himself to get up. It wouldn't do to have Finn wake up while still unfettered. Stefan was too weakened by blood loss to overpower him again.

He grabbed the boy's hands and shuffled backward through the double doors into the darkened sanctuary. Only a diffuse glow from the city's night lights filtered through the stained-glass windows, enveloping the nave in a dim purple hue. Stefan dragged his ward down the center aisle and up the steps of the chancel to where the lectern stood. Dropping the boy's hands, he walked to the altar table and shoved it out of the way. The candelabra toppled, but he caught it before it struck the floor. Replacing it, Stefan turned and squatted. A key reader lay in the spot where one of the table's feet had stood.

The pastor extracted the key from his pocket and swiped it. A red LED switched off, and its green neighbor illuminated. A hatch retracted, exposing a set of well-worn stone stairs. Louvered lights near the base of the walls guided the way. Stefan took the first few steps backward before reaching across the opening and snatching Finn's hands. He pulled the boy across the floor and thudded him down each of the steps. The boy grunted quietly on the last couple of stairs. Stefan would need to hurry. At the landing, he let go of one hand to swipe his card against another reader, causing the retracted door to slide back into place.

The pastor flipped on a light switch, nearly blinding himself with the glare. *Need to install a dimmer switch*, he thought. He squinted as his eyes acclimated from the gloom that had preceded the brightness. He pulled the boy, who was now semi-conscious and making moaning sounds, to the far wall and propped him to a sitting position. As he straddled over the boy to position him, Stefan looked up. Though he could not see it, he knew the cross hung above them.

"Finn, lad, help me stand you up."

The boy mumbled incoherently, but complied. They had to get this done before the boy awakened enough to resist.

"Raise your arm, Finn."

He raised his arm, and the pastor clasped an iron cuff around his wrist.

"Good boy. Now the other."

The other arm and another couple of clicks.

Finn slumped but yelped at the pressure that the posture applied to his wrists. The pain brought him around somewhat, to the point that he pushed himself upright and started apprising his stone surroundings. Stefan turned and walked back to the stairwell wall and flicked a second switch. The exhaust fans activated. That would help to alleviate the dank smell that pervaded the room.

As he returned to Finn, the youth accumulated enough wherewithal to croak, "Where …?" He reached for his throat and was brought up short by the manacles. He looked up to where his wrist hung above him, and a groan escaped him.

That was the look the pastor coveted. Helplessness. Comprehension of their fate, to be followed by despair. But it was the shock and awe of the sudden terror that deeply moved him. A sense of power swelled within him. The shepherd lost all empathy for the member of his flock.

"Where am I?" Finn finally pushed out through the fear.

"You are the last place you will ever be." It sounded overly dramatic when he said it, but he took a minute to let the statement resonate with the boy. "Now, I have to go wash up. Do not yell. I will become very displeased, and it would be a vain effort anyway."

Stefan turned his back to the boy. He walked past the stairwell to a room on the other side, which housed a wall of cabinets and a rudimentary sink. Opening one of the cabinet doors, he pulled out a first aid kit and set it on the countertop. With his good left hand, he unbuttoned his shirt. He shrugged it off his left shoulder, then peeled it off his right arm. The sticky, coagulating blood held tight to the fabric in places, causing him to wince. The blood flow had mostly stopped now. He dropped the shirt to the floor and ambled to the sink, supporting the injured arm in front of him. Turning the water on to a gentle, warm flow, he methodically rinsed away the crimson stain to reveal the extent of the gash.

The wound was as long as his palm was wide, running in a jagged arc along his forearm. Even after he washed the blood away, it tinged the water pink as it continued to seep. A glance into the mirror above the sink revealed a torso cross-stitched with scars, the work of decades of self-loathing and punishment.

Going to another cabinet, he retrieved a plastic container housing several small spools of thread and various sewing needles. He placed it on the table that sat against the far wall, opposite the stairs by which he had entered the basement. Stefan returned to the cabinets for a towel and rubbing alcohol, a grim expression on his face for the task that was ahead of him. Having to use his left hand was going to make it all the more difficult. *Could the boy help? Sure, he'd love to poke a few holes in you. Nein, you must do this yourself.*

Stefan sat down and inhaled deeply, the scar tissue constricting him as his chest expanded to accommodate the inflated lungs. He unscrewed the cap on the alcohol container and poured the liquid into the divider holding the needles. With his right forearm laid flat on the table, a towel underneath it, Stefan exhaled slowly as he dowsed the laceration. A thousand wasps stung simultaneously. His controlled exhale faltered. Tears sprung to his eyes involuntarily.

He retrieved a needle and a spool of fine black thread, and began running off more than twice as much as he expected to need, knowing that he would double thread the needle. No sense in taking a chance on the strand breaking as he punctured his flesh and pulled it through his arm again and again. He brought the end of the string up to his mouth to lick it. The acrid smell of alcohol flared in his nose.

Threading the needle required both hands. As he flexed his right hand and bent the wrist, the wound gaped, and he could glimpse the cords of muscle working until the blood washed over them and spilled again.

He laid the arm flat and wiped the blood away again when he was ready to begin suturing himself. Stefan ground his molars against each other as he pushed the curved needle through several layers of skin, first on one side of the wound and then the other. He discovered soon that the punctures were not the worst part of his chore. The coarse fabric tugged at his flesh as he pulled it through dozens of times. The feeling left him nauseated and tense.

When he finished, he poured alcohol over the arm again and dabbed at it with a towel. His arm looked like something borrowed from Frankenstein's monster. *Well, that's fitting. Am I any less of a monster than that creation?* He wrapped the arm in a cloth bandage and stood to go check on the boy.

"Ach mein gott," Finn whispered upon first seeing the hundreds of ivory slashes on the pastor's chest that bore witness to his years of self-inflicted penance.

Stefan looked down at himself. His shirt was a blood-soaked mess. He couldn't put it back on and did not have any extra articles of clothing. Modesty would have to wait until he could return to the rectory. *Besides, who is the boy going to tell?*

He redirected the boy's attention. "Finn, do you know when the nave of this church was completed?"

"What am I doing here?" Finn demanded.

Ignoring the question, Stefan continued, "1603. Only a couple of generations removed from the Peasants Revolt. Shall I tell you why that is significant, Finn?"

Finn scowled and made a point of being non-responsive.

Stefan shrugged, "The thing about the nobility killing a quarter million peasants is that it gives the peasants cause to have places to hide." Stefan held his arms out and rotated in semicircles showing off the dimly lit room.

Finn jangled his shackles at Stefan. "It's hard to be super receptive to whatever you're talking about when you've got me hanging over here like a side of beef."

"Do not be hyperbolic. It is a less effective device than you might think. Back to my point. Because of the slaughter, the peasants and the clergy worked together in building catacombs under their churches. They served as both a place of refuge and one of imprisonment. But as you might have surmised, you should not expect to find refuge here. This is rather more like," as he considered an analogy, Stefan rubbed at the chin that he had allowed to grow salt-and-pepper scruff, "the Apostle Paul's Mamertine Prison in Rome. Except that you are no disciple of Christ."

Finn looked shocked at the assertion and protested, "I've been a member of this church since I was little."

The pastor waved him off. "Your church membership is of no consequence when you are irredeemable."

"What are you talking about?!" Finn shouted through his confusion. "You taught us that the only unforgiveable sin is dying in a state of disbelief. I am a believer!"

"LIAR!" Pastor Stefan roared as he leapt forward and slapped Finn's face. A rosy handprint accompanied the welt that arose on his right cheek. "You are a born heretic. An abomination whose kind should have been wiped from the surface of the earth thousands of years ago. Yet somehow you persist. For now."

He remained close enough to Finn that the spittle from his excited speech landed on the boy. The musky fear rolled off Finn in waves. It was intoxicating. He stepped backward lest he get overly aroused and act rashly. He became so bloodthirsty in these moments. It was nearly painful to restrain himself.

Stefan backed away further and began pacing. He needed to figure out what to do with the boy. He had not been part of the plan. Stefan was such a deliberate man that spontaneity and improvisation unsettled him. He needed time. Time to think. Time to plan.

"You're the one, aren't you?" Finn asked timidly.

"What one?" *It had only been a matter of time until he put those pieces together. He'd have been disappointed in the boy if it had taken him much longer.*

"The serial killer."

Stefan scoffed. "Such a pedestrian term. Do not trivialize my work by connoting it with the likes of those mere murderers. I have been entrusted with a divine purpose. I am a prophet. A zealot. Both the protector of my flock and the eradicator of the Nephilim."

A long silence drew itself out between them.

Finn shook his head slightly and smirked in spite of his situation. "Thomas has a phrase for what you are. Hang on. I have to think about it. It's one of his weird American things. Oh, right — crazy as a bessy bug."

Something broke inside Stefan. He would not be belittled by this creature. The pastor lunged at Finn and smashed him against the wall. He pummeled the boy with several strikes from his left fist. Finn kicked at his pastor, but he was in too close for the kicks to carry any force. The nuisance only angered Stefan more. He lost any sense of preservation for his right arm.

He struck with both arms, landing punches against the boy's stomach and ribs. Finn tried to evade them. There was nowhere for him to go. When a solid blow landed against Finn's stomach, the air left him in a gust. He resorted to gasping while still absorbing the shepherd's fury.

Stefan would drive the courage out of him. If Finn could talk at all after this, he would be nothing but compliant. There would be no more mocking. He would have to remind the little heretic of what happened to the gang of boys who mocked Elisha.

Stefan's arms tired. He was not accustomed to this level of exertion, and that was besides the blood loss from earlier. His bandage was stained red with his own blood, while the rest of him was speckled with Finn's.

He struck the boy several times in the face. The final blow caused the boy's neck to turn at a severe angle, and his body went slack. Stefan leaned forward with his hands on his knees, heaving air in and out in great gulps.

The pastor took in the pulpy bleeding mass hanging by its wrists. He considered unshackling the boy and tethering him to the eyebolt anchored to the floor. He slapped himself. *No compassion. They are not worthy of it. You will purge yourself of this weakness, or they will use it against you.*

Stefan looked at his watch. He needed to get to the rectory while it was still dark. Some rest would do him good.

24

THOMAS

As Emma sat scrunched up against Thomas, she asked, "So nobody's heard from Finn?"

The other three shook their heads.

"His mom called me freaking out yesterday afternoon," Luka said, "because he'd never come home from the night before. But I told her he was probably still at your house." The last bit being direct to Thomas.

Thomas shook his head again and added with agitation. "He was never here."

"I know that now. I didn't know it when I told her."

Thomas added, "His brother texted me. I told him that Finn was probably with you."

"You two," Lea said in exasperation. "If she wasn't terrified before they talked to you, she sure as hell was afterward."

The boys looked at each other, trying to figure out what they could have done differently. Luka tousled his hair and tried to put his arm around Lea.

"No," she said flatly.

He straightened his arm back out and raised the other one to match it, acting like he had been stretching all along. He dropped his hands back into his lap as the silence stretched out among them. When he couldn't take it any longer, Luka asked, "Do you think something's wrong?"

Lea's mouth fell open, and she turned to face Luka directly. "Of course something's wrong, dummkopf. No one's heard from Finn in like almost forty-eight hours. How dense are you?"

Luka flushed brightly as Lea moved to the other end of the sofa. From their places on the opposite side of the room, Emma and Thomas shared amused grins at the dysfunctional couple. To break the tension, Emma asked, "Is he dating anybody?"

Thomas' gaze shifted to Luka, who looked to be on as uncertain of ground as he was. But Luka was clearly not inclined to answer due to so recently being chastised. The corners of Thomas' mouth turned down. "I don't know?"

Lea looked back and forth between the boys. "You're just a wealth of information, aren't you?"

Having finally had enough of being mocked, Luka said, "Oh, like you know."

"Actually, I do know. He's — before I enlighten you about your friend, let me ask you this — what is it you three talk about when you are together?"

Again, two shrugs.

Emma's giggle was laced with anxiety.

Lea shook her head in dismay. "The answer is that he's not dating anybody. There's a girl he likes, but she doesn't have any idea. And he's never going to do anything about it."

"Who is it?" Luka asked eagerly.

Lea furrowed her brow at him. "If he'd wanted you to know, then you'd know already. Besides, if he winds up in a body bag like the others, it won't matter."

"Wow. That got dark," Luka whispered.

Thomas' face reddened. He pushed himself up from his place on the floor beside Emma and pointed his finger at Lea. "You don't know what you're talking about. If my parents had assumed I was dead, nobody would have come after me, and I'd just be a pile of bones in an abandoned mine. Or worse. Finn is alive. We are not giving up on him."

Thomas stalked out of the room into the kitchen on the other side of the wall that the couch rested against. He flattened his palms on the countertops and blew out a lungful of air. He knew he had overreacted. But it just kind of burst out of him.

From the other room, Lea whispered coarsely, "What the— what just happened?"

He would have to go back in there. No one but Luka knew. He'd have to tell them now, though. And what did it matter anyway. Twelve years later. If any of that was going to follow him here, it would have reared its head already.

"Do you know?" Lea persisted.

A rustling sound on the sofa told him that Luka was fidgeting uncomfortably. It brought a smile to one corner of his mouth. That girl could be relentless. Thomas should go rescue Luka, but like any good friend, he let him dangle a little longer. He needed a couple of minutes anyway. He had to figure out how to tell his story without spilling his secret. Even Luka didn't know that. Not that he believed he fulfilled any sort of prophecy. But he couldn't deny the things he could do. And he was old enough now to understand its rarity.

"I'll go check on Thomas," Luka offered.

"Sit down."

Another brushing sound, then light footsteps, and after a moment, Emma rounded the corner. She smiled compassionately at him, and he turned to face her fully. She crossed the kitchen and pressed herself against him. He wrapped an arm around her.

Emma patted his chest as she asked, "You okay?"

Thomas nodded, his scruffy chin mussing the auburn hair on top of her head.

She leaned back, and he used the opportunity to let his arm

slide down to her waist. "It sounds like you have a story to tell, Herr Wande."

Thomas sighed, "You could say that."

"Are you ready to share it?"

"I guess now's as good a time as any."

Emma took him by the hand and led him back to the living room.

"I didn't say a word," Luka said, his hands out in front of him, staking a claim on his innocence.

"I know you didn't."

"I mean like ever. I never told anyone." Luka beamed with pride. "Do you know how hard that was?"

"It's his secret," Lea said. "Of course, he knows."

"Yeah, but he's not … he's…"

"Not a loudmouth?" Lea offered.

"I was going to say discreet, but whatever."

They dropped the bit when they realized the moment that was in front of them. Thomas sat back down on the floor and recounted what happened to him. He left out some pertinent details, but told them about being abducted at the lake and being held prisoner in the mines of Red Mountain when he was six. How Vulcan killed the pegasus and his own crony in front of Thomas. When he told them about the multi-dimensional panda, which had come to feel imaginary as time passed — so much of it had — the other three were all equally shocked.

"That's amazing." Luka became excited. "Hey, that's all you need to pick up girls is just to tell them you have two können. They'll be falling all over you."

Emma glared at Luka.

Picking up his cue, he added, "Well, you know, if it doesn't work out between you."

Lea slapped his leg. "That's not better, dummy. Stop talking." She turned her attention to Thomas. "What happened next?"

He told as much as he knew about the rescue and as much as he dared about the rest. In this version, Agatha was the hero, fighting Vulcan to a standstill and forcing him into his portal exit.

"But why you?" Emma asked.

He had to navigate this carefully. "It wasn't just me. There were about twenty of us kids and magical creatures. The rest of them died. I mean, they didn't just die. They were murdered. He thought one of us was supposed to fulfill some prophecy or have some power. But none of us did." It felt bad to lie to them so directly, but there was no other way. *This is the way*, the Mandelorian's tinny voice echoed in his head.

"What was it?" Lea asked. "What was he looking for?"

Thomas shrugged. "No one ever told me."

Luka held up his hands, palms out. "Hold up. I think we're losing sight of the important thing here — Thomas' mom is both super hot and a badass who fought off a god."

Thomas grabbed a throw pillow that was within arm's reach and slung it at him. Luka knocked the pillow aside but left his ribs exposed. Lea landed a punch that resonated with a thud. Luka grunted, and the laughter left his face.

Emma placed a hand on Thomas' arm and brought things back around. "I'm sorry about your dad."

"Yeah, me too." Thomas said quietly before trying to shrug it off. "It was a long time ago."

"Still, I guess that's not something you ever get over."

"You learn to live with it. But if I ever come across Vulcan again … I'll kill him." There was no warmth left in his voice.

Even Luka didn't have anything to say.

After that lingered for longer than was comfortable, Thomas redirected the conversation. "We need to find Finn."

"How?" Lea asked.

Thomas mulled it over and looked at Luka. "Has your dad said anything about Finn's disappearance being related to the …

uh, other stuff." He couldn't bring himself to consider the possibility.

"I haven't seen him. That other girl was attacked the same night. He's been pretty covered up dealing with that and all the townsfolk calling for his job."

Emma said, "Has he said anything about that girl's attacker?"

Luka reiterated, "He hasn't said anything to me. I haven't seen him."

Thomas fidgeted in frustration. "We need more information. We can't help him if we don't know anything."

"Has anyone tried to call him?" Lea asked.

"I sent a couple of messages, but didn't call," Luka said.

Thomas shook his head. "Same."

Lea leaned over the arm of the sofa and rummaged through her bag until she found her phone. She punched at it a few times and held it up to her ear. Seconds later, she brought it back down to her lap and disconnected the call. "Straight to voicemail. He must have it turned off."

"It was a good idea, though," Emma said.

"But how are we going to get more information?" Thomas asked.

"They're going to hold a town hall meeting tomorrow. We could go to that?" Luka said.

"Actually, that's not a bad idea," Lea said.

Luka crossed his arms. "Thanks for sounding so surprised."

"I mean, your track record today isn't great. The town hall meeting probably won't give us a lot, but let's see what we find out between now and then, and get together after."

Everyone else nodded in agreement with the plan.

25

THOMAS

THOMAS TOOK Emma's hand after he closed the front door behind them. "You're okay with leaving them in there?" Emma cautioned. "Do you know what they're going to do to your couch? Or your bed? Or your mom's bed?"

"Surely not ..." Thomas stopped himself, recognizing his own naivety. He couldn't allow the house to be desecrated like that. "Yeah, you're definitely right."

Thomas disentangled his hand from Emma's, stepped back toward the house, and pushed the door open. Luka popped his head up in surprise and climbed off Lea, who reclined on her back on the couch. Luka's face turned the same color as it had the time that he'd eaten watermelon and discovered he was allergic to it. When Emma stepped through the door behind Thomas, he looked back at her and found her to have an expression that very much said, *I told you so.*

"Umm, excuse me," Lea fussed at Thomas. "We're kind of in the middle of something. Actually, we're at the very beginning of something, trying to get to the middle."

Luka's red face blossomed into a color of embarrassment

Thomas hadn't known was possible. "Dude, we hadn't even got to the sidewalk yet. And we were just talking about Finn."

"Coping mechanism?" Luka shrugged.

Thomas rolled his eyes.

"A man has needs, Thomas," he said.

Lea added, "A lady does too."

"Y'all *need* to go do this somewhere else," Thomas said.

Lea sat up, and Luka extended a hand to pull her up off the couch. Once on her feet, she said, "Come on. We can go to my house."

"Won't your aunt and uncle be there?" Luka asked.

"Probably. Maybe. Doesn't matter. He'll be drunk and she'll be strung out. They won't bother us."

"Oh," Luka's eagerness turning to concern. "Are you sure? Do you want to tal—"

"No, I don't want to talk about it. Do you want to wreck this by having a therapy session about my messed-up family situation?"

Luka was on uncertain ground. "No?"

"I didn't think so. Let's go."

She walked out ahead of Luka, whispering something to Emma, who blushed and laughed in response. Luka shrugged at Thomas and padded along behind Lea until he caught up to her at the front walk. She pulled him against her hip and shoved her hand into the back pocket of his jeans. He did likewise. They walked alongside each other with awkward gaits to maintain their contact, as if they would otherwise become untethered.

Emma turned her head to Thomas, "Don't even think about it."

He raised his hands in surrender.

Thomas pulled the door shut behind them a second time. "I want to show you something."

Emma raised an eyebrow at him.

A fair response, considering the exhibition they'd just witnessed. "There's someone I want you to meet."

"Is that all the information you're going to give me?"

"For now," he said. "It's a complicated story, and I'm not sure how to tell it."

"Okay," she said, taking his hand. "Lead the way."

When they turned onto the street that led to Stephanus-Haus, Emma asked, "We're going to a nursing home?"

Thomas nodded.

Emma knitted her eyebrows together in confusion. "I thought your oma lived next door to you."

"She does. We're not here for her."

"You know it's just a myth that girls like it when guys act mysterious, right?"

"Is that true? That might explain some things," Thomas said. "But just give me a couple of minutes, and I'll explain as much as I can."

They walked through the facility's front doors and were greeted with a "Guten tag, Thomas."

He smiled and waved at the woman behind the reception desk.

"You brought a friend today?" Marta asked with a wink.

"This is Emma," he offered.

"That's it?" she asked. "Just 'This is Emma,' with no indication of what her relationship to you is, when you've never brought a girl here before?"

"Jeez, Marta. You're worse than my mom. Do we need to sign in?"

The woman flicked her hand back and forth as if she were shooing a gnat. "I think they were just about to take her for her afternoon walk. You might catch them in time to do it yourself. You know Emilia is going to take any opportunity she has not to work." Thomas waved and led Emma down the residence corridor.

"You seem to know her pretty well?" Emma prodded.

"The people here have practically seen me grow up. We've been coming here every couple of weeks — sometimes more — since I was a little boy."

Emma slid her hand into the crook of his arm. "Who are we here to see, Thomas?"

He pointed to a door to their left. He walked through the doorway into the room, but Emma got no further than its frame. Thomas spoke to Emilia and leaned forward to kiss Elle on the forehead. Only then did he realize Emma hadn't followed him into the room. He turned to find her standing with her hands covering her mouth. The pallor of her face was several shades too pale.

"What's wrong?" Thomas asked. "Are you going to be sick?"

Emma shook her head slightly. She looked unsteady on her feet. Thomas stepped back to her, and taking hold of her arm, guided her to the chair in Elle's room.

"I've seen her before," Emma said weakly.

"Here? She's been here a long time. So I guess—"

"No. She comes to me."

Thomas scrunched his eyes in confusion and ran his hands through his hair, trying to figure out what was going on. "Emma, she doesn't go anywhere. She's catatonic and has been ever since … well, since before I was born."

Emma shook her head again. The initial shock had worn off. Her color was better and her voice stronger. "Not like that. She appears to me in my dreams."

Emilia, who had been absorbing all this with eager curiosity, finally said, "I'm going to step out. I'll be at the front desk if you need me."

Thomas acknowledged her with a nod, but without turning away from Emma. He squatted down in front of her, placing his hands on her legs just above her knees. "What does she say to you?"

For the third time in the last couple of minutes, Emma shook her head, looking down at her lap. "I don't know. I always thought it was just a strange recurring dream, or I was being haunted or something."

"Think," Thomas urged. "This is important."

Emma looked directly at him with smoldering eyes. "Do you think that I do not understand the importance of what is happening? Or that if you prod me about it, I am more likely to recollect it?"

Thomas retracted his hands from her legs. "No, you're right."

She nodded, and the intensity dissipated from her expression. "I never focused on remembering the words before. It always felt too misty and far away when I woke up. I didn't know then that it was important. I'm sorry."

"It's fine," Thomas said, trying not to show frustration and disappointment.

"Help me up." Emma lifted a hand, and Thomas offered his as he stood. After she was on her feet again, she clung to his hand. "I know it's not fine. I'll try to remember. And if I can't, maybe she'll come see me again soon. It's been happening for years, since I was little — I don't know when it started, but I bet it was after you moved here — so there's no reason to think it will stop now. Okay?"

"Okay," Thomas said without any conviction.

"Come on," she prompted. "Let's take her on that walk. And Thomas?"

Thomas was having difficulty wrapping his head around this and what it meant. "Hmm?" he responded after being called out of his daze.

"I still don't know who this is or what her name is."

He smiled through the chaos that enveloped his brain. "This is my aunt, Elle. My mom's older sister."

"Oh, I can definitely see that now. I've only seen her much younger, and wearing sweatpants and a long-sleeved shirt."

Thomas laughed from behind the wheelchair as he pushed it forward into the corridor. "What?"

"I'm serious. That's what she's always wearing in my dreams. Sweatpants, a George Strait concert shirt, and flip-flops. With her hair pulled into a ponytail. It's always the same. It's how I learned who George Strait was and started listening to country music."

"I did always think it was peculiar that you liked country. But don't you think it's odd that you remember details of what she was wearing but not what she was saying?"

Emma shrugged, "Maybe. Dreams are weird."

"I guess," Thomas conceded doubtfully.

The trio exited through the automatic doors. Thomas pushed Elle through the garden and out onto the walkway that ran parallel to the Gutach. He walked without speaking, not knowing what to say. Had it been a mistake bringing Emma with him today? Had fate intervened, making it inevitable that she would be here? He didn't know. But whatever resulted from it, he didn't think this was a mistake. It felt too heavy for that. Maybe heavy wasn't the right word. Consequential.

"What happened to her?" Emma asked quietly, timidly.

"I will tell you. It's why I brought you with me today. Or at least, that's why I thought I was bringing you. I don't know now. It kind of feels like someone else, some*thing* else, is pulling the strings. Anyway, I'll tell you after we take her back from the walk. It seems like bad manners to tell her story in front of her like this."

The river on their right flowed quietly, carrying away the summer as the seasons prepared for their autumnal turn. Thomas was glad for the babbling. It quelled his tempest somewhat. He also appreciated about Emma that she didn't require constant chatter. Sometimes he just needed some time to think. And there was no shortage of things to work through right now. One calamity had been piling onto another for weeks now.

When they reached the end of the walk and got to the bridge, Thomas brought the wheelchair to a halt, preparing to turn it around. Emma held up a hand. She leaned down toward Elle, then looked up at Thomas. "I think she's trying to say something."

"She can't talk. Sometimes she makes noises, like a moaning sound. The folks at the nursing home say it's just the air moving over her vocal cords as she breathes."

"I don't think so, Thomas. It sounds ..." Emma trailed off. She picked up again, addressing Elle, "Aunt Elle, are you okay?"

She placed her hand over Elle's. The woman snatched her wrist and clutched it like a vice. Emma wrenched her neck toward Thomas, her face blanched with terror. When she spoke, the voice did not belong to her.

"He is coming, boy. He is coming."

Panic rose within Thomas' chest and spread outward, filling his body like a gas fills an empty space. With a dry, hurried voice, he asked, "Who is coming? When?"

But the moment had passed with the same sudden ferocity that it had arrived. Elle released Emma, who nearly fell to the ground. Thomas rushed forward and helped her to sit down on the pavement. Emma began crying. Thomas sat beside her and wrapped an arm around her shoulder.

"I don't know why I'm crying," she said through the tears. "I don't even know what happened. Not really."

"Honestly, I think it would be weird if it didn't upset you."

"Please, don't tell anyone," she requested. "I feel like a freak as it is. I don't want anyone else looking at me like that."

"I don't think ..." She looked directly into his face. Her eyes pled with him in a way that her words could not express. "Okay.

I won't tell anyone yet. But we need to figure out what that means. What she said."

"Thomas, look inside your heart. I think we both know what that meant."

Instead of looking inward, Thomas looked at Elle, who sat is her chair, still as water. Just as she had for the last twenty-five years.

26

AGATHA

AGATHA CLACKED the door knocker again. About the time she concluded that the occupant wasn't home, she heard a noise coming from within the house. It was followed by a deadbolt sliding against wood as it retracted. The pastor opened the door.

"Can I help you?" he asked in what was clearly not a tone that was offering help to anyone.

Frazzled. That's definitely the word for it. Agatha let the rude greeting hang in the air for a minute as she considered her response. Even though she was certain she'd caught him in the middle of something and his terse response wasn't intended as a personal offense, she met fire with fire. That was kind of her thing, after all. "Do you know who I am?"

He considered her for a long minute as he ran a hand through his disheveled hair and tried to fix it, resulting only in tufts that protruded at odd angles. "I'm sorry?"

Agatha noted his untucked shirt and one sleeve that was rolled up. It revealed a bandage that was in serious need of changing.

She responded, "I asked if you know who I am. But it looks like you really did a number on yourself there."

He looked down at his arm and began unrolling the sleeve. He smiled at Agatha, "Ja. I should have called the repairman rather than attempting to manage things myself."

"That looks pretty bad. Would you like me to change the dressing for you? Or take you to get some treatment. We could go see Frau V—" Agatha brought her sentence up short as her breath caught in her throat. "I'm sorry. I keep forgetting."

The pastor nodded solemnly. "Yes. It has been a terrible loss for the community. And personally too, for those of us who knew her well. It will take some getting accustomed to."

Agatha nodded her agreement.

"I do recognize you," he said.

She waited for him to continue.

"You asked if I know who you are. I do. You are Thomas' mother? Agatha?"

"That's right," she said.

"I'm Pastor Stefan. It's nice to finally meet you. Thomas has stopped in to talk a couple of times over the last few weeks. Seems like he's had a lot on his mind."

Agatha wore her alarm on her face. "He's come to your house?"

"No, no." He placed a reassuring hand on her forearm before quickly withdrawing it. "We have only met in the sanctuary. No one is permitted in the rectory. It is a matter of propriety, you understand. Avoiding the appearance of evil, as the Apostle Paul put it."

"Okay," she said. "I was curious why we were still standing here on your stoop. Should we go inside the church to talk?"

The pastor flicked his eyes to the church building and back to Agatha. "Not at all. It's a lovely afternoon. Let's occupy one of the benches here in the courtyard."

He was right about that, at least. The sun warmed her skin as they sat. The bees buzzed around the flowers in the planters, preparing for the soon-changing season and winter beyond. All merriment on the outside and turmoil on the inside. She needed to get to the heart of what she was here about. But how to do that tactfully. When her mother's words resounded in her head — *"Agatha, you're about as prickly as a cactus."* — she decided to forgo tact. "What is it that Thomas has been talking to you about?"

"I fear you will not like my answer. But it is not for me to tell. Are you familiar with priest-penitent privilege?"

"Excuse me? I am the boy's mother. If he's having a problem, I need to know."

The pastor tried on a disarming smile. Agatha thought it made him too closely resemble a fox to be at all comforting. "I'm sorry," he said. "I am unable to disclose the substance of our conversation. While I can understand why that might be unnerving to you, I would ask you to consider it from another perspective. If those who confided in me had to worry about me discussing their concerns with others," he gestured with his hands palms up, "I would soon be out of business. I am not so different from a lawyer or a psychologist in that way."

Sensing that his resolution wasn't going to yield, Agatha changed her approach. "What about you? Are you from here?"

Pastor Stefan shook his head. "Not originally, no. I grew up near Stuttgart, though we moved around a good deal during my childhood. Following work wherever my mother could find it. It was difficult for an unmarried, uneducated woman. She was a devoutly religious woman, so I guess I followed in her footsteps. I didn't have roots anywhere, so it was not a problem for me that the church elders might assign me to a different parish every few years. But when my mother died, I felt a calling to this place, to this town. My grandmother was from here. I believe I was looking for somewhere to connect to."

"Can just anyone be assigned to Hornberg? That seems ... problematic, all things considered."

A genuine smile this time. "Quite not. I was uniquely qualified. Both my mother and her mother were zauberin, though my mother had not been trained in it. I had seen what my grandmother could do, however. She was very gifted."

"And you?"

"Sadly, no. It seems to have skipped a generation. Or maybe the magic ran out of the bloodline. I do not know. But I'm just a muggle."

Agatha smiled despite herself. She realized he was younger than she had always supposed him to be. Maybe only a few years older than herself.

He continued, "So when the church here needed a new pastor about twenty-five years ago, I received the assignment."

She did some quick mental math. "You were young to pastor a church, weren't you?"

"This is beginning to feel like an inquisition, Frau Wande," he said, feigning the lightness of a joke. Agatha did not relent, so he continued, "Assuredly, I was. As you might imagine, there is a decided lack of qualified candidates. So I got the call, and I have been here ever since. In many ways, I grew up here. Or at least grew into myself."

"You're kind of forthcoming about personal stuff for a German, aren't you?"

"An occupational hazard, I have found. How can I expect people to open up with me so that I can shepherd them, if I am unwilling to do the same?"

"And Thomas — is he an open book, too?"

"Thomas is trying to identify who he is and what he can divulge. It is clear he has been through something traumatic that has left lasting impressions. He did not tell me what it was, if that is your concern. But if I can be so presumptuous as to suggest it, he may find it beneficial to counsel with someone about it."

Agatha stood up suddenly. "You were correct to think you

presumed too much in suggesting it. I have been tending to that boy's needs as I deem best for a long time. And I will continue to do that for a little while longer. After that, he can make his own decisions. But until then, I would caution you not to embed yourself too deeply in Thomas' affairs. Into my affairs." Agatha backed up a step, realizing that she was uncomfortably close to the pastor, who still sat placidly on the bench.

Redness crept up Pastor Stefan's neck and into his cheeks. "Frau Wande, if I have somehow offended you, I—"

"Oh, you and your apology can go kick rocks. I'm not offended. What I am is encouraging you not to further interject yourself into Thomas' life." Agatha paused for half a second, considering. She decided that was a good place to end the conversation. She turned on her heel and strode away. *That could have gone better. Of course, it could have gone worse too. Prickly as a cactus*, she thought again and shrugged to herself.

As she walked back to the house, something gnawed at her about the man. His arm. The way he guarded it, then tried to cover it up after she'd seen it. He almost recoiled when she offered to put a new bandage on it for him. But maybe that was a normal response. She'd be hard pressed to let a stranger help her. Heck, she wasn't too keen on letting people she knew well help her.

And he was just so salty when he first answered the door. Not at all what she'd expected. *Maybe he'd been in the middle of something. Yeah, like planning his next murder. Let's not get out our jump-to-conclusion mat and start making leaps just yet.*

Agatha pulled her phone out of her bag. When she reached the arched viaduct that split the town into disproportionate sections, she turned to look back over her shoulder. She was out of sight of the church and rectory, and no one was behind her. She paused where she stood and searched for a name in her contacts.

"Pereira," the voice answered dispassionately.

"It's Agatha," she announced.

"Ah. What can I do for you, Frau Wande?"

"What did the victim from the other night say about pulling a knife on the guy who attacked her?"

Pereira sighed on the other end. "I am helping the Polizeidirektor prepare for the meeting tonight. I do not have time for you to play investigator right now."

Boy, he's ornery. And obstinate. And … she couldn't think of any other mean o-words right now, but when she did, she knew they would apply. "Look, I'm sure you're an invaluable asset to his speech prep. But either you can take about thirty seconds and help me out here, or I can come down to the station and search for the information myself and we can hang out for a while. I can be there in a couple of minutes if that's your preference." What she wouldn't give to be on a video call with him right now and observe his unfiltered contempt for her.

"Please wait," he said. "I will look at my notes."

Agatha leaned against the stone viaduct while she waited.

"I have found it," he announced. "She says that she was carrying a kitchen knife. When he attacked her, she used her können to knock him away. When he came at her a second time, she pulled the knife and swung it at his face. She hadn't been sure whether she had made contact, but we found blood on the knife. We have sent a sample off for DNA testing. We do not have the results back yet. And there's no guarantee that the attacker will be in the database."

"Is she right-handed or left?" Agatha asked.

Pereira clacked a keyboard on the other end of the line.

"It does not say."

You mean you didn't think to ask. She decided not to antagonize him further.

"Are you onto something, Frau Wande?"

"Not sure yet. I'll let you know. Hey, give Markus a message for me."

"Nein."

The line went dead.

"Rude," she said to the martins nesting under the viaduct. *Who pissed in his muesli?*

27

AGATHA

HORNBERG HADN'T HELD a town meeting for at least as long as Agatha had lived here. So she hadn't known what to expect. Would it be a couple dozen people who showed up? Or would most of the town's four thousand residents try to cram themselves into the school gym?

Before Agatha turned the corner to walk through the metal double doors, the din from the crowd resonated through her feet. Hundreds had turned out. They were anxious and scared and angry. As much for themselves as for their children. Three murders, one attack, one missing teenager. All within the span of a month. Of course they were wound up. Even she was on edge walking here from the rectory as elongating shadows cascaded the sidewalk around her. Every footfall or unexpected noise whose source was unseen caused heart palpitations.

There were no chairs in the gym. The citizens of Hornberg clumped together in clusters across the floor. She couldn't imagine the rumors and theories that would grow out of this congregation, as people roved from one pack to another. She remembered a TV show that used to run called *Truth, Lies, and Democracy*. This was its living embodiment.

Agatha nodded greetings to people, but didn't seek anyone out. No one knew her involvement in the investigation, and she would rather avoid sticking her whole foot in her mouth by saying something that would betray her. Best just to be the quiet spectator for now. She secured a place against the wall near the door through which she had entered.

She spotted the pastor among the crowd, making his way from one parishioner to another. Presumably offering words of encouragement. She noted that he wore a long-sleeve shirt. As he scanned the crowd for others to speak to, their eyes met. Her expression remained stony, suspicious. He broke eye contact and smiled reflexively at someone near him. *Yeah, I'm watching you, buster.*

Agatha checked her watch. Two minutes until time to start. Not having chairs was a mistake. Chairs would have anchored the crowd, settled them. This too closely resembled a reverberating mob. All they were missing were pitchforks and torches. And maybe a tree to lynch Markus from. She looked up and noted the rafters. *That might do in a pinch if they have a long enough rope.*

At exactly seven o'clock, the Bürgermeister stepped to the microphone at the front of the platform. She had truly come to appreciate German precision.

"Guten abend," his baritone voice welcomed the assembly. "Polizeidirektor Fischer has prepared a statement. After he finishes, he will take some questions." The Bürgermeister moved to the side and waved Fischer forward.

Precise and concise, Agatha thought to herself, appreciating the rhyme.

Despite the earlier clamor, the room was now astoundingly quiet. Someone cleared their throat on the far side of the gym. A shoe squeaked against the basketball court. But beyond that, the quiet anticipation and anxiety were nearly palpable.

Oof. He looks rough. Agatha grimaced for Fischer as he took his place behind the microphone. *Those overhead LED lights aren't doing him any favors either.* She hadn't seen him since this most recent attack. It looked to have taken a toll. His face was unshaven and haggard. He appeared to have lost some weight, too. The stress was getting to him. *I'll cook him a good meal — well, I'll cook him a meal. Good may be a bridge too far.*

"We are a small town accustomed to small-town problems. Graffiti, shoplifting, domestic disputes. We have felt safe for many years. But now that has changed. Not since the threat of the Soviet Union has dread so completely permeated this town.

"As you all know, there have been three killings in the last four weeks. We have evidence that leads us to believe that these murders are related to each other. A few days ago, a young woman in town was attacked. Fortunately, she escaped. Based on the details she provided, we believe her attack may be connected to the others. She has been treated for her physical injuries and is expected to make a full recovery.

"On the same evening, a local teenager, Finn Brandt, turned up missing. We expect to be able to pinpoint his last known whereabouts soon. We do not yet have any evidence that Finn's disappearance is in any way related to the other occurrences.

"Our investigation into each of these incidents is ongoing. We will not be releasing any information about suspects or persons under suspicion at this time. We will release additional information as it develops. I will now be glad to field any questions."

You might have interjected a little personality, Markus. Not even a lot. Just the tiniest fraction would have been nice.

The silence persisted long enough that Fischer appeared hopeful that he might avoid a public skewering. Then a small-voiced woman at the front asked, "Are you going to get my boy back?"

"Frau Brandt," Fischer acknowledged with a father's tenderness. "We have not ruled anything out as it pertains to Finn. We are still hopeful that he will return of his own accord. Sometim—"

"He did not run away," Finn's mother asserted more firmly.

Fischer smiled and course-corrected, "Of course. We are attempting to develop evidence that will establish the time and location of his disappearance. That will enable us to establish additional leads and move the investigation forward. If anyone recalls seeing Finn three nights ago or any time since, please reach out to me or to Detective Pereira." Fischer gestured to his right, where Pereira stood attempting to appear approachable. It was a vain effort. He was every bit as docile as a crocodile.

From the middle of the audience, someone asked, "Is the killer targeting certain people?"

Agatha turned away from Fischer to find Shafer, whom she refused to call Pastor Stefan, like he was trying to be the cool youth minister.

He looked cool as a cucumber. Had she misjudged him? Hard to say. She didn't have to decide right now. She returned her attention to Markus. "...certain characteristics that each of the victims has in common. We endeavor not to ascribe correlation to what might be coincidence. But it is undeniable that all the victims to date have been zauberin."

Murmurs rumbled throughout the assembly. A man in the back shouted, "It's the Beast of the Black Forest!" The murmuring erupted into a panicked cacophony.

Even from this distance, Agatha witnessed Fischer's face reddening in frustration. Watching someone else have to deal with the public in this way affirmed some of her life choices — though to be totally self-effacing, some of those things weren't choices as much as things she'd been conscripted into. But she'd come to terms with that a long time ago, and even had the personal satisfaction of ... eliminating the decision-maker. Thinking about how the Warden had begged brought a wry smile to a corner of her mouth. She shut off the memory before it could turn bitter. She hadn't taken pleasure in any other killing, but he'd had it coming. For a long time and for a lot of reasons.

"Quiet!" Fischer demanded. When the clamor ceased, he resumed, "Heinrich Pommerenke died in Hohenasperg prison in 2008. At the time of his death, he had not killed anyone in nearly fifty years. I will not hear any further absurdity about the Beast of the Black Forest."

"What if it's a copycat?" a woman yelled.

Fischer looked to Pereira, who shook his head. Fischer turned back to the assembly and raised his arms as if he were at a loss for how to proceed. "You have read what is being reported. Each of you has a dozen ways to look up Pommerenke's murders on the internet. I can't stand here and tell you there are not similarities between what we are seeing now and what was done in 1959. But speculation and rumor-mongering help no one and do nothing but stir up more tension and fear. We deal in facts and evidence, not conspiracies. If any of you have questions along those lines, I have time for a few more."

"Have you considered calling in the Bundespolizei?"

Fischer fidgeted with his watch before answering. Agatha thought, *He probably wishes the killer would just come in and murder him at this point. It would be better than this death by a thousand questions.*

The polizeidirektor cleared his throat. "In short, no. The BPOL is an effective policing organization. But most crimes of this nature are solved by local police. As this one will be. I will not defend my own credentials, but I will brag about my team. Detective Pereira is a formulaic and devoted detective. He and the others who are working with us have made significant strides with the available evidence. And now that we have a survivor of one of these attacks, we have an additional means of gathering evidence and establishing a profile of the person we are dealing with.

"Let us not forget. It is a person we are looking for. Not a myth. Not a legend. A man. Likely from this community. Possibly in this room. Someone you know. Someone you work with. Go to church with. Someone you see every day. You are as important to this investigation as we are. Be vigilant. Do not be outside alone after dark. Comply with the curfew we have imposed. And above all else — to borrow an expression from our American friends — if you see something, say something. Now if you will excuse us, my team and I have some work to get back to."

Agatha wanted to do a fist pump. For as much as that kind of got murky and uncertain in the middle, he closed it out like a champ. She thought of a few good sports analogies about being clutch, but she didn't think either Mariano Rivera or Brett Favre would really resonate with Fischer, and she still knew nothing about futbol. So she'd have to let that lay.

The crowd seemed split between wanting to leave and staying to spread more rumors. None of those who left walked out alone. At least they had heard that, if nothing else. *To be fair, most of the rest of it was official non-statements.* A couple dozen people congregated around Fischer and the mayor. She still couldn't call him Bürgermeister without being as amused as a ten-year-old boy making a fart joke.

There was no way she was wading through that mess of people to talk to him. Nor was she inclined to wait for the crowd to thin out. She needed to get home to Thomas. One of his best buddies was missing, and she'd hardly seen him to talk about it. She had been so glad to have something meaningful to immerse herself into again that she had let being a good mom slide a little bit. She'd give him a couple of extra hugs when she got home, whether he wanted them or not. That was a sign of good parenting, right? Embarrassing your kid with affection, especially if his friends were around.

Agatha stepped across the threshold into her home to discover two teenagers on the couch. One on either end. Their legs folded up against each other, feet intermingled. A reminder that there were still good and wholesome things in the world. She stepped over to Thomas, placed her hands on the side of his head, and kissed his forehead.

"Alright," he complained and playfully pushed her away.

"Do you need a kiss too?" she asked Emma.

The girl sat upright and leaned forward to receive her kiss. Agatha obliged and whispered loudly to Thomas, "I like her."

He sighed. "Please go away."

Always the contrarian, Agatha stayed to make conversation. "What are you reading, Emma?"

Emma held up her book, *"Harry Potter and the Deathly Hallows."*

"First time?"

"Third time," Emma said.

Thomas chimed in, "She practically has them all memorized."

"I remember reading them with Thomas for the first time."

"Please, don't do this," the boy pleaded.

"He was petrified of the basilisk. That was only, what, a year or two ago?" Agatha asked innocently.

"No. That's not true or funny."

Emma smiled. "I think it's funny."

"Please, don't encourage her, or I'll have to ask you to leave."

Agatha spoke to Emma, "He hasn't begun paying rent yet, and until he does, I get to decide who comes and goes. And I say you can stay for as long as you like."

Thomas made a point of trying to ignore them and re-immersing himself in his book.

"What are you reading?" Agatha asked Thomas.

He kept his attention on the paperback that he was three-quarters finished with.

Emma answered, *"Stranger in a Strange Land."*

"Interesting choice," Agatha said. "Fitting, in a way. But best if you let some of those things fly right past you without getting any ideas."

Thomas looked up with widening eyes and flushing cheeks. "Please, go away."

Agatha took them in a minute longer before turning to go to the kitchen. Her work here was done. She said over her shoulder, "Emma, we'll have to take you home before too long. Curfew."

"Mom, can't she—"

"Not my rule," she called from the kitchen. "You'll have to take it up with Polizeidirektor Fischer."

She received only a grunt of protest in response.

28

THE SHEPHERD

STEFAN WOULD HAVE to get rid of the boy. He could not chance whether the police were able to pinpoint the location of his disappearance, like the Polizeidirektor had said. How could they determine that? He considered this as he strode back to the parsonage.

Stefan pulled his phone out of his pocket to check a notification. A weather alert. He realized that's how they would find Finn. His cell phone. Had he turned the phone off? Yes. He must have. Otherwise, they would have found him already. Still, once the phone company turned over the records, they would scour the area for the boy. Tonight, he would decide on a plan to get rid of the boy's body in a way that could not be traced back to him. That would be far more difficult than the other exterminations. He had ended them where they were. There had been no transporting of bodies. At the time, those events had seemed like random killings to the investigators. They understand now that was not the case, even if they'd been unable to state it outright.

Then there was the wench Agatha to deal with. *Should never have answered the door.* She would have to be next. She was far too interested in him. The way she scrutinized him at the meeting, like she could see into him. She tried to hide it, to appear more casual. She could not. He looked forward to the challenge, uncertain whether he was up to it. This was the first time he had doubted himself on this front. That came as somewhat of a revelation.

As Stefan neared the rectory, he deviated from his course to go check on the boy, who would need food and water. Holding a captive was considerably more work than he preferred. But what else was there to do? He could no more have killed that boy in the moment than left him alone there. Finn had put him in a terrible position. And he had reacted accordingly. If only he hadn't fouled up the killing of the girl.

But there was no point in revisiting all that now. He had to make do with circumstances as they existed. And for the present, that included tending to the boy's basic needs.

He unlocked the church door and entered, making his way through the darkened building to the altar table. He moved it backward and scanned his card to open the basement door. It retracted. He listened. The only sound was the hum of the lights below. He was uncertain what he was listening for exactly, but nothing sounded amiss.

Stefan descended the stairs. He rounded the corner to the left and called, "Fi—"

Something smashed into his chest. His breath expelled from his lungs in a blast. Stefan stumbled backward into the wall and fell against it with a concussive thud.

Finn's wrists were still shackled. The chains hung from the cuffs but were no longer affixed to the wall. Ancient blocks rested at Finn's feet. Correlating holes pocked the wall he had been chained to.

Finn made an arcing motion. Another stone became an artillery shell. Stefan lurched to the right in time to avoid a direct hit. The stone crashed into the wall where Stefan had just been and pummeled him with gravel and chunks of stone.

Stefan crawled around the corner of the wall back to the stairwell. The stitches in his arm tore away from the skin with the flexing and twisting motion as he got to cover. He sat with his back against the wall. Breathing was excruciating. The boy may have broken several of his ribs with that first barrage. Stefan smirked through the pain. Broken ribs were the kind of thing that Frau Vogel had been good at tending to.

"Finn," he said through the pain. "Stop this now, and I will be merciful to you."

A thunderous blow shook the wall. A wordless answer. "You will kill us both if you keep pulling blocks from that wall. You will collapse this entire building on top of us."

The boy responded, "I'm going to die anyway. Might as well go out like Sampson."

"You are not Sampson, Finn. You are one of the Philistines. A scourge to God's people. I am the prophet who is eradicating you."

Another volley of blocks crashed against the opposite side of the wall that Stefan sat against. Mortar and dust trickled down onto him. Stefan pushed himself up, clutching his chest with his mangled arm. He steeled himself and stepped into the open. "Enough!" he raged.

Finn did not cow to his anger, even though most of his face was still swollen and purple from the abuse the pastor had delivered a couple of days before. There was mettle in the boy. It wouldn't do to allow him to further resolve himself.

Stefan stepped toward the boy, then another. Both opponents were tensed. The pastor extended his left arm toward Finn, maintaining eye contact with him. When he clenched his fist, Finn collapsed to the floor and curled into a ball. The shaking began immediately. He covered his ears. It did no good. The shrieking was coming from within.

"Stop. Please, stop," Finn begged.

"Stop? I have not even begun. Besides, is it not fair that I use my können when you have already done the same? Did I fail to mention that I too am an abomination?"

Finn's screams intensified in their volume and desperation. His hands whitened as he grabbed his legs and strained to pull them in tighter against himself.

"What do you most fear, Finn?" Stefan yelled over the terror. "Is that what you see? What you are immersed in? Can you feel it and taste it? Is it the death of your parents, your brother? Or being skinned alive? Can you distinguish that reality from this one?"

Finn writhed in agony. Clawed at the floor, breaking fingernails and paying no heed to it. Stefan continued to pour terror into him. This could not happen again.

The screaming devolved into whimpering over time. Finn became a puddle of a person, non-responsive to further stimuli. Stefan withdrew his arm, which ached from being outstretched for so long. He rubbed his eyes with the heels of his hands. He was tired. His brain felt groggy. It had been a long time since he had done that.

He did not regret it. What other choice did he have? His remorse lay with having the ability at all, not with the using of it. Yet, he would have to do penance for it, nonetheless. It was the only way to cleanse his spirit. How could he be expected to purge his flock if he did not atone for his own shortcomings? *Later.*

He took hold of Finn and dragged him across the floor to the eyebolt that was anchored in the stone.

Stone. The boy could manipulate it. Stefan could be setting himself up for another ambush the next time he came down. But the way the boy was now a moaning mess, Stefan thought he had sufficiently broken Finn's spirit that further rebellions wouldn't be a consideration. Stefan had no way of knowing what he had superimposed into Finn's mind. But he knew his können allowed him to extract a person's worst fears and overwhelm their senses with them in an experience so immersive that it was inescapable. A thing like that could break a person. Irreparably.

Or was it irreparable? He could conduct an experiment. He should know how long-lasting the effects were. There was so much more extermination to be done. If his können were a gift that could aid him in his work, then he would be a fool not to use what providence had bestowed upon him. Stefan climbed the stairs and closed the door behind him, thinking about how best to draw the boy out to measure his level of brokenness.

AGATHA

THE PHONE WAS ALREADY in her hand when it started buzzing at her. *Could her timing be any worse?* Agatha punched the green icon to answer the phone. "Hey, mama. What do you need? I'm kind of rushing around." *Markus was already going to kill her for waiting a day to tell him about the pastor. But she hadn't wanted to overreact. Maybe it was coincidence.*

Nothing is ever coincidence.

"Oh? What are you doing?"

This wasn't going to be the succinct call she was hoping for. "Fixing dinner."

"For you and Thomas?"

"No," she answered flatly, attempting to discourage further inquiry.

Gertrude was either missing the signals or just running right through them. "Oh. Who for?"

Agatha sighed. "Me and Markus."

"Oh!" After her initial enthusiasm, Gertrude paused. "Dear, if you're still trying to impress him, are you sure you should be cooking?"

"Uhh ... rude. I can cook a meal."

Gertrude said, "Yes, I'm sure you're perfectly adequate. Let's just hope you're better in bed if there's any chance of you keeping him around."

"Oh, my gosh!" Agatha's cheeks flushed with heat. In her entire life, her mother had never said anything like that to her. Not that she was wrong. Agatha's cooking skills were ... well, adequate was probably the best word for them. She looked in the mirror that hung on the wall above the dining table. If she were going to rely on her other features, she had some more work to put in on that front, too. *At least I already have some color in my cheeks.* "Did you have a particular reason for calling?"

"Oh. I'm sure I did. I just have to remember what it was," Gertrude answered. Agatha heard a grumbling noise — maybe a deep voice — in the background. "Right. Do you want to meet your daddy?"

Agatha ripped the phone away from her ear and stared at it. Even as she did it, she realized it was a nonsensical reaction. Looking at the phone would not make what she just heard any more or less likely. She shoved the phone back up to her face. "I'm sorry. What?"

"I asked if you want to meet Vik. He's surprised me with a visit, and I think it's about time you two meet." Despite the buzzing sound that reverberated through her head and the sudden nausea in her belly, Agatha heard Gertrude's cheek scratch against the phone. She whispered, "He's not as hand-some as I thought. But he's as big as life itself. And now I remember what I liked about him," she added, giggling.

A booming voice called to her through the phone, "Come on over, Agatha. It's about time you met your papa."

"Mama, don't go anywhere. I'll be right there." She looked around the kitchen for weapons. Nothing stood out. She walked resolutely to her bedroom at the back of the house. Agatha stood on her tiptoes as she reached onto the shelf at the top of the closet and felt around blindly for a minute before latching onto what she'd been searching for.

As she brought it down, a raw groan heaved within her. She backpedaled slowly to the bed and sat against the edge of the mattress. The last time Joseph's Ka-bar had been used, Joseph had plunged it into the Warden's shoulder while the Warden was in the form of a chimera, just before it had crushed Joseph's throat. Before that, she'd shoved it into a sentinel's head, scraping through bone on the way to his brain. She could still hear the gloopy sound and the resistance of the suction as she tried to extract it. A shiver ran down her spine, pulling her out of her reverie.

When they'd moved here, she had put the knife and the few possessions of Joseph's that she'd had shipped over at the top of the closet and tried her best to ignore them. She thought she'd been too busy settling into a new life and raising a grieving child who'd just lost his father, met his oma, and been uprooted from the only world he knew, to give herself room to mourn. But it had found its way out anyhow, in unexpected ways. Fits of anger. Clothes that still smelled like him when she pulled them out of a drawer, which brought on sobbing spells. But all of that had subsided. It had been a long while since she'd reacted to something as strongly as to the knife. She looked down at the Ka-bar that lay in her hands across her lap.

The knife was mostly a reassuring gesture for herself. The actual weapon was the power that she could summon with her hands. Even now, energy swam around her, an invisible cloud of radiance that resonated while waiting for deployment. It grew denser, sensing the moment.

Yet she knew something that the kinetic cloud did not. It would betray her. Not out of malice, but because it could not do otherwise. His power was so much greater than anything she could muster. All of this was futile. That thought triggered a childhood memory of a *Star Trek* episode, "Resistance is futile."

That may well be, but resistance is necessary. She understood the cost. Today she would discover what Joseph already had — what's on the other side of the veil.

She pulled out her phone and typed a message. "I love you, my beautiful boy. No mother could ask for a better son. You are strong and bold like your father. You have been the great joy of my life." He was going to think she'd been day-drinking again.

Agatha stood up, walked back to the closet, and grabbed one of the belts that lay on the shelf, coiled like a leather snake. She threaded it through the loops on the left side of her pants and ran the belt through the belt loop on the sheath, and cinched everything snug.

"Alright," she said to an empty room before wiping the moisture that had accumulated at her eyelashes when she was texting Thomas. She put behind her sentiment and everything else that wasn't bottled fury.

She didn't hesitate again until she touched Gertrude's door handle. So few knowingly open the door to their own death. She recognized the choice she was making. Though it didn't feel like a choice. It was the accumulation of events that had led to an inescapable eventuality. She welcomed it. As much as her heart ached for Thomas, life had been hard. Just so hard. All the time. And she was tired. To go out waging war against Vulcan was about as much as she could ask for. There would be pain. He wouldn't kill her quickly. But she would give as good as she got. So let it begin. Agatha twisted the handle and pushed the door inward.

Gertrude was in rare form. All giggles and greetings. Vulcan, meanwhile, played at a smile that didn't touch anything beyond his lips. He was wary as a bobcat. He hunched somewhat to keep from raking his head against the ceiling. The pairing of them was totally absurd, as he appeared to be nearly double her height. Her mother babbled away, but Agatha caught none of it, until Gertrude grabbed her by the hand and dragged her across the room. Agatha finally tuned her back in, "… shy, Agatha. He is your daddy, after all."

He raised both hands, palms outward. His voice rumbled. "I'm not here for a fight, Agatha."

Agatha barked a rueful laugh. "You're going to get one whether you're here for it or not."

Vulcan grinned down at her and wagged a finger. "This is what I like about you. Always ready to brawl. And I suspect you're itching for one. Twelve years is a long time to act domesticated for a feral thing like yourself. That bloodlust is how I know you're mine. And you can't say I didn't try to tell you."

Agatha looked at him incredulously. "You what?"

That's all she got out before Gertrude laid a hand on each of their forearms and beamed up at them. "Look how well y'all are getting on. I'll go get us some tea."

Agatha's mind was turning itself inside out while she worked at figuring out what he was talking about. Tried to tell her? They'd only ever interacted once. And there wasn't all that much conversation involved.

"How do you take yours, Vik?" she asked, still so beautifully oblivious. Lost in a time and place that did not exist.

"However you like," he answered without taking his eyes off Agatha. When Gertrude left the room, he asked, "Figure it out yet?"

"No."

"That's a shame. When we were in the mines of Red Mountain, I said to you that we could make it a family affair."

Agatha looked bewildered. "That's it? That's you telling me you're …." She couldn't even bring herself to finish the sentence. *Why are we even talking? Let's just get to it.* As she began sliding her hand around to her back, a question occurred to her. "How did you find us?"

His expression was almost pity. It stoked the fires of loathing and hatred within her to receive such a look. "Agatha," he said, "you thought changing your last name and moving a couple thousand miles away was sufficient? Please think more highly of me than that. I have known almost since you arrived. But what I learned in the few days that the boy was in my care was that I didn't want to raise him. Any more than I wanted to raise you. As I had long suspected, children are all but intolerable. So kudos to you for bringing him up. So I let you be, rather than having you run all over the planet like a scared rabbit. I watched from a distance as the boy grew. Now, he is almost a man, and it is time for me to retrieve him."

That was all the provocation Agatha needed. She bared her teeth and snatched the knife from her belt.

Gertrude bustled through the door as her daughter advanced forward. "Agatha, no!" She dropped the tea service. Silver clattered on the floor, and bits of porcelain burst around the room.

IT TOOK SOME EFFORT, but Luka pulled his eyes away from Lea, who sat across the room pretending not to notice the lingering gaze. He asked Thomas. "Are you going to tell us why you wanted to meet, or are you just going to make us guess at it?"

Thomas chewed at his bottom lip. "Which of those options would annoy you the most?"

Lea sighed. "Maybe you could start by telling us why you and Emma weren't at the town hall meeting. Because if you're not going to follow through with plans, then I don't even know what we're doing. I'm going home."

"No," Luka said a little too desperately, and waved his arms in frustration at Thomas.

Thomas said, "I want us to go to the church to pray for Finn."

"Umm, I'm Jewish," Luka countered. "Well, not like goes-to-synagogue Jewish, but you know."

"Yeah, and I'm atheist," Lea said. "So I'm going to give it a pass. Besides, when did you get religious?"

Thomas squirmed at the uncomfortable turn the conversation had taken. He had thought they would be more agreeable to the suggestion. He decided to be more assertive to see if they would respond differently. "I've gone up there to talk to the minister a couple of times about things. He was nice and helpful. So we *are* going up there to pray for Finn, because there's nothing else we can do for him. And I can't just sit around doing nothing. Look at it this way, if there are no deities, then you've wasted part of an evening making wishes for your missing friend."

Lea said, "Luka's excuse doesn't hold up. The Hebrew God and Christian God are both Yahweh. It's Jesus they disagree about. So he could just pray to Yahweh and leave Jesus out of it."

"Whatever," Luka said, clearly out of his depth on the topic. "I don't think it's quite as simple as what you just said, but I'll go. For Finn."

The boys looked to Lea. She untucked her legs, clomped her Doc Martens to the floor, and stood up adjusting her leather skirt. When neither boy moved, she crossed her arms and glared at them. "What." It was more of a demand than a question.

Thomas said, "I guess I was expecting more of an argument than that. I had other points prepared in case I needed them."

"Well. Are we going or not? I need to know if my heathen self is going to start smoldering the minute I darken the doors of that church."

"I think you're smoldering hot," Luka said with a grin.

Lea nearly allowed her annoyed exterior to crack. "Shut up."

Thomas rose and reached down to pull Luka up.

Luka asked, "Is Emma coming? This can be like a double date."

Lea rolled her eyes. "Dude, you have to tone it down. But no, she has some family thing."

Thomas nodded his head.

Luka hollered across the house, "Mom, we're going to the church to pray for Finn."

A confused voice called back, "Umm … okay. Just be back before curfew so your father doesn't have to arrest you … again."

"Too soon. That's not funny."

Lea said, "It is funny though because you two are morons."

The trio stood looking dumbfounded at the front door of Evangelische Kirche. Thomas said, "It's never been locked before."

"Do you think the side door is unlocked?" Luka asked.

"Just to be clear," Lea said in a tone that dripped with mockery, "you think they bothered to lock the main door, but left the side door unlocked for any random person to come in?"

"I don't know. Maybe?"

She shook her head at him and looked around. No one was in their vicinity. "You two keep an eye out for a minute."

"Why?" Luka asked.

Instead of answering, she squatted down and dug through her purse. She pulled out a folding knife and flipped it open. Luka asked with concern, "Why do you have a knife?"

She pointed it in his direction. "First of all, you can't be keeping a lookout if you're watching me. Second, I don't know if you've heard, but there's a murdering bastard on the loose, and if he lays a hand on me, he's going to catch a blade. And third, for reasons like this." She shoved the knife point down under the bolt that dropped into a slot in the stone below the door and started trying to leverage it upward. "Some of these old doors have more give to them than they used to, and the stone has eroded enough so that … okay, pull on it. Slowly."

Thomas leaned forward and gently tugged on the door's handle. It opened outward with a grinding sound as Lea maintained pressure against the bolt. When it had opened wide enough that the three of them could squeeze through, he stopped pulling and waved them in.

"That was incredible!" Luka asked excitedly. "How did you know how to do that?"

Lea looked down at her boots and fiddled with the hem of her skirt. "There may be a few apparel items I need to ask forgiveness for possessing while we're here."

Luka's jaw dropped. "That's not just a little shoplifting. That's totally breaking and entering." He reached into his pocket. "Hang on. I have to call the authorities."

"Shut up," she said, punching him in the arm. "I know, alright. It's just … I just like nice things. I don't do it anymore."

"Since when?" Luka asked with a grin.

"Since I just decided." Lea looked around the church's entryway, realizing they were the only two present. "Where's Thomas?"

Thomas had had enough of their banter. They had come here for a specific purpose. Maybe they weren't supposed to be here. Not maybe. They definitely weren't supposed to be in here. The door was locked, after all. But they were here for Finn.

Before Thomas made his way up the center aisle, he looked for a basin of holy water. He'd seen it in Catholic churches, but he didn't know if that was a thing Protestants did. He was relieved not to have seen one, since hei wouldn't have known what to do with it if it were here, which was more or less the same way he felt about Emma most of the time. Things had been simpler when they were just friends. This new thing was good, and he liked it. But it was not simple.

Thomas' watch buzzed at him. A text from Agatha. He scrolled through it. *Weirdo.* He allowed his hand to tap the tops of the pews as he walked to the front of the church. Lea and Luka entered the sanctuary behind him, cackling but shushing each other as they failed to gain their composure. Thomas tried to ignore them, to keep his frustration from boiling over.

Agatha's voice sounded in his head, *You can't control others' actions, only your reactions.*

Considering his surroundings, Thomas wondered, *Where am I supposed to pray?* He didn't know *how* to pray either, but he hadn't come to that bridge yet. He wished Pastor Stefan was here to talk to. He had a way of making Thomas feel better about things. Thomas hadn't met anyone else who had so many similarities to himself, who could really understand what he was going through. Except his mom, but she didn't count. It's not like he could talk to her about this stuff.

It came as something of a revelation when Thomas realized that he and the pastor had never really talked about God or prayer or anything like that. Wasn't that kind of his job?

Thomas felt a hand on his back. He jerked his head to the right.

"You okay?" Lea asked. "You stopped walking and just stood here in this one spot."

"Yeah, fine. I guess."

Luka called from up ahead. "Come look at this."

Lea and Thomas caught up to him. One of the tables on the platform had been pushed to the side and stood askew. There was a gaping rectangular hole in the floor with stone steps leading downward.

"Has this been here before?" Luka asked. "Seems kind of weird."

Thomas raised his arms. "I've only been in the church twice, and I've never been up here. Maybe we should go. Something doesn't feel right."

"Listen," Lea whispered.

The three teenagers stood motionless. A small primal noise crawled up the steps. Thomas couldn't discern whether it was human or animal.

"What the heck was that?" Lea whispered.

Luka suggested, "Maybe it was a boiler."

"Oh, because of all the hot water that's being used right now?" Lea said.

Luka shrugged.

"Or maybe we need to leave," Thomas said.

The sound emerged from the darkness again. This time, it was more readily discernible as moaning.

When Lea descended the first two steps, Thomas grabbed her arm. Her eyes blazed at him when she whirled around. "What are you doing?" Thomas asked.

She shoved his hand away. "There is someone or something down there."

"Yeah, no kidding. That should be all the reason we need to leave."

"Do whatever you want," she said. "No one is making you come with me."

Thomas looked to Luka for backup. The other boy offered none. He wasn't wading in. Thomas turned back to Lea to find that she had taken two more steps. This wasn't an argument after all, just his own ineffective protest. He couldn't very well let her do this alone. He admitted to himself that Lea was probably more daring than he was, so he followed in her wake. Luka's feet scuffed the steps behind him. Whatever happened, they were all in it together.

The darkness wrapped around them like a quilt as they descended. Thomas held up a hand above his head and formed an orb of fire that he sent above and ahead of Lea. It cast a roving orange light around the space and illuminated a light switch at the bottom of the steps. When Lea reached the bottom and flipped the lights on, Thomas recalled his fire to himself and extinguished it. Florescent lights popped on and flooded spaces to their right and left.

"No. Please, no. No. Please," a pitiful voice whimpered from the room to the left.

Instead of hesitating, Lea bolted into the room. Thomas and

Luka were on her heels. They found Finn huddled on the floor, cradling his legs to himself. His eyes were glassy and unfocused, and he didn't seem to recognize them right away. Lea knelt in front of him. "Finn," she called softly. "It's us, Finn."

Nothing.

She looked back at Luka and Thomas, who might as well have been statues.

Lea turned her attention back to Finn. "Finn, can you hear me?" She placed her hands on his cheeks. Finn flinched and tried to scramble away. He got only an arm's length away before his shackles stopped his progress.

"He has had some traumatic experiences of late," said a fifth voice in the room.

Finn groaned. The others whirled almost simultaneously.

"Pastor Stefan." Thomas recognized the man with some relief. "Something's happened to Finn. You've got to help…" His voice trailed away as realization crept over him.

Lea spoke it aloud. "He's what happened to Finn."

Thomas' eyes pled with the minister to contradict her. Instead, he observed a darkness in the man's expression. One he hadn't seen before.

"I had been contemplating how to dispose of this particular problem," Pastor Stefan flicked the back of his hand dismissively toward Finn, who had stilled himself again as if playing dead, "when my phone alerted me that the security cameras were picking up movement. Imagine my frustration when I turned on the live feed and saw you three nosing about. Magnifying my problem many fold. As difficult as it is to get rid of one body, I cannot fathom how I will manage four."

"You're going to kill us?" Thomas asked, still harboring disbelief and having difficulty coming to terms with this new reality.

"Hey, dummy," Lea said with unrelenting attitude, "he's the one who's been killing everyone."

Thomas was dumbstruck. He returned his attention to Pastor Stefan and awaited a denial.

None came.

"But I thought … but you said …" Thomas stammered through his confusion. "You said you weren't like him."

Luka asked, "Weren't like who?"

Thomas pointed an accusing finger, "His grandfather is Pommerenke, the Beast of the Black Forest."

Lea glared at Thomas. "You didn't think that was important information to share with anyone?!"

"He said he wasn't like him," Thomas defended himself.

"So the next time a viper tells you it's not poisonous, you're going to believe it?"

"Venomous," Luka interjected, "not poisonous." He quickly realized his poorly timed correction. He shrugged, "I'm just saying."

"He's … right," Finn croaked.

In a halting effort, Finn pushed himself to a sitting position.

"Finn!" Luka exclaimed. Thomas and Lea also turned to him with what approximated smiles under the circumstances.

Finn pointed behind them, "Go."

They looked back to see the pastor disappearing up the stairwell. Thomas and Lea fled after him. But Finn snatched Luka's arm, "Stay." Luka tugged against the grip. Tears formed in Finn's eyes, causing Luka to consent.

31

AGATHA

AGATHA HADN'T BEEN SCOLDED like this since she was a child. She had always despised the part of being in trouble where she was getting chewed out and had always wanted to say, "Either punish me or not, but let's just skip you fussing at me." The yelling part was rarely for the kid's benefit anyway. It was just so the parents could hear themselves say it. She'd done the same with Thomas — still did — and observed many half-constrained eye-rolls.

Gertrude was waggling her finger in a full fit about the etiquette that older Southern women care so much about. *After their children and looks leave them, manners are all they have left to fret over.* Maybe that was too harsh, but she didn't particularly care right now. "... and Vik is a guest in my home and is entitled to all the protections and customs that affords him. I will not have that blood on my hands. Do you understand me?"

"Uh-huh."

Vulcan grinned like the cat who ate the canary.

Agatha tucked her hand back behind her back as if she were replacing the Ka-bar in its sheath, although she had no such intentions. She maintained the pressure on her forefeet. She would not be lulled into any casual stance.

"Now, I've got to get the broom and dustpan to sweep up this mess. Do you think you can mind your manners until I get back?"

Agatha didn't answer. But Gertrude just stared at her, awaiting a response.

"Fine. Whatever. Yes."

Gertrude flipped her switch back to a chipper and delightful demeanor, her voice sickeningly sweet. "Wonderful. I'll just tidy up this little mess, and we can get back to our reunion."

Neither Vulcan nor Agatha moved nor spoke for the several minutes it took for Gertrude to retrieve her cleaning supplies, use them, and return them to the closet. She came back into the room futzing with her apron. Agatha thought in this moment that her mother could have been pulled right out of *The Stepford Wives*.

With a smile on her lips, Gertrude suggested, "Shall we all sit together for a while?" She sidled up next to Vulcan and sat on the sofa he stood in front of. She patted the seat beside her, and Vulcan lowered himself onto it. The furniture creaked under his immense bulk. The disparity between them was a ridiculous sight. It only became more so when Gertrude put her hand on Vulcan's leg, well up and on the interior of his thigh.

"Agatha?" Her mother gestured to the highback chair to Agatha's right.

"I'm good."

"Agatha." The tone had changed from invitation to warning.

Vulcan patted her knee. "Let her be, Gerty. Our girl is just having a moment."

Rage swelled within her like a hurricane. She hadn't been aware that she could layer so many levels of fury on top of each other. He looked Agatha full in the face when he asked, "Now tell me, how's sweet Elle doing?"

Agatha roared and launched herself across the room. She raised the knife overhead and clasped it with both hands. She would plunge it through his chest and be done with this. The usually-black blade glowed a vibrant orange with the heat she applied to it. Vulcan's eyes grew fearful in realization, and his smirk fell away.

Before Agatha landed her blow, she was struck by a blast of energy that changed her direction and sent her crashing into the adjacent wall. The plaster and slats cratered with the impact. She fell in a heap, dazed. She quickly yanked herself off the floor, expecting Vulcan's counterattack. But when she looked up, his mouth was agape as he stared at Gertrude. She remained seated with casual grace. Finally, Vulcan looked at Agatha. She wondered if her expression was as bewildered as his.

"Agatha, we will not have that again. Do you understand? Now, you apologize to your daddy."

Agatha ran a hand up to the back of her head, where a goose-egg was already forming. She pulled the hand away to inspect it. No blood. It was only then she realized she was no longer holding the knife. She saw it lying among the rubble from the ruined wall. *That's a shame*, she thought. He was on guard now anyway. Any attack had almost no chance of succeeding.

"I told you to apologize." Gertrude stood as she spoke, her voice carrying an edge to it that Agatha hadn't heard in a long time. "And I won't say it again."

"The hell I will." Agatha felt every bit the defiant adolescent, even as the words escaped her mouth.

Gertrude clenched her fists, and her arthritic knuckles whitened with the strain.

"Now, now." A smug, bemused Vulcan pushed himself to his feet and rolled his shoulders back, stretching, giving Agatha an opportunity to recognize exactly what she was up against. "Agatha's just a little riled up. We've all been there. Let me get her a chair, and we can finish our chat."

Two steps brought him parallel to Agatha. They stood shoulder to shoulder, or what would have to pass for that with the dramatic height difference. He looked down at her, then abruptly turned his back. He was daring her to attack again. She knew from their last battle that her fire could do little more than singe the elephant hide he called skin. An attack now would only give him justification to snuff her out. Agatha doubted that her apparently witless mother would so much as bat an eye. She was trying not to take it personally. She'd known that Gertrude was deteriorating; she just thought she had more time. Agatha had even considered looking into putting her in Stephanus-Haus with Elle.

Vulcan opened a portal, reached in, and pulled something through. He pivoted to face Agatha and clear her line of sight.

It was the chair. Elle's chair — the Savanarola. Inlaid with mother-of-pearl and the gold overlay accents. Agatha took an involuntary step backward. Vulcan sauntered back to where Gertrude still stood in front of the sofa. He put his arm around her shoulder. But rather than it being a gesture of affection, he nudged her toward himself until she stood directly in front of him, shielding him from Agatha.

Vulcan pointed to the chair. "Sit."

That chair brought back so much horror she had tried to keep buried. In this moment, she did not trust herself to speak. Agatha shook her head, trying to look resolute, confident. She knew what would happen if she followed his instructions. She'd watched Elle, who had never come back from whatever happened to her. Well, her body had, but the most important parts had not.

"Sit down, Agatha."

"You'll have to kill me to get my body in that chair."

Vulcan laughed. "As much as that would delight me ..." he paused, reveling in the prospect of it, and withdrew one of his chisels from the pouch beside the massive forging hammer that hung from his belt. The chisel was nearly the length of her fore-arm. "Let me tell you what's going to happen if you don't get your ass in that chair. I'm going to kill your mother here in front of you. Then I'll maim you and beat you nearly to your death, so you can lay there in misery knowing that when I walk out that door, I'm headed to finish off your sister and take your boy."

Gertrude stood quiet as a church mouse in front of Vulcan, still oblivious to the reality she was drenched in. "Ags, be a good girl, and do what your daddy says, won't you?"

Agatha's stomach was in knots. There was no right decision, only bad options. Oberhaupt used to tell her, "The hard decisions in your life will not be choosing between right and wrong. Those decisions are pretty easy, even if you don't always choose to do the right thing. The tough choices are when you have to decide between the known and the unknown, both of which seem to be good options." He was wrong. The hard decision was between letting yourself become a captive so a monster could torture you and fighting the monster, knowing it was sealing the fates of others. But even her compliance didn't guarantee their survival.

"What's to stop you from killing them anyway if I do what you say?"

"Nothing." Vulcan shrugged and put on his most disarming expression. "I guess you'll just have to trust me."

Agatha wanted to spit. She looked down at her hands and flexed them. Energy swirled around them, waiting to be trans-formed, ignited.

"Uh-uh." Vulcan tutted and raised the chisel to the back of Gertrude's head in warning.

Agatha relaxed her hands, and the energy dissipated. Her whole body slumped, dejected. She didn't know what else to do. This was everyone's best chance. She walked to the chair. Before sitting down, or even touching it, she said, "Mama?"

Gertrude's eyes followed the path she'd taken and met her where she stood.

"Do you hear me?"

"Of course, I hear you, baby girl."

Agatha couldn't tell whether she was permeating the fog that had descended on her mother. "I know I wasn't a good daughter, but I tried to be a good mother."

A veil parted, however briefly, and Gertrude said, "We're all just doing the best we can, Chipmunk. These last years have been everything to me."

Her mother hadn't called her that since she was small, when everything was still right with the world. Or seemed to be. Before her friends started dying. Before she had begun killing to protect other people's ideals. Before her husband's throat had been crushed and the lifeblood poured out of him. Before her boy became an orphan. Because that looked to be what would happen next. She was giving herself up to give him a chance.

She breathed in slowly, deeply, and put her hands on the arms of the Savanarola, expecting to feel something more than the tight-grained texture of the varnished walnut. When nothing extraordinary happened, she sat down, the portal still shimmering to her left. With her hands gripping the armrests, she pressed herself fully into the chair. Vulcan watched with greedy eyes.

When Agatha fully situated herself in the chair, gold chains slithered out of the legs and armrests, coiling tightly around her appendages. The metal was cold against her arms, but that wasn't what made her shiver. She had placed herself at his mercy now, but she wouldn't beg, or even ask, for it. Ever. More chains weaved themselves around her chest and abdomen. She took a deep breath and held it, expanding her lungs and chest so the bindings wouldn't be so tight when the binding stopped. Once she was thoroughly imprisoned, everything stilled.

"Now," Vulcan said, looking pleased with himself. "I think

you more fully understand the situation. So let me ask you a question — where is Thomas?"

Agatha did spit this time. It didn't make it to Vulcan, but the message did. He glowered at the viscous fluid lying between Agatha and himself. He turned Gertrude so that she faced him and placed his hands on the sides of her face. The metal of the chisel pressed against her cheek. His hands were so large that his fingers overlapped at the back of her skull. As he tilted her head back, he leaned down and kissed her on the mouth.

Something awakened within Gertrude, fighting through the faulting synapses to the surface. She grabbed his wrists and struggled against him. Energy vibrated around them as she tried to force him away from her, using her können against him, but she was too frail to create any separation.

Vulcan pulled his face away and smiled down at her. "Fighting to the bitter end. Just like our daughter. I'm glad to see you still have that in you." He removed his right hand from her face. The chisel had been pressing so hard against her cheek that a line of bruising had already formed.

Vulcan drove the arm upward, smashing the chisel through the base of her skull into her brain, until it protruded from her forehead like a devastated unicorn. Her body slackened and became dead weight in his arms.

Agatha screamed. Not words. Just a scream of horror.

Vulcan spun Gertrude around so her back was to him. He held the extruding base of the chisel like a handle and applied upward pressure. As it slid out of Gertrude's head, he allowed gravity to tug at her body. She collapsed with a thunk. Blood leaked from the voids left by the chisel and spilled to the floor. He wiped the chisel on his leather pouch and dropped it back in.

Agatha still screamed. But her horror had become rage. She thrashed and bucked against her confines, her face nearly purple. Veins stood out on her forehead and the tendons in her neck strained. She summoned flames, but nothing happened. She tried again. Nothing.

Her chest heaved with a sob when she inhaled and drew in a ragged breath. She had thought that acquiescing to his demands would give them a chance, but it just made things easier for him to dispatch with them. The chains bit into her arms as she strained against them. They were so tight now that her hands were going numb.

Vulcan watched quietly from the other side of the room. He waited for her to exhaust her efforts. Agatha grew still. In a voice that was barely more than a coarse whisper, Vulcan asked, "Where is Thomas?"

Agatha closed her mouth. No amount of terror that he could rain down on her would coerce her to answer that question. He saw that too.

"That's fine," he said. "Where is a pen and paper?"

Agatha wrinkled her brow in temporary confusion, but still did not answer. Vulcan sighed. Stepping over Gertrude's body, he walked past Agatha into the kitchen and out of her vision. Cabinet draws opened and closed, their contents clattering. She heard an "Ah" as Vulcan opened the correct drawer, followed by scrawling. He entered the living area with a rectangle of paper that he laid on the side table.

"He can come find us then." Vulcan looked around the room and nodded to himself. "I think we're about done here." He walked around behind Agatha, tipped the chair backward, and dragged her through the portal, just as he had done with Elle so many years ago.

32

THOMAS

THOMAS TOOK the stairs two at a time. He was more than halfway up when the pastor reached the top and whipped something out of his pocket, kneeling hurriedly and swiping at the floor. Thomas heard a mechanical noise and pumped his legs even harder. He dove up the last couple of steps to tackle Pastor Stefan, who hadn't yet retreated from the lip of the opening.

The man reacted to the attack by shifting to his left. Thomas flailed past him and landed hard on his belly. He shoved himself up to his feet and turned to face Stefan. Lea burst through the opening before it clanged shut.

The pastor grabbed Lea from behind and wrenched her toward himself. He wrapped his good arm around her throat and held her tight against his chest. With his bad arm, he retrieved his knife from its sheaf and pulled it toward Lea, pricking the skin between two of her ribs. Making sure everyone understood the stakes. Lea grunted in pain and stopped resisting.

Thomas was spinning out of control. Two friends locked in the basement. Lea in danger. Someone he trusted is the serial killer. "You said you weren't like him!" he yelled. "You said it."

"That is what you heard, but it is not what I said, Thomas,"

Pastor Stefan said in a condescending tone. "What I told you was that I am not like Pommerenke just because he is my opa. I do not do the things he did because his blood runs through my veins. I do them by choice. I am continuing his mission to eradicate the zauberi plague."

"No. No, no, no. That's not what you said. It's not what you meant." The foundation of the world had shifted under his feet again, and Thomas was unwilling to accept it. He tugged at the energy that surrounded him and formed fire in his hand.

"Nein, Thomas. I will stick her like a pig." Lea grunted with pain as the shepherd twisted the knife several degrees and the point opened a hole in her skin. A small red flower blossomed on the side of her shirt.

Thomas held the flame, not knowing what to do. He noticed Lea looking at him intently. She flicked her eyes downward and slowly withdrew her left hand from the bag that still clung to her side. She clasped something. Her knife. It was still folded shut. He looked back at Stefan, not wanting to alert him. Thomas needed to divert his attention without getting her killed in the process.

"Thomas, we can all walk away from this."

The boy laughed. It was an ugly sound, devoid of joy. "No, we can't. No one is walking away from this. It only ends one of two ways."

"If you do not release that flame you're holding, you will certainly seal the girl's fate."

Thomas had to bring the standoff to an end. He did not trust himself to hit the pastor and miss Lea. He just needed to get close enough to give her a chance.

In a flurry of movement, Thomas pitched his fiery orb sidearm over the right shoulders of Lea and Stefan, who flinched to the left, pulling her with him. Lea's knife opened with a click. She swung her arm downward and back, aiming to lodge it in the man's thigh. Like a burst of lightning, Stefan shoved Lea forward by the neck. She went sprawling to the ground without making contact. Stefan stumbled several steps to the side before recovering his balance. Thomas helped Lea up off the floor.

The trio resumed their standoff. Thomas and Lea on the platform, their backs to the cross that hung on the wall. Along the wall, a crackling sound grew stronger, and an orange yellow glow brightened. The pastor's shadow danced on the floor around him. Thomas' fire had found something to consume.

Lea still held the knife in her left hand. She looked down at her ribs to assess the damage.

"You okay?" Thomas asked.

"I will be. After we deal with this—"

Thomas' vision erupted with terrible images and sounds. Things that had fueled his nightmares for the past dozen years. Sounds of screaming and death. His father's voice in agony. His mother wailing. He grabbed his head, trying to squeeze the horror show out. Through clouded vision, he saw that Lea, too, was afflicted. But she fought it. She screamed, not in pain, but in fury. The sound pierced through the racket in Thomas' head. He began searching through the noise to find Stefan.

The pastor had his arms outstretched towards the two teenagers. No knife in his hand. Had he lost it somewhere along the way? He was the source of the terrors. Despite his concentration, concern showed through on his face. Thomas realized the pastor had expected to immobilize Lea and Thomas with whatever this was. But they were battling against it.

Stefan leaned forward. His hands shook with the strain. A fresh wave a dread flooded Thomas' senses. Lea roared. She shrugged off the attack, like a mantle that she forced to the floor. The intrusion into Thomas' mind dissipated as the pastor's attack faltered.

"We've already lived through our worst nightmares," she spat at him between heaving breaths as she recovered from the bout. "We live them every day. I see my parents burning to death in the car that I escaped. Your little barrage is nothing compared to that. Nothing compared to lying awake at night fearing the next time my wasted uncle is going to come in to cop a feel."

Stefan paled. He had lost his advantage. This must have been what he had done to Finn, who had lived a life devoid of tragedy. What he had witnessed must have been devastating to him.

Lea launched herself off the platform, her knife raised overhead, clutched in both hands. Stefan stepped up to intercept her. He caught her mid-air and used her momentum to fling her to the side. She swung the knife wildly as she sailed to the side and crashed through a flagpole and into a pillar. Wood cracked and splintered under her. She landed in a heap. Stefan turned his attention back to Thomas.

"Looks like it's just us now, boy."

Thomas almost didn't recognize the voice. How could this be the same man he had talked to before? Who had counseled him and given him advice? It seemed impossible.

But the time for words had passed. There was no reasoning with a monster. But what did that mean? Would he have to kill the man? He didn't know if he could do it. He didn't know if he would be given a choice.

Thomas jumped down from the platform, positioning himself on the opposite side of Stefan as Lea. He had to keep the pastor's attention away from her; she hadn't yet moved again since smacking against the stone pillar. Thomas filled his palms with flame and pitched the first of his fiery orbs at Stefan, who swatted at it with the flat of his knife. He succeeded in making contact, but rather than deflecting the projectile away, it burst into a hundred smaller spheres, splattering Stefan's torso with magma. He yelped and slapped at the fire as his shirt burned away in blackening curls that revealed a chest and stomach layered with hundreds of scars.

Thomas' eyes widened. Stefan looked down to see what the

tattered remnants of his clothes had revealed. "My burden comes at great cost, Thomas. We all have our cross to bear."

Thomas was unmoved by the speech, focusing on his next attack and what came after that. He didn't know what he was doing. He had never been in a proper fight before, much less something like this. The closest he'd come was his stupid duels with Luka.

That kindled a thought. Luka had tripped him up by pouring ice at his feet. Maybe he could do the same with fire. Back the shepherd into a corner and hold him there until help arrived. How long until that happened? Thomas glanced at the fire that was growing along the front of the sanctuary; hopefully, not too long. A sustained fire might roast Stefan alive or catch the rest of the place on fire. Of course, that would resolve the problem as well. But how long could he hold it? He had no idea.

Stefan charged at Thomas, driving through the boy and tackling him like a linebacker. The full weight of the man landed on Thomas' chest as they crashed to the stone floor. Thomas grunted as the air exploded from his chest. He lay on his back, trying to gasp for air as his uncooperative lungs convulsed without drawing in air.

Stefan leapt on top of Thomas and straddled him, pinning Thomas' arms at his sides. He held the tip of the knife against the soft flesh behind Thomas' chin. "If you try anything, I will shove this upward and drive it through your brain. I will be the last thing you see as you descend from this hell to the next."

Thomas resolved not to speak. To give Pastor Stefan no satisfaction. Several deep thudding noises rose from the basement stairwell. "I will deal with them next." It didn't sound like a threat as much as a statement of fact.

Thomas panicked. But thoughts of his mother pushed through his frenetic state. She had lost so much already. Would he be next? What would that do to her? His memory flipped back to their last training session in the woods. He had told her about meeting with Pastor Stefan and the trust he had in the man. The man who was now jabbing him with a knife because he wasn't paying attention.

"...my successor, Thomas. I had plans for us. With no son of my own, you could have been my apprentice, my heir. ..."

The memory from the woods triggered something else. He looked away from the ceiling, where black smoke gathered in great billows. Without turning his head, which was anchored to the floor by a steel blade, Thomas cast his eyes around as much of the sanctuary as he could see. With such a limited field of view, he did not find what he was looking for.

Thomas closed his eyes. He felt around the church with his memory. He found it.

The pastor yelled at him, demanding that he open his eyes.

Thomas scrunched them tighter. He had to focus. He reached out to the potted plants clustered under one of the windows on the far wall and called them to himself.

A hand pawed at his face. Trying to force his left eye open. He shook his head. The hand gripped his face and squeezed. Still, he called.

Tendrils slithered across the floor.

"Look at me, Thomas. Look at me! See me. Hear me."

The hand was ripped away from Thomas' face. He opened his eyes just as suddenly. A half dozen vines had coiled around the pastor's wrist and forearm. He inspected them with disbelief, as they suspended his arm out to his side. He strained against the restraint to little effect. Another set of tendrils struck his knife hand and yanked it away from Thomas. More came on, wrapping themselves through the crooks of his arms and around his neck.

Pastor Stefan's already wild face became feral. The tendons in his neck strained with exertion as he fought against the backward pull of the vines. He squeezed his knees to hold on to Thomas like a bull rider. He couldn't maintain his grip. The plants pulled him off Thomas, who scrambled backward and to his feet.

Stefan tugged forward and gathered his feet under himself. He flipped the knife around in his hand and tried to cut at the vines. The vines constricted around his arm like pythons. Stefan flinched at the pain but continued cutting until there was a crack. The man screamed and dropped the knife. It clattered to the floor at his feet. In his burned away clothing and draped with plants, he was more creature than man.

Stefan lunged toward Thomas. He dragged the plants with him. They didn't weigh enough to root him to the ground. With enough effort, he could overcome them. Thomas backed up several steps and smacked against the stone wall of the church. Nowhere left to run. The shadows around him deepened as the blaze within the church grew.

Thomas raised his arms in front of himself and put the heels of his hands together. A brilliant light formed between them. The heat of it touched his face, while his hands remained unaffected.

Stefan halted his cumbersome forward trudge. "Do it, boy. Do it!"

Everything around Thomas seemed to wink out of existence except the man in front of him. He recalled the pastor's words from their last meeting. *Only you can choose your path.* Thomas' hands shook. The fire within them faltered. The man deserved to die, certainly. But the boy couldn't do it.

The pastor grinned with renewed hope. He lurched forward. "That's what I thought, boy. You are too wea—"

His words became a guttural sputter. He looked down in shock. Several inches of wood protruded from his abdomen, just below his sternum. It was stained red from where it had skewered him.

Stefan whirled around to find his attacker. An arm's length of wood trailed behind him like a rudder. "You," he accused.

"Me," Lea said. She held in her hands the top half of the broken flagpole, her makeshift spear. Germany's banner trailed to the ground in front of her.

The pastor tottered where he stood. He reached his arms behind his back, trying to grab the pole that impaled him and whimpering with the effort. When he gave up flailing at it, he lurched toward Lea and opened his mouth to speak.

She drove the splintered rod forward with all the force she could muster, using his forward momentum against him, to push it through the space between ribs on the left side of his chest. Lea dodged as Pastor Stefan fell forward. The eagle adorning the top of the flagpole struck the ground first, embedding the pole further into Stefan's torso until it struck his spine with a thud. After balancing precariously for a moment in a ridiculous propped up posture, Stefan toppled to the side and slammed to the ground.

The German flag that appeared to flower from his chest fluttered around him until it fell still and covered his lifeless face like a shroud. The tangle of vines withdrew from him and scurried back across the floor.

33

THOMAS

LEA HUNCHED over with her hands on her knees. Beyond that, she didn't move for several minutes. Thomas pushed away from the wall and staggered over to her. He placed his hands on her shoulders and urged her upright. Tears dripped from her eyes, and he pulled her into an embrace. "You saved me," he said into her tangle of hair. "I couldn't do it. I froze."

"Yeah, you kind of did," Lea teased in a strained voice, then pulled sharply away and shoved him. "You lied." Her indignation had enabled her to recompose herself in short order.

Thomas recovered his balance but not his understanding of the change that had just come over Lea. "I — what?"

"What was that with the plants?"

"Oh, yeah. That. I didn't lie exactly. I just—"

Several loud concussions came from the platform.

"Finn and Luka," Lea said, taking off in their direction.

"The key. Is it up there?" Thomas called, as he squatted down beside Pastor Stefan and prepared for the grim task of rummaging through the newly dead man's pockets.

"Got it," she yelled back, picking the rectangular card up off the floor where the pastor must have dropped it a few minutes earlier.

Thomas ran to join her. She rubbed the key card over the scanner and the door retracted. Luka and Finn stood eight feet below them, with Luka supporting the other boy.

"What took you so long?" Luka asked with a smile.

"Shut up," Lea said.

One slow step at a time, Luka helped Finn up the stairs. Finn winced with each step. When they got to the top, Thomas leaned in and took over assisting from Luka, who stepped toward Lea. He looked at the burning destruction around him. "You kind of made a mess of the place."

Lea punched him lightly before grabbing him by the shirt and pulling him in for a hard kiss. Thomas and Finn turned away. When Finn caught sight of the impaled body, he shrank back. "It's okay," Thomas whispered. "It's okay." He wrapped his arms around Finn. The boy buried his face in Thomas' shoulder.

The stained glass window nearest the fire burst into a glittering rainbow of shards, pulling Lea and Luka out of their embrace. "Guess that's our cue," Luka said.

Thomas helped Finn down the two steps from the platform to the floor. When they came alongside the shepherd's body, Finn spit on it and ambled toward the center aisle.

The double doors at the entrance to the sanctuary burst open. Fischer and Pereira surged through, guns in hand. The sight of the four teenagers brought them up short. There was a long pause as everyone assessed the situation.

"Hey, dad," Luka said casually. "We found Finn."

Thomas shook his head at his friend, who was confirming something Thomas had long thought true of him — the boy would try to weather any situation with humor.

"The pastor?" Fischer asked.

Thomas and Finn shifted to one side of the aisle, Luka and

Lea to the other. They left a line of sight that led to the impaled body of Pastor Stefan. Fischer nodded to Pereira to check on the minister. He strode past the group of four, gun in both hands, pointed toward the floor.

Luka said, "Unless he turns into a zombie, Pereira won't need that gun. Lea kabobed him like a Turk … I lost my analogy."

"Please stop, son." Fischer wrinkled his nose at the acrid smell of the smoke that roiled across the church's vaulted ceiling. "We need to get out of this building." He stepped out from in front of the doorway and waved the kids past him.

Thomas was the last of the four out. He placed a hand on the door frame and turned to look over his shoulder. Pereira signaled to Fischer, confirming that the pastor was dead. Fischer holstered his pistol. Thomas was … conflicted. Too many things welled inside for him to identify them. He turned back and followed his friends out of the sanctuary and through the foyer.

Once they were outside, Fischer had the four teenagers sit on a bench. They waited while he made several phone calls. After he'd hung up from the final call, he pocketed his phone and squatted in front of them, pulling a notepad and pen out of his shirt pocket. "The fire department will be here soon, and an ambulance is on the way. At least two of you appear to need medical attention. Finn, I've called your parents. They're on the way." The boy tried to keep himself together. He made several terrible noises that Thomas suspected were barely-constrained sobs, before dropping his chin to his chest. Thomas put an arm around him and kept it there while Finn's chest heaved in and out. Fischer looked at Lea and continued, "I didn't reach anyone at your house. I've sent someone over. Thomas, I've texted your mom that you're with me. I'll take you home when we leave here." Fischer took a deep breath. "Before everyone gets here, I'd like to get answers to a few of the seven hundred questions I have. So let's start with this — why are you here?"

"Well," Luka said, "Finn got kidnapped." He looked around, pleased as a peacock with his own wit.

Fischer leveled a fierce stare at him. "Enough."

If Luka had a tail, it would have been firmly tucked between his legs. Lea answered, "We came here to pray for Finn."

Fischer raised an eyebrow at her.

"It's true," she said. "It was Thomas' idea."

Thomas nodded to confirm her statement.

"Okay," Fischer said in a tone that wasn't sure whether it was a statement or a question. He scratched some notes into his pad.

"Can I ask a question?" Thomas said.

Fischer nodded.

"Why are *you* here?"

He gestured toward Pereira, who was emerging from the church, walking backward and dragging the pastor's body by the hands. He was backlit in the twilight by the glow of what was now an inferno. Smoke poured out of eves and broken windows. Sirens screamed in the distance. "We finally got the GPS records for Finn's phone. The towers showed it was last on right around here. When we got close, we saw the fire."

Fischer stood up to meet Pereira as he approached. The detective leaned in to whisper something to the polizeidirektor. Fischer nodded. He knelt in front of Finn. "Finn, look at me."

The boy looked up slowly.

"Did he have you in that basement?"

Finn shook as if he were freezing, but he nodded.

"Was he the one we've been looking for?"

He broke eye contact and nodded again.

The sirens drew closer. He pivoted to his left, back to Lea. "How's your head?"

She started to protest being hurt. Fischer held up a hand. "One of your eyes is dilated more than the other. There's a knot on the back of your head that is evident even through your hair.

What I need to know is whether you can tell me what happened in there. I can talk to these two after the ambulance takes you."

"I'm not—"

He held up his hand again. "You are. It's not a discussion."

Lea sighed at him. "I can tell you."

Luka leaned over to Thomas and whispered, "I need to learn how to do that."

Ignoring the interruption, Fischer said, "Good. As quickly as you can then."

She recounted everything that had happened since they arrived at the church, attributing her breaking-and-entering skills to luck rather than experience. In the failing light, Pereira shined a flashlight over Fischer's shoulder so he could scribble into his notepad. Lea finished her telling of the events of the evening as chaos unfolded around them. Before they got wrapped up in it, Fischer instructed, "Do not talk to anyone except me and Pereira. It is imperative that we handle this well."

Each of them nodded their understanding.

Finn's parents swept in and engulfed him in hugs. He groaned in pain at the pressure being applied to his ribs. They released him, their worried faces growing darker still. His older brother hovered in the background. Thomas nodded to him, remembering the day several weeks earlier when he had carted Luka off on the back of an ATV, burns stretching across his chest and stomach. That seemed a lifetime ago. Paramedics dropped in, inspecting them and peppering each of them with questions.

A hand gripped Thomas' shoulder. He started and looked to his left. Fischer beckoned him away from the mass of people who had accumulated. "Are you okay?" he asked.

Thomas shrugged, "I guess."

"Are you hurt?"

Thomas swiped his hand across his throat and looked at it. The bleeding had stopped and dried up. "No. I'm okay."

"Okay. Let's get you home," Fischer said.

"Don't you need to stay here?"

"Pereira can handle it from here." He called for Luka, and the boy bounded over.

"Am I going with you?" Luka asked.

Fischer pointed across the crowd. Luka's mother was looking around for him. He grunted, "She's just going to make a fuss over me."

"She's a mother," Fischer replied dispassionately. "That is one of her primary occupations."

"Can't I go with you and Thomas?"

"No. You two can catch up later."

Luka stalked off in the direction of his mother. Fischer pointed the way to his car, but all Thomas saw was a hoard of onlookers. As they slid through the crowd, several people asked Fischer how the fire had started. He uttered no response whatsoever.

Once they were inside the car, Thomas asked, "Does my mom know what happened?"

Fischer smirked at him before putting the vehicle in gear. "Do you think she'd be waiting patiently at home if she knew what happened here?"

Thomas returned the smile. No, she certainly would not.

"I suspect your mother would have dragged every heilerin in town up to that church and made them bring the pastor back to life just so she could kill him all over again."

Thomas nodded. "That sounds about right."

"We were supposed to have dinner tonight. I texted her that something came up that Pereira and I needed to check out, so I was going to be late. She was cooking for us."

"She was cooking?" Thomas said incredulously, being pulled out of the stupor he had felt himself sliding into as the illumi-nated windows of the town floated slowly past. "You're probably better off dealing with dead bodies."

FISCHER STOPPED his car in front of Thomas' house. "Do you always keep it this dimly lit?"

Only the faintest glow reached the front window that was obscured by a shade and blinds. "No. She's usually got every light in the house on."

"Okay," Fischer said as he opened his door.

On the walk up to the house, Thomas asked a question he wasn't sure he really wanted the answer to. "Are y'all dating?"

Even in the darkness, the surprise was visible on Fischer's face. "We ... uhh ... it's not ... later."

That was all the answer he really needed. And he was certain he didn't want any details. It almost would have been worth asking follow-up questions just to mess with him. That's what Luka would have done.

At the front door, Fischer raised his hand to knock. Thomas looked at him quizzically. "It's my house too. We don't have to knock."

"Right," he said, holding his hand out in an invitation for Thomas to open the door. It swung open to reveal a darkened living room to the right. The lights in the bedrooms to the left were off as well. The only light in the house that was illuminated came from the kitchen, which Thomas and Fischer found in disarray.

A metallic smell clung to the back of Thomas' tongue. He took a couple of steps toward the oven and turned it off. The counter tops were littered with opened boxes of ingredients, a mixing bowl whose contents had partitioned themselves into distinct layers, and a pan that had been buttered.

He turned to face Fischer, who raised both eyebrows at him. Thomas shrugged. It wasn't unlike his mother to create a colossal mess like this, but she wasn't one to just leave it that way. "Mom?" he yelled loud enough to wake the dead. Then more quietly to Fischer, "Sometimes she wears her noise-canceling headphones."

There was no response.

"I'll go check her room," he offered.

He walked down the hallway and found her door closed, as usual. Not because she wanted privacy, but because the place was such a wreck. She kept the rest of the house tidy. At the end of every day, everything had to go back in its place. Thomas had hated clean-up time as a kid. If he were just going to get the same toys out again the next day, why did it matter if he put them away now. It made more sense to him now. He always kept his room picked up. But not her. This room was her messy sanctuary, where she let everything unravel. It's like her brain needed a place where it could be totally unkempt.

He knocked briefly and pushed the door open while keeping his eyes obscured with his other hand. He really didn't want to walk in on her getting dressed. But no lights were on, and there was no movement. He returned to the living room, where Fischer was inspecting things. *What's he looking for? Does he think something is wrong?* Thomas didn't ask. The flutter in his chest told him he didn't want to hear the answer to those questions.

"She's not here," Thomas said as he thought of something.

"Maybe she went next door to see my oma. She's been having some trouble lately."

"Let's go check."

Thomas took the lead, heading back out the front door and making a left. He crossed the lot and stutter-stepped in front of Gertrude's house, seeing that it too was unexpectedly dark. He started toward the door when Fischer grabbed his upper arm. Thomas turned back to him with fear inscribed across his face. Fischer held on to his arm and pointed to the door. It stood open several inches. Darkness spilled out. Thomas tugged at the man's grip.

"Stay," Fischer instructed. He searched Thomas' face. "Can you do that? Can you stay here while I go check it out?"

The boy's nod was nearly imperceptible. Fischer maintained their eye contact, assessing whether Thomas meant what he said. Thomas gave a more reassuring nod.

Fischer released his arm. "I'm going to grab a flashlight out of my car." After he had taken several steps toward the vehicle, he looked back over his shoulder.

Thomas remained where he had been left. As much as he needed to know what was in that house, he did not want to know. Panic seized him. His breaths came in rapid, shallow bursts. He kept his back turned to the open door, even through the fear that a shadow slipped in. A shadow shaped like a lion with a serpent's tale. He closed his eyes, waiting expectantly for the claws to shred his shoulders and the teeth to tear into the exposed flesh of his neck.

Instead, what grabbed his shoulders was firm, reassuring. Thomas opened his eyes again.

"Deep breaths," Fischer said.

Thomas complied. His first breath was a gulp. As the air hit his lungs, the oxygen-starved veil that had occluded his vision gave way. His second breath came easier. He steadied, only now realizing how wobbly he had been.

"Can I let go of you now?"

"Yes," Thomas said.

"Have you had a panic attack before?" Fischer asked.

Thomas shook his head.

"Are you going to be okay if I go in there?"

"Yes," Thomas said, trying to project more confidence than he felt. It must have been enough.

"Just take some deep breaths for me," Fischer said as he pulled the flashlight from his left back pocket and unholstered the pistol from his right hip. He looked at the boy one last time before leaving him standing in the middle of the front yard.

Fischer sidled up to the front door that stood ajar. As silently as he could manage, he pushed it open with his hip. He swung the gun and flashlight inside. The beam came to rest on the far side of the room. "Scheisse," He whispered, flipping the switch on the wall to illuminate the living room. Fischer cursed again and stepped back outside the door, then took several more steps away from the house. He looked at Thomas but said nothing. Fischer returned the flashlight to his pocket and retrieved his phone.

As soon as Fischer began punching at the screen, Thomas bolted past him. Fischer dropped his phone to the ground and tried to grab at the boy with his free hand. Thomas knocked his arm away and sprang toward the open doorway. He disregarded the "Thomas, no" that Fischer flung in his direction. Thomas grabbed the doorpost and swiveled right as he dashed in.

He faltered. His grandmother lay in a heap on the floor, enveloped in a black pool of coagulated blood. A gaping hole in her forehead appeared to be one of its sources. Thomas crawled the rest of the way to her, wading into the quagmire of blood. He grabbed fistfuls of her dress and buried his face against her chest.

Sobs did not come to him, nor did tears. Nothing came to

him. Everything fled, leaving in its wake a storm of quiet desolation.

After an indeterminate time, Thomas stood. His vision blurred from his eyes having been pressed so tightly against Oma. He brought his hands up to his face, intending to rub his eyes, but found that his palms had been painted with his grandmother's blood. He doubled over in pain and revulsion.

Fischer rushed to his side and grabbed him to keep him from collapsing to the floor. He stood upright again. If he'd had anything left, he would have been embarrassed about the trend he was setting. Thomas noticed something crinkling between his arm and Fischer's hand.

"What's that?" Thomas asked. "What's in your hand?"

"Let's get you washed up first," Fischer said.

Thomas demanded, "Show me what it is."

Fischer sighed and held up a clear evidence bag with a piece of parchment inside. There was writing scrawled on it. Thomas snatched the bag from him, smearing bloody fingerprints onto its outside edges.

Dearest Grandson,

I have borrowed your mother for a bit of father-daughter time. We would love to have you join us. That is, if you can find us. To do so, you will have to seek out the places of the old gods. Maybe then we can attend to our unfinished business.

Until then, best wishes,

V

Thomas stared through the message long after he'd read it for the third time. Heat coursed through his arms and into his fingers. He was on the verge of losing control again. He pulled in a coarse breath and blew it out slowly. The plastic bag was tacky and rippled where it lay against his fingers. He handed it back to Fischer.

"Thomas," Fischer prompted, "what does this mean? Who is V?"

The boy met the man's gaze. "She didn't tell you?"

Fischer shook his head. "Your mother isn't much for sharing."

Thomas gave him a knowing look. "There are some things I need to tell you. But can we go outside?"

"Of course."

"Give me a minute with her?" Thomas asked.

He saw the conflict in the police officer's face. Concerns about evidence and further disturbing the scene. But the human inside him carried the day, and he relented. "I'll be just outside. There will be a crew arriving momentarily."

Thomas nodded and turned back toward his grandmother. He knelt down as Fischer's feet scuffed across the floor and out of the house. Thomas leaned forward and whispered. "I can't make this right, but I can finish it. For you and Daddy and Elle." He reached out a hand and closed her vacant eyes.

THOMAS

THE MONITORS beside Finn's hospital bed displayed a continuous stream of data. "They said I'm normal," Finn said with a smile.

"I knew this wasn't a reputable hospital," Luka said. "No doctor in his right mind could reach that conclusion. We're going to have to break you out of here."

"They said I'll probably be discharged today," Finn said, looking in turn at each of the four friends who gathered around his bed. He reached out and placed a hand on Thomas' arm. "I'm sorry I couldn't make it to your grandmother's funeral."

"Don't worry about it." Thomas gestured at Finn's arm cast and the other hardware leading back to the persistently beeping monitors. "It's not like you had a choice in the matter."

Finn shrugged. "Still, I wish I could have been there."

"It was so cool," Luka said excitedly.

Lea smacked his arm with the back of her hand.

"What? It was."

"You are the least situationally aware person on this whole green earth," Lea fussed, shaking her head.

"It's fine," Thomas said. "You can tell him about it."

"Okay, so first we went to this place way out in the woods where Thomas and his mom — sorry, can I mention her?"

Lea sighed in exasperation.

Thomas nodded, looking bemused in spite of everything.

"We built this big funeral pyre, like in the old days. Then they brought in his grandmother, carrying her on a stretcher from the cars to the pyre. And Thomas wanted his aunt there—"

Finn turned to Thomas. "You have an aunt?"

"Yes, it's a story for another time."

Finn nodded, shifting his position in the hospital bed and turning back to Luka.

"Careful. We don't want to see your wang," Luka said.

"Speak for yourself," Lea said.

Luka looked incredulous as he swiveled his head in Lea's direction. She shrugged at him, "Finish your story."

"So Thomas' aunt was there. And after everyone said their words, Thomas walked up to the pyre, where his oma was covered in a white sheet. And out of nowhere, he starts growing these flowers in the palms of his hands — what were they called again?"

"Trillium," Thomas said.

"Yeah, trillium. It was like magic. Well, I mean, obviously it was magic. You know what I mean. I've never seen anything like it."

"I have. But only once," Lea said, giving Thomas a look that demanded an answer.

Thomas knew what he had to do. All the secrets that he and his mother had stockpiled for the last twelve years had finally outlived their utility. "I am a schöpfer."

The group drew quiet. The only sound in the room was the cycling of medical equipment.

"Well, that's ..." Finn's sentence petered out.

"I'll tell you what it is ... hang on," Luka consulted his mental rolodex of words, looking for the right one. "Thomas, what's that hillbilly word you like to use when you say something isn't true?"

"Hogwash."

"Yeah, that's the one. It's hogwash, Thomas. No one is a schöpfer. It has to be something else. Do you know how rare that is?"

"I do," Thomas said solemnly. "And I'd give anything for it to have been otherwise. If I were anything else, I would still have a father and a mother and a grandmother."

Emma took his hand and squeezed it. "You haven't lost your mother."

"Yet. I haven't lost her yet. You all know the deal. Vulcan took her, and now I have to go find her."

Emma put her other arm on his forearm and started to object. Thomas cut her off. "I know it's a trap. I know he's smarter, stronger, and more experienced than me. But it doesn't matter. I have to go find her. She would do it for me, come hell or high water — that's another country expression for you."

Luka smiled. "I like it. I'll have to practice with it. Also, I'm going with you."

"No. You're not," Thomas said. "I can't put you at risk like that."

"The hell I'm not. My bag is already packed. I knew this was coming. I may be a loudmouth, but I'm not an idiot."

"I'm going too," Lea said.

Thomas opened his mouth but didn't get further than that. Lea leaned across Finn's bed grabbed Thomas by his shirt. "You don't get to tell me no. I saved you from the priest who was about to murder you." She let him go and patted the wrinkles flat on his chest. "Besides, the alternative is to keep living with the dope fiends until I wake up one morning to discover they overdosed on fentanyl or something. So I'll take my chances against your super old Roman grandpa." She finished her sentence and kept her eyes leveled at Thomas, daring him to oppose her.

Finn raised his arms up like an inverted Pinocchio. "Obviously, I'm not going anywhere."

Thomas turned to Emma. "You should stay, too."

Her cheeks were a bright red, and the tears that had already been sitting atop her eyelids spilled over the ledge.

"I'm sorry. It's not that I don't want you to come," Thomas added frantically.

Emma waved him off with one hand and wiped away from the tears with the other. "It's not that. I already talked to my parents. They said no."

"Oh. It may be just as well. I mean, you're the only one who can … I mean, never mind."

"It's okay," Emma said. "They might as well know everything since we're already telling secrets."

"Okay. If you're sure," Thomas said. "You're the only one who can talk to Elle."

Emma nodded as though she had already anticipated this, too.

"Wait," Luka said. "Your aunt Elle? The comatose one?"

"Catatonic, not comatose, dummy," Lea corrected.

"I'll fill in the details later. It wasn't talking. That's not the right word. It was …" Thomas didn't know what it was, but Emma was the only person who'd communicated with Elle in years.

"Weird," Emma finished his sentence. "It was weird."

Luka thought of something. "So, I guess, that's decided then. But how are we paying for this?"

Thomas reached into his back pocket and pulled out a couple of credit cards. "I … uh … pulled a play out of Lea's book and went through my mom's wallet. So I guess we have until we max these out. Then we'll have to figure something else out."

"I want to be offended at that," Lea said with a shy smile.

"But really, I'm just proud of you. Important question though — where are we going?"

Thomas dropped his head and said quietly, "I don't know."

"Rome," Finn said with certainty. "Vulcan was a Roman god. So you go to Rome. At the very least, it's a good starting point. From the time you get on the train, it'll take you about twelve hours. That's plenty of time for us to do some quick research and figure out where to start looking."

"That makes sense," Thomas said.

"Last question," Lea added. "When do we go?"

"Now? I guess?" Thomas shrugged.

"Alright!" Luka said, "Let's go Vulcan hunting. But let's get my mom to pack us some food first."

Lea shook her head slowly and asked Thomas, "Are you sure bringing him is a good idea?"

Thomas said, "I'm not sure about much of anything right now."

AUTHOR'S NOTE

Writing *Seeking Sanctuary* was such a different experience than *Vulcan Rising* had been. For starters, I knew that I wanted to set it in the Black Forest of Germany, but there was one problem – I've never been there. And in the midst of a global pandemic, there was no chance of me doing so. I did know what I was looking for, however.

I was searching for a quaint town in the Black Forest that wasn't overly well known or touristy. After doing some research, I landed on Hornberg.

The setting in my debut novel, *Vulcan Rising*, is Birmingham, Alabama, and there are times that it becomes nearly a character of its own. I wanted Hornberg to be that for *Seeking Sanctuary* despite my not having set foot in the town. This meant that I needed to do more research. Fortunately, my training as a historian and a lawyer has instilled in me a deep appreciation for the treasures that can be uncovered with diligent research.

Using maps, photographs, and a couple of 3-D tours, I learned as much about what Hornberg looked like as was possible in my situation. But I stumbled upon one limitation that I hadn't been expecting — Germany doesn't allow Google

Street View, which was a tool I had expected to use. I was concerned this would limit my ability to immerse myself in the town, but I used as many resources as I could to fill those gaps. I feel comfortable now that *Seeking Sanctuary* paints a good picture of Hornberg and its surrounding areas.

The more onerous problem with the book was that I had significant difficulty in figuring out my antagonist. I wrote several chapters of the book without knowing who the bad guy would be or what the major problems within *Seeking Sanctuary* would be.

I knew some of the plot points and how I wanted to structure the novel. We would finally learn about what happened to Agatha's sister, Elle. The story was also going to reveal that Vulcan was Agatha's father, and she was going to struggle with that knowledge. I knew Vulcan would be a current that ran through the book, even though he wouldn't make an appearance until the end.

But what I didn't know is who was going to be my antagonist for this story. Having written as much as I could without knowing who that would be, I leaned into my research again to see if I could sort things out. And what I learned was extraordinary.

I had been looking for and thought I had found a sleepy, little town in the Black Forest. But as I dug into Hornberg's past, it didn't take me long to strike gold. I learned that in 1959 a serial killer named Heinrich Pommerenke went on a killing spree, and over the course of three-and-a-half months, he committed the following atrocities before being captured: 65 total crimes, including 4 murders, 7 attempted murders, 2 rapes, 25 attempted rapes, 6 robberies, 10 break-ins, and 6 thefts.

As soon as I read about Pommerenke, I knew his atrocities were going to make it into the dark fantasy story I was writing. How could they not? It also seemed like immediate affirmation that the sleepy, little German town with an insidious past was the perfect setting for *Seeking Sanctuary*.

This bit of history also gave me what I needed to figure out that my antagonist would be a serial killer who was riding Pommerenke's coattails. At that point, I just had to figure out who the killer would be. It didn't take long for me to determine which character fit the role and how the story would develop.

In many ways, *Seeking Sanctuary* was a more challenging book to write than *Vulcan Rising*. But in the end, I think it became a compelling story that set up the end of the first trilogy within the zauberi chronicles and has given me ideas for the next couple of books beyond the trilogy.

Here's hoping that I can give you (and myself) a satisfying ending to the trilogy as Thomas and friends go Vulcan hunting in search of Agatha.

October 2, 2021

ABOUT THE AUTHOR

Seeking Sanctuary is the second book in The Zauberi Chronicles. It follows *Vulcan Rising*, the debut novel for J. W. Judge.

Judge lives in Birmingham, Alabama, also known as The Magic City. In his day job, he is a lawyer, practicing civil defense litigation.

If you enjoyed *Seeking Sanctuary*, sign up for Judge's newsletter for information about the The Zauberi Chronicles and other stories he's working on. You can also follow him on social media for updates, developments, and news about other projects. If you'd like to reach out to him by email, please do so at jwj@jwjudge.com.

Please help others find and enjoy *Seeking Sanctuary* by leaving a rating and review on Goodreads or your preferred retailer, or by sharing about it on your own social media.

WORKS BY J. W. JUDGE

Fiction

Vulcan Rising (The Zauberi Chronicles, Book 1)

Seeking Sanctuary (The Zauberi Chronicles, Book 2)

Forging Bonds (The Zauberi Chronicles, Book 3)

The Murder Tree (A Short Story)

Non-Fiction

Write Your Novel One Day at a Time: How to Write a Novel While
Having a Career, a Family, and a Life